WHICH STARS ARE YOU TALKING ABOUT?

A SCI-FI NOVEL

Ahmad A Rahaa

Which Stars Are You Talking About?
By: Ahmed A Rahaa

To contact the author

ISBN: 979-8-89965-680-4

FIRST EDITION
2025 JUNE

CONTENTS

Prologue (006)

Chapter One: (010)
Open Your Days with the Prayer of the Uprising

Chapter Two: (038)
Does the Liar Err at Dawn?

Chapter Three: (076)
Featherless Birds Bring Down Dreams

Chapter Four: (142)
A Flame Whose Color Marks the Sail of Tragedy

Chapter Five: (188)
The Glow of Disappointment at the Banquet of Silence

Chapter Six: (236)
The Funeral of the Stars, Its Time Has Come

Chapter Seven: (282)
A Painting for the Lost Ones with a Brush of Sand

Chapter Eight: (328)
The Chrysanthemum Wreath Makes the Sky Bloom

Dramatis Personae

STAR
ONE

STAR
TWO

STAR
THREE

STAR
FOUR

STAR
FIVE

STAR
SIX

STAR
SEVEN

STAR
THIRTEEN

Prologue:
Which Stars Are You Talking About?

The time has come to disclose the words within me. The feeling of being lost was the best thing we experienced on that planet—or at least, it was for me. For with every step, we took searching for a way out, we harvested a story that consoled us, gave us the lessons we needed, and even adorned the darkness of perseverance for us. Perhaps the fall wasn't as random as we first thought; perhaps the journey itself was the story we would present to you, O Mother Sun.

What led me to think this way is that this experience carried, deep within its folds, the answers to all the questions that had come to us up above. But no one else cared about such things; no one cared about anything except trying to survive in the darkness and return to your light. Were we previously this reckless to embark on a journey of this kind? Dull of feeling? Lacking experience? Perhaps the story itself was asking from the beginning: which stars was I talking about? Us? But we were never worthy of playing that role. And now, we have departed; no trace of our existence remains but the wreckage of a ship and this story, left as a legacy for the coming Stars, so they might realize that the world outside also carries meanings of sorrow, and that it is intensely dark. That the world outside is nothing but a vibrant life of being lost, and its inhabitants are in no better state than you up above. Perhaps you will realize it's time to return to the sky without argument, for writing stories is nothing more than a long solace, an unending lament, and much that should not be conveyed to a lofty lady like her, through you, Stars. So, return whence you came.

Which stars am I talking about? If this is the question you asked me, O my story, then this is what I will try to answer in the coming pages. And although I am incapable of capturing words like breaths, poor in what the world contains, weak of body, frail of stature, simple of mind, and the worst one who might answer such questions, the answer was always on the tip of my tongue, awaiting the moment of its release. Are you ready to hear it? These stars are us, and only us. But this answer alone is not enough. The time has come for me to tell you who we were and who we became. And will even that be enough? For all answers in themselves are merely the chatter told by a star about to breathe her last, hoping the meaning will become clear. Like the illusion of a dream that hadn't begun before ending as a nightmare. Like a fire that ignited and set its surroundings ablaze by itself, without an agent. Rather, my story must begin side-by-side with their stories. And I think the best beginning for me is to return once more to the incident of our ship's fall—the moment the story of the Stars, and no other, began to be recorded—and for them, to the moment of Nazi defeat in World War II, when the final era began to be written. Perhaps in the end, we will find the sufficient answer, and present it to you, O Story.

And in another era, long, long ago:

We bring you breaking news this evening, as the United States officially announced today the failure of a previous experiment to develop a nuclear bomb. This experiment, conducted in complete secrecy in Los Santos, had its full details revealed after secret files confirming its existence were leaked yesterday. Joining us now live on air is Professor Sharon. Professor, it's clear there is much controversy swirling behind the scenes since this announcement was made, especially since you were one of the most prominent participants in the project, indeed one of the staunchest defenders of the necessity of its success and of this bomb entering the American weapons arsenal before anyone else. Despite this, around the same period, you strongly criticized the Soviet Union's development of a similar bomb and repeatedly warned of its danger to the human race and the catastrophic consequences of its use. The question that now arises is: Did those fears stem from the actual danger the nuclear bomb truly represents, or because the Soviets were the ones who succeeded in developing it, and not the United States of America?

Chapter One:
Open Your Days with the Prayer of the Uprising.

O Sun of ours, O illuminator of the sky... ♪

[Everyone holds fast to your places, no one move]

We, your children the Stars, are going... ♪

[What happened?! Everything was fine just a moment ago!]

On a journey lasting thousands of years... ♪

[Does anyone know where we are? It seems like a planet
abandoned long ago. Star Two?]

Passing like a day for us from afar... ♪

[Where is Star One?! Mother appointed you leader for this
journey, what should we do now?!]

O Sun of ours, return us safely... ♪

[Let's retreat far from the ship as a precaution, and sit by that
tree to discuss what happened]

And be for us a guardian and watcher... ♪

[Believe me! We will overcome this ordeal quickly, but you all must calm down first]

So, we may tell you tales of spring... ♪

[Ha! What a ridiculous jest!]

(1)

In a new adventure, the dilapidated Ship of the Stars sailed again far into the depths of space, soaring high, reflecting whatever light had not yet been devoured on its sides. Its white wood appeared luminous from afar, an optical illusion drawing all eyes like an artwork carrying many meanings. It represented hope and the new dawn whenever it passed by the dark rocks; it even granted them a wish. And sometimes it reflected distant worlds, an endless song appearing on its huge sail, chanted by its passengers tirelessly, without boredom. It represented ancient glory and pride, and unending thanks to a Mother of great esteem seated amidst the circle called space, a towering center for this universe surpassing the significance of steadfastness and might. This time, the ship embarks on an adventure entirely different from its predecessors. It sails far not for the adult Stars to find their place in this kingdom on a journey of separation, but rather for the little Stars to learn some lessons on their own, and to seek answers to questions endlessly repeated in their minds and on their tongues, until the Mother decided to organize this trip. Curiosity, nothing more.

A sharp collision in the atmosphere was like a violent earthquake for everyone on the ship, stopping it instantly. In a moment, it was sucked downwards, as if an octopus arm had embraced it tightly and begun pulling it with tremendous force. The command tried hard to pull the ship out of its stasis, but to no avail. Their only option was to close the sail and surrender to sinking into the depths of the unknown, hoping for a landing that wouldn't claim their lives. Deep down it went, plunging amidst resistance from the atmosphere, like a burning meteor forging its path downward. With the engines focusing all their power upwards, the ship finally managed to float for a single second, but that lifeline wasn't enough to guarantee life. It collided horizontally with all its might against the trees of the sky-reaching forest. Luckily for them, this lessened the severity of the fall slightly, making it less fatal than it could have been. It continued for a few more miles, harvesting trees before it, until it reached the ground with its nose completely crushed, black in color, and its engine burnt out. It immediately sank a few meters down into the mud, hiding its flaws, finally settling, alone, beautiful despite its wreckage, with the remains of the destroyed forest behind it, and a green, flowering plain before it.

Everyone remained frozen in their places until things calmed down, then panic dominated the scene. One screaming with what breath remained in her chest, another yet to comprehend that her companion in her arms had departed from life, and a third smiling madly, leaning back against her chair after a superhuman effort, with trembling hands and a pale face, before striking the steering wheel with her bloody fist. And only one, who had moved away from the window in her terror, anxiety, and fear, began giving orders to them wisely and calmly as the song concluded.

(2)

They surrounded the tree as if in a courtroom, everyone considering themselves guilty until proven innocent, which is precisely why they wanted to pin the blame on one star in the end. Although everything now depended absolutely on the responsible one and her perspective. And what if there truly was a guilty party? It no longer mattered after this moment. Star Three began speaking in a high, sharp, reprimanding tone: "Star Four, you and your crew were responsible for monitoring the ship's indicators. Why didn't you report any problems during observation?"

"Because there was nothing worth reporting! All indicators were perfectly normal, and the ship was in excellent condition until the moment of impact. Perhaps the problem was in *your* piloting method, Star Three?"

"I am certain we were sailing in a gravity-free zone, and there was nothing different from usual. I tried with all my might to avert the disaster; that was all I could do."

Star Four flared up, her voice angry, almost breaking: "And what are we going to do now?! Are we going to ignore what happened and continue arguing? My entire crew was crushed under the ship's nose, yet you're still thinking of blaming me!"

Three replied, having calmed down slightly, trying to control her nerves: "I'm not blaming anyone. All I'm saying is that we are now officially stranded here forever!"

(3)

Everyone fell silent, the quietness a clear declaration of the court's adjournment. Although the cessation of hostilities seemed positive on the surface, it left all ears and eyes hanging, awaiting the words of the responsible one—words she didn't actually have. For a moment, she wished the earth would swallow her to spare her such a situation, an utterly unenviable position. But finally, she gathered her courage, resolved herself, stood in the center with her confident, reassuring smile, and said in a steady voice: "The Sun did not put us here without reason. So, until we can repair the ship and get it running again, let's adapt to this new life, learn some lessons from it, and spend this time together. I know what happened is a tragedy for everyone. Those who left us midway, their names will be immortalized in the sky when this journey of ours ends. But now we must move past it, focus our efforts on survival and return, instead of blaming each other and creating animosities that will serve no one."

Convincing words, as usual, which no one opposed. Yet, they weren't enough to banish the fear from their hearts. The responsible one turned towards one of them and asked calmly: "Star Two, you with the wandering gaze, did you notice anything distinctive about this planet? You must have come across something about it while reading in the Celestial Library."

Star Two hesitated slightly before answering cautiously: "I haven't read anything about it, but I'm sure I've seen it somewhere before, near the Sun. Its greenery, mountains, and buildings... this is not a dark planet at all. There is a civilization living here."

The responsible one nodded understandingly, then said firmly: "Alright, let's conclude this quick word here. As we learned before, you will split into pairs and disperse to search for anything that might be useful to us—tools or information. As for myself and Star Three, we will examine the ship's condition, the extent of the damage, and what it needs to be able to fly again. If any star among you encounters something strange or runs into any trouble, send up a light signal into the sky immediately."

All the Stars replied in unison: "Acknowledged, Leader!"

(4)

They were walking beside what remained of the ship. Although they had been walking steadily for minutes, one of them stepped forward a few paces as they drew near. From her comical gait, she seemed entirely unserious, until she finally arrived and touched the charred wood at the ship's nose. She pressed it, and it turned to dust between her hands. She then turned towards the other, who was frozen, staring intently at her. She threw the ash from her hand with a sarcastic smile, then opened her arms wide, gesturing to the poverty of options before them.

"I don't expect junk like this to ever fly! You are clinging to your illusions, nothing more."

Then she kicked the sand in a foul mood, her hand aching and a headache almost splitting her skull, her feet uncovering the remains of some crushed Stars' fragments beneath the mud. She looked at them seriously, accompanied by a sadistic laugh, and said: "And soon we will all meet the same fate as her. How lucky she is. You must tell them that."

"Get out of her what you can. We will bury them near the tree."

This wasn't the answer she expected from her, and she knew she could never bring her down to the base level she was trying to push her towards. So, she contented herself with a sarcastic laugh like her previous words to the ship and began digging in the dirt to retrieve the body. However, Star One unexpectedly continued: "We will exert every effort to repair the ship and return it to its course. Perhaps in the remnants left behind by the ancients here, we will find something to help us achieve this goal quickly. That's why I eagerly await the report from

Star Two and the others about what they find. And if we cannot do that, the Sun must come to rescue us in the end, for the Mother never forgets her children."

She stopped digging as soon as she finished speaking, her expression changing to clear anger. She clenched her fists and rushed towards her until the distance between them completely vanished, saying with her head held high and in a sharp tone: "The Sun! The Sun! She doesn't care about you at all. How long will you continue to flee from this reality?!"

"Then what shall we do?! What can we possibly do but believe that now?! What..."

Tears began streaming down her cheeks after that last cry. She grabbed the front of Star Three's shirt with her weak grip, looking at her with pained, weak eyes. It was an unforgettable scene of a false leader crushed by pain from within. She collapsed gently onto the other, who merged with her for a moment. Star Three could only drop her own insistence as well, embracing her tenderly, patting her head gently, sharing the pain with her.

When Three finished digging the grave, One placed all the remains and fragments she had retrieved from under the ship's nose inside it. Before covering it with dirt, she silently recited a final prayer, only to be surprised that the other standing beside her was sharing in it too. They finished the burial process in silence, neither uttering a word. Afterwards, she stretched her arms towards the sky, tired from the effort she had exerted, and sat down to rest under the shade of the tree. Star One followed her and sat beside her again.

"I didn't mean to offend you or mock you. I know we are all in the same mire, but you bear a greater responsibility than all of us. I don't know how to describe it exactly, but you are trying to maintain more than sixty stars and ensure their safety."

Star One looked at her gently, then said calmly: "Your problem with the Sun, is it because she chose me as the responsible one for the Stars and the journey, even though you are older?"

Star Three then smiled a faint smile, shaking her head in denial: "Quite the contrary. I understand very well now that piloting the ship is harder than leading the Stars. It just relates to different problems we faced along the way, differences in viewpoints, nothing more. And frankly, I don't like sharing these matters with you."

Star One suddenly laughed, saying playfully: "Differences in viewpoints? Perhaps I can share my real opinion about these differences sometime, you liar!"

Their loud laughter quickly spread through the surroundings, erasing with it every trace of the previous argument. But the laughter didn't last long, as the sky suddenly lit up with a clear sign to the north. This definitely meant that a star from the exploration team had found something important.

They stopped suddenly after climbing the hill and remained standing like that for some time. Eventually, they decided to part ways with their leader, Star Two, leaving her immersed in her thoughts. Only Star Seven remained beside her, sharing contemplation of the world from that towering height. The view from there granted the mind some tranquility and enthusiasm, and many questions. What does this vast, abandoned world hide for us? And what will we find inside its towering iron buildings, its black roads, and its huts covered by grass and trees? It is the mystery and magic of the unknown, that influence which pushes you to embark on the adventure, overcoming all your fears for the sake of uncovering what lies beneath. Star Two broke the silence, asking Seven with clear curiosity: "I don't know if our falling onto an inhabited planet like this is good luck. Among all the ill-fated, unknown rocks and planets we passed in the sky, fate chose for us to fall here, upon this wondrous world. What is your opinion on the matter, Star Seven?"

She answered then, calmly and contemplatively: "The surprises of the future are what will reveal that to us. Haven't you found out the name of this planet yet?"

"I don't understand why knowing the planet's name matters so much to you all, but I am about to identify it. It's one step away from this exhausted one's mind."

Star Seven turned around, placing her hands behind her head, slowly walking away. Then she stretched out on the ground near Star Two, gazing at the deep blue sky, at the great light of the Sun that no one can mistake, and at the birds migrating from east to west, then said: "We aren't far past midday. The Sun's light is still bright, and hot. Have you reached anything?"

Suddenly, Star Two jumped up with obvious excitement and said in an enthusiastic voice: "Yes! I found it! They call this planet "Spoiled Paradise". I saw a report about it previously in the Mother's library. It must be it! And this means there are many important and dangerous details we must tell Star One immediately. Come on, let's return quickly!"

(6)

As soon as the sign flared, everyone gradually returned to the gathering point around the tree. This time, the leader was with them, and behind her, a distinctive rocky star was planted in the ground that hadn't been there before. With Star Two's arrival, she appeared raising one finger to the sky, her head lowered as usual, as if declaring she was the one who sent the signal. From among the crowd, Star Four suddenly appeared to whisper something in Star One's ear. After she finished, the latter took a step forward, concluding the first day on the planet: "Welcome back, Stars, and blessed are your efforts this evening. Let's conclude the report for the first day. Each squad will announce what they found during their roaming. We begin with you, Star Three and the Command Squad."

"After reviewing the ship's damage up close, with you of course, we confirmed that the damage sustained from the incident is extensive and serious. The ship needs restructuring, which could take weeks, perhaps months, meaning we will remain on this planet for quite some time. We still need to ascertain the condition of the engines, wings, and the controller."

"Star Two and the Exploration Squad?"

"The planet we fell upon is nicknamed Spoiled Paradise, and it is the Earth previously inhabited by humans. Therefore, I am sure we will find many valuable things that could help us return quickly, but it also holds great risks. So, I request that touching objects be forbidden for all squads except the elites of Engineering and Exploration until we ascertain the general condition of the surface."

"You have it, Star Two. And from this day forward, you will be responsible for gathering and documenting information about this planet, and Star Seven, Deputy of the Engineering Squad, will assist you in this. What about you, Star Four and the Engineering Squad?"

"We found many strange materials that might be useful, most importantly a red liquid that ignites quickly upon contact with fire, making it a good option for fuel in the future. Besides that, as Star Two mentioned, there is a lot of damaged heavy equipment scattered around; we might find useful parts for maintenance in it."

"Star Five and the Protection and Health Squad?"

"We found many deep caves in the south, empty and safe. We didn't find any minerals in them, but with the stores, houses, and damaged equipment mentioned by Star Four, there's no need for excavation deep underground. The environmental condition is indeed disastrous, and it worsens within the cities, but it's not dangerous to us. As for the atmospheric condition, it's unexpectedly suitable, and there is no risk of deadly diseases spreading."

"Thank you all. And before we return to the ship, I remind you not to despair. We will get out of here as soon as possible, and we will live together in comfort on this planet without worry or hardship, I promise you that. Let's eat now and go to sleep; tomorrow will have its own word."

Although all circumstances seemed, in their view, set for a quick return, anxiety still gripped everyone; even the most positive among them was the deepest in thought. What surprises did this hazy future hold for them? A single question now terrified them all. The questions multiplied until their hearts were consumed, and sleep found no easy path to their eyes that night.

She could barely close her eyes after hours spent contemplating the cracked ceiling and thinking incessantly. Even counting sheep was of no use to her; she must have surpassed eighteen thousand, nine hundred and thirty-five sheep. And when it was the next sheep's turn to jump over the fence accompanied by tranquility, a girl with long, dangling white hair suddenly appeared from above, blocking the window light, making her features in the darkness look like a terrifying ghost. The other flinched in terror, so the visitor quickly covered her mouth before she could let out a piercing scream. Then she sat beside her on the floor, with an enigmatic smile and scattered glances. It was Star Two. She whispered: "You can't sleep, can you? I don't know how that leader thinks we'll sleep after discovering such a wondrous world. I don't think I'll close my eyes until I roam all its lands and see all its shores. Don't you feel the same, Star Seven?"

"Actually, I was one second away from sleep! We have hard work tomorrow; it's better for you to rest too. Get those crazy ideas out of your head; no one will join you in them!"

Star Seven thought her talk was just a joke or part of some game, so she pulled the cover back over herself, this time covering her head completely. Moments later, she lifted the cover again looking for her, only to find the space empty, as if Star Two had vanished into the darkness.

It is said that hatred and revenge might break a few barriers, but not as powerfully as the desire for knowledge and curiosity. As for knowledge, one might reach a stage where they realize the futility of their pursuit and return empty-handed, yet still wiser. But when the motive is curiosity, accompanied by a firm, unwavering will, there is no way to return empty-minded. That's why she was walking through the pitch darkness with determination, alone, holding a lamp in her right hand, and a notebook and quill in her left. And to grasp the extent of her madness, it suffices to know that she preferred carrying more paper and extra inkwells over taking a flask of oil or even a weapon to protect herself. Thus, we reach a simple conclusion: The pursuit of knowledge can be dangerous for some people, just as the pursuit of blood is dangerous for others.

"Wait a moment. Where do you think you're going like this? Alone, and before dawn!"

"Changed your mind?"

"Just a minute… let me catch my breath… then I'll answer you."

She bent over sharply, hands on her knees, panting with pride that she had managed to shout despite her condition. Clearly, library-goers aren't the best at running or raising their voices, and it showed plainly here!

When her rest break ended and she finally straightened up, she grabbed Star Two's hand and pulled her as if she were a small child, heading back towards the ship. But the other stopped her with a serious look before saying: "There's no place for me on the wrecked ship anymore. Everyone will play the part they excel at, while I will be out there, documenting everything. I think I got the best job on this trip."

"But you know we need to get permission before going out! If Star One finds our sleeping places empty, we'll be in big trouble."

"Don't worry, it's a short tour in a nearby area, and we'll be back before dawn arrives. I'm sure you realize it's not right to waste such precious time sleeping."

"And I'm sure tomorrow will definitely not go well."

"Stop being pessimistic; nothing will happen. On the contrary, I'm sure everyone will stay asleep until we return, and no one will notice our departure. What could possibly happen in just two hours? I spotted something from the hill, and if what I'm thinking is correct, it will be the greatest building your eyes have ever seen."

She stood no chance against this insistence in the end; she was the defeated one, dragging the tail of disappointment behind her. She took hesitant steps behind her, while a star with fiery eyes lit her path, eager to explore every inch of this land. But one question began to echo in her mind, the answer to which she would only know when the time came: Will we really return before dawn?

(9)

A great cement dome, surrounded by decorated classical columns, topped by striped blood-red banners fluttering on its four sides. On its facade, a statue of a man carrying a rock on his back, and scales in his hand. Fake stars adorn the blue square on the flags—that which symbolized a sea that was once the last line of resistance against their settlement. It was a point of pride that half of it remained without holes, except for the huge hole in the middle. And although the trees had declared their occupation of the place, spreading their pure green banner, this specific spot remained cursed; neither rain nor tree could erase that curse, or even pass through it.

Star Two stood at the entrance, beside the statue, imitating its unique stance, which made Star Seven laugh at her as she continued her tour around the place. She was stepping over rubble and scattered puddles of water until she heard Two call from afar: "Look closely at this building. They call it the Legislative Center. Right here, laws were signed, imposed, and constitutions amended. Huge, solid, fortified, and possessing great awe."

"But, what's the point of constructing a building with such grandeur and fortification, if its purpose was only to issue laws to organize and facilitate people's lives?"

"I was waiting for that question from you!"

"I take it back…"

"No! Wait! I'll tell you. Because the laws transformed from a tool to organize life into a means to feed and fund the government, a means to steal production and extort others. If you were on the government's side, you were above the law, above the constitution itself. For centuries, this wasn't clear, but as time passed, the pockets accustomed to stealing began wanting more, and with each success, their appetite grew. They assumed the old methods would always work, and indeed they did, but one day the people would discover the truth and refuse to comply. At that point, this place was no longer a center for laws but transformed into the main arena of confrontation against the government."

"The law transformed from a pillar for organizing the state into a means to support factions, parties, and ideas, justify injustice, and reinforce the ruler's dominance. What a quick way to destroy an entire nation."

While they were talking, Star Seven found a pile of worn-out papers, books, and disks. Most were unusable, but she decided to give them a chance anyway. Amidst that chaos, among the rubble, her gaze fell upon one book that caught her attention more than the others. Its cover was torn, but the title was still prominent in bold script: Uprising. And below it, in finer, sharper script: How to Apply One of the Middle East's Most Famous Concepts for Resisting the Occupier within the United States of America. She lifted it off the ground, finding some papers attached to its cover, stamped with a high-level government seal, centered around a picture of a person who looked like he had been imprisoned on charges of incitement against the government. Here, in this book, and in these papers, his story was written. Seven said, extending the book: "I found some interesting things here. Do you want to take a look? I think they'll give us a deeper understanding of what humans were like before their extinction, and coincidentally, they connect perfectly to our main topic of discussion."

"Uprising… What a dazzling title. But we don't have time to read it now; we need to document the details of the place so we can return to the ship early. Or would you prefer to read it aloud while I take notes?"

"Alright, I'll leave the documenting to you, while I dive into the depths of this book. Ahem! Ahem!"

She took a deep breath, then opened the first page and began to read: "Someday…"

(10)

Someday, a weak and solitary people will decide not to remain silent forever under the occupier's injustice. They will await their chance to rise up ignited, shaking the dust from their exhausted body, burdened by the wounds of the past. Its spark will likely begin, as narratives will probably later recount, with the killing of a few men, and it will continue despite the waterfall of blood that will mercilessly sweep through it, until that weak one, possessing an iron will, finally sits at the negotiation table, opposite a superpower seemingly formidable, but fragile in reality—a fragility exposed only at the first thorn that blocked its path. There, he will realize that what bolsters it is nothing but myths, and that his enemy who actually triumphed over it possessed nothing but his will and his patience. And yet, he stood against the most modern weapons arsenal in the Middle East.

Uprising. This is the name given to the method that forced the occupier, despite its impudence, to submit to the demands of the resistance. It is the path of opposition in this example. But what if we represent the opposition? What if we are the ones who possess the weapon, whatever its type? It doesn't have to be material to be powerful, for how many non-material weapons were far more lethal and impactful? We are the ones who move the country. What is the army without its soldiers? What is the factory without its workers? So why haven't we mobilized yet? How long will we remain silent? Rather, in my opinion, what we lack is one single thing: an answer to the famous question, and how to mobilize. The time has come for us to learn from the East how they rise up against us.

"Here, this is your salary for this month."

"Excuse me, are you sure you didn't miscalculate? There's a shortfall in the transferred amount."

"No, there's no mistake. The government increased the income tax this month."

[If we want today's operation to succeed, we must follow the plan exactly, without discussion.]

"It's gotten late, aren't you sleeping?"

"I'm trying to figure out how to organize the bills."

"Things will get better tomorrow."

"How? Will money suddenly grow in my account?"

[After entry, a secret unit belonging to the Chinese army will support us from behind. We just need to keep advancing.]

"I won't be able to sleep at home tonight. We can barely afford this month's rent."

"You work day and night! And now you won't sleep either? You need to recognize your limits!"

[This operation will determine not only our fate but the fate of the entire uprising American populace. We must succeed no matter what, even if we have to sacrifice ourselves to do it. Is that clear?]

"This recording is yours. Do you object?"

"No, Lieutenant!"

"And with this, the charge of incitement against the government through your book is proven against you, along with recruiting terrorist elements to support an armed coup. What do you think you are, insect?!"

"The people, thanks to me, will change your policies and restore freedom and democracy to the arena."

"What a funny clown you are! Do you still not know who was supporting your plan from the beginning?"

When the book spread in the region, I found widespread support among the youth, especially older teenagers. Calls to take to the streets to overthrow the government soon began, and I saw my only chance gleaming amidst the chaos. I decided to lead my group amidst this rebellious tide, to become the hidden hand strangling the government from the shadows. I actually succeeded in establishing it, and it wasn't long before we received generous financial support from Communist China. It was surprising, but not suspicious; given they were one of our government's most prominent enemies, their support for us was natural within the context of the political game.

"Your attack on the weapons depot, surely you still remember the events. What happened there?"

"The supporter instructed us to target that area first, even specifying the ideal attack strategy for us. We infiltrated inside as planned for us and stole a huge quantity of weapons and ammunition, necessary to arm the group. Then we seized the box of secret files; we were told it was invaluable to the government and that they would pay any price to get it back."

"And coincidentally, after you left the depot, Iranian drones—source initially unknown—launched a suicide raid on it and completely wiped it out. It turned out they were launched from a Russian aircraft carrier, and the operator was a Chinese army agent. Let's move on to the second operation."

The second operation was almost simultaneous with the first. We had to demonstrate our strength to the government before informing them we had the box. Therefore, we chose the Legislative Center as the main target for the attack. The goal wasn't sabotage, but rather to control the building, establish a position within it, and then invite the government to negotiate with us in exchange for returning the box.

"The operation failed due to the betrayal of the Chinese forces who claimed to support us. As soon as we entered the building with the box, we found ourselves surrounded by American forces, and we had no choice."

"And now you will be executed as a traitor and enemy agent."

"No doubt about it."

"But, unfortunately, it's not that simple. You will be imprisoned for ten years for incitement, and for life for attempting a military coup. And this is only because you saved the army from a great disaster. Didn't you know what was in that box?"

Time stopped then for seconds. The box?

"All along, you were carrying the core of a huge nuclear bomb. And now, you will watch with me how it falls on Taiwan. Thanks to you, we will start our war against China. And lest I forget, we were the ones supporting you all along."

After everything I did, I was just a game in the government's hands without realizing it. I didn't move the masses; rather, I myself was being led, a tool in their schemes instead of being a dam in their way. I never realized I was a shepherd tending their sheep for them wherever they wanted. What a fool I am. But, at least, I achieved my final goal: The American street will rise up against them forever.

(11)

As Star Seven finished speaking, Star Two watched her silently, having noted down the last sentence. She said quietly, gently reaching out her hand to brush strands of hair from her eyes: "He appeared to me as an important figure. Is that really all that was mentioned about him in his judicial record?"

"Almost. Not much was written about him, just a few concise words. But he seems truly pitiful; abandoned by his comrades, secretly led to help his opponents without knowing, and then the Uprising stopped immediately upon his imprisonment and the declaration of war on the China alliance. Even though all he wanted was a better life."

Star Two turned with a serious gaze towards Star Seven and said calmly: "Humans are ignorant, even if many of them possess a unique vision. I don't know why they always insist on falling into the trap of politics, entering games that require a cunning they'll never possess."

"Perhaps they measure things by simple scales. In his case, he thought the Uprising was easy, as he explained in his book, but he discovered that resisting an entire government and army is not like confronting an occupation. It's a nearly impossible task for civilians without strong backing."

"That's plausible. Anyway, I've finished documenting. We need to return quickly before we're late."

[I knew my day of death was not far off, even if I distanced myself a little from this burning world, death would await me as punishment for the sin I committed. I regret everything I did. Farewell, world.]

"Let's leave then. There's nothing more for us to do here."

They left the place with cautious steps, leaving behind a new story whose pages had closed on regret and a final confession, in a world that quickly becomes preoccupied with the next wave of dreamers and rebels.

The ship was lit up with a decoration of lights, standing out in the darkness in a way that made you wonder how they managed to power them in such a place, and where they got the energy to start their day with exaggerated activity even before sunrise. But as they approached, they noticed something strange. The movement inside was agitated in an unnatural way; not a situation causing extreme worry, but not familiar either. Maybe they're looking for us, was the first thing that crossed their minds. They clung to this idea until they arrived, only for their conviction to shatter upon seeing the burnt wood, and when their eyes collided with Star Five, covered in blood. They rushed towards her quickly, and Star Seven asked her in a worried voice: "Five! What is this blood?! What happened?!"

But another voice answered this time, the voice of Star Three, who rushed towards them, sharp with anger: "Where were you two?! Who allowed you to leave the damned ship at night!!"

Seven tried to maintain her composure despite the rapidly escalating tension and said seriously: "We apologize, but we need an explanation now! What happened in our absence?!"

Five wiped the blood clinging to her forehead, then answered in an exhausted voice: "Packs of wolves attacked the ship. But they weren't ordinary wolves, not at all, rather closer to savage beasts, likely attracted by the smell of stored food. We didn't see any of them during the morning rounds, and we don't know how they approached so quickly."

Three spoke again, this time her tone saturated with accusation: "And we expected our adult sister, Two, to stand by our side, to help us protect the Stars. But we didn't find her, because she was strolling outside without informing us, while we were trying to save each other here!"

Seven's eyes widened, and she quickly confessed: "I was the one who asked her to come out. Enthusiasm blinded my heart. This was my fault."

Three didn't waste a moment. She advanced with angry steps towards Seven and grabbed her shirt, as if the argument would change what had already happened. Seven didn't try to struggle, just remained silent, frozen under the weight of conflicting emotions. As for Star Two, she stood at a distance,

watching them from afar. She secretly wanted to confess the truth but couldn't get the words out; her tongue froze from fear of their gazes. And she wasn't wrong in her feeling of fear, especially after glimpsing Star One, standing among them, silent, commenting on nothing, her gaze empty as if she were no longer present with them in this place.

But luckily for them, their argument was interrupted by the arrival of Star Four, who emerged from the ship to announce her report in a rigid tone: "The ship inspection is complete. Seventeen stars inside now. Most of the rear section was destroyed after the fuel explosion during the fight… Nineteen, counting the two runaways."

Three inhaled deeply, trying to control herself, then said calmly: "Thank you, Star Four, for the report. Let's rest a little now, and we will discuss the remaining matters at dawn today, including your issue, Star Two and Seven."

And with that, the matter was closed for now. No one could object; none of them had the audacity to protest. They just left the meeting amidst suffocating tension, burdened by worry and pain, while the two runaways remained standing in their place, clinging to their fear, unable even to approach the ship. Their eyes were fixed on the entrance, on the broken ramp whose eroded structure the wolves had crossed, on those dark stains that dyed the ground where their sisters had fallen. A voice still echoed in their memory, how they were told yesterday that tomorrow would be better. But how could it be, when only a quarter of them survived to see the morning sun?

Chapter Two:
Does the Liar Err at Dawn?

(1)

Hands were cuffed and bonds tightened until the flesh grooved beneath them. My soft arms stretched out, helpless and powerless, reflecting the darkness of space and its harsh rocks onto their chains. I was aimless, without reference, trapped amidst trapped tears, like the suspect standing in a vast square, accused of a brazen daylight murder. This time, the police were the weeping eyes, and the killer was my heart, and no one else's. I prayed the earth would swallow me when I realized returning to the ship was no longer an option after I had uttered my reckless words before them, trying to salvage Star Two's situation. I found I had led the spotlight directly towards myself, like the prime suspect, as if our leaving the ship at night was the sole reason for losing some of them, as if my presence or absence would have affected them in any way. Ah, and the overflow of mixed feelings from their wounded hearts reached me; I even understood its words: perhaps I had become one of those who lost the thread of life instead of one of them. Could another truly have survived if I had been in her place in that imaginary scenario? Had misery penetrated their hearts to this extent? And if I had to blame someone, it would be Star Three, who stopped us from the beginning with her ridiculous question. What did she expect me, or any other star confined to a library or observing a lab, to do?

Then, after some time had passed, I realized that prayers alone are useless, just like wishes, and that thinking rationally, if you possess enough wisdom, leads you to only one solution: correcting the misunderstanding diplomatically, without blaming anyone. This begins in two stages: First, to understand the previous catastrophe down to the last detail—all its causes, consequences, and lessons; to comprehend who fell, who endured, who tried, and who gave up. And second, to re-extend the broken lines dangling from the sky between myself and the squad leaders, for they alone possess the ability to explain the picture anew to our sisters, giving the truth a voice that can be heard amidst this rubble.

(2)

Her mark was a cup of tea on a wooden table, a cup that never left her, no matter what, and always full wherever I met her. Sometimes she sipped it as if it were bitter medicine, and other times she enjoyed it like a beast accustomed to eating only one main meal for endless years. Her seat wasn't inside the ship, but atop the surface of its nose, where she had habitually sat since we set sail. And always beside her rested her sword made of gold dust and ash, glowing with its unique sheen under the moonlight, the trace of frozen blood upon it showing like silent scars. On her thick leather jacket, inlaid with heavy metal, our insignia stood out. Sometimes the shadow of her long, straight, silver hair covered it, and sometimes the number five—written by the Sun's hand in honor—was revealed. She wore it over the sailor's uniform, making her the only one among us dressed differently from the others. She was the fiercest in competitions, the most savage in games, and the strongest build among us. I still remember the words preceding every ball game: *If you want to stay unharmed, never stand in Five's way when she wants to score!* I was always annoyed by that phrase, but we never cared; how lucky was anyone who played on her team. And you wouldn't believe it if I told you she was completely the opposite in classes and lessons, suddenly transforming into a considerate, helpful star, quick to smile and rarely still. Perhaps that's why she became the leader of the Protection and Health squads.

I approached her, and she raised her eyes from her teacup: "Star Five, could I steal a minute of your break time to catch a word?"

"Depends on the kind of talk, but how could I refuse a request from our gentle writer, Seven. Please, sit down while I prepare a cup of tea for you; I have some biscuits too."

Although I was only asking her to listen to me for a minute, I sat on the opposite chair, my eyes contemplating the spilled tea stains on and around the table. This didn't usually happen, until I noticed the ship's tilt. Luckily, she hadn't been thrown from the ship with her table during the fall, otherwise, that would have been the most grievous loss we would have suffered. She is safety, and what else besides safety could we need here?

"What specifically did you want to talk about?"

"Some questions about tonight's incident."

"But I already explained the matter to you earlier."

She raised her cup to her lips, her hand trembling. Her agitation was clear, and I could be certain that this smile of hers was undoubtedly fake. There were more details she was hiding from me, no doubt about it.

"Star Four said you detonated the fuel stored in the ship's rear. I don't think that was your plan to drive off the wolves; judging by the blood staining you then, you were in the ship's corridors protecting the Stars. Was it Three, then, who ordered it?"

Her heart refused to answer before her tongue did. This wasn't her habit, and this silence was nothing but confirmation of what I suspected. There had been a disagreement, a collision, another fall. The impact of what happened that night was more severe than just wolves invading the ship during our absence.

I deduced something new: when they needed Star Two then and didn't find her, they knew she wasn't on the ship, meaning the story precedes and goes beyond the wolves.

"I don't like how Star Three portrayed Two as having an important influence on us, when she actually has no connection to defense or organization, nor do I. The matter bothers me."

Five furrowed her brows and answered sharply: "That doesn't change the fact that it was wrong for you two to leave the ship at night without anyone knowing. If you're trying to find an excuse for me to overlook your violation, I will never participate with you in that!"

As expected, I can read Star Five easily, but she is extremely cautious. She believes some matters must be kept confidential from the others, and therefore, it's difficult to lure her or push her to disclose details of what went on in closed rooms. But I knew exactly who could help me with that; she alone could give me the answers I seek.

(3)

I retraced my steps outside after being dismissed from the tea table. It was then I realized that, instead of resolving part of the conflict, I had placed another barrier between us, widening the distance. This wasn't what I had sought, but I found no other way to talk with her without my words colliding with a wall of silence and refusal. I walked away until I reached the tree, and there, I sat beneath it. I placed the lamp beside me and began flipping through the pages of the book I had stolen from last night's adventure, my eyes gleaming with the reflection of its faint light on its glass cover. I lifted my gaze for a moment, contemplating the perfect engraving carved on the rock beside me. Star One must have made this grave, and she must have been in a good enough mood then to transform pain into a masterpiece immortalizing those who fell. How I wish we wouldn't have to make another. That was her hobby; she loves drawing and sculpting, loves immortalizing moments by creating landmarks that remain witnesses to what we've experienced. Even when she first saw me, she drew me as a child hiding behind a great light. I didn't realize then that she meant me, until later, when I looked at the drawing through her eyes and recalled the memories.

Then *she* appeared. She approached slowly, hesitantly, hiding a feeling of shame and disappointment behind her impassive facial expressions. I didn't need to hear her words to know what she would say; I knew it beforehand, as if I had read it in an old book a thousand times. Therefore, I didn't listen to her, didn't even lift my eyes from the book, letting it reflect the lamplight on its glass surface. When I decide on my actions and choices, I don't like anyone blaming me. I live my life like a novel, and the words I write are those I have chosen carefully, to extract from them the meaning of absolute rightness—rightness as *I* see it, not as others do.

Her hesitation didn't last long. She sat down quietly, without looking at me or the book, and said: "You shouldn't have done that then!"

I didn't look up, didn't change my position, left no room for doubt in my reply: "Weren't you the one who told me before that there's no use talking about matters that have passed? Indeed, the mistake was mine when I didn't extinguish the flame of your enthusiasm at the start. If blame must be cast on someone, my personality makes me the ideal candidate for that, unlike you. Everyone knows I'm the one drawn by adventure, the one defeated by curiosity in every day and every tale."

Silence fell for a moment, but she didn't back down, didn't get up to leave. Instead, her response came quickly, carrying the weight of the truth I hadn't yet dared to face: "But they won't just blame you for going out with me; they will hold you responsible for the deaths of all those stars."

Her tone was harsh, merciless, but it wasn't empty cruelty; it was the truth in its harshest form. I finally raised my eyes and looked directly into hers. There was something cold in her gaze, something I hadn't seen in her before.

"What will you do then? Will you just apologize? Will you kneel to them for forgiveness?"

I didn't answer because, for the first time, I didn't know the answer. I had put myself inside a net I couldn't escape from. That's what I thought for a moment. But what was hidden from her was that I *can* find a way out, I *can* create a path of escape. For when I discover the truth of what happened that night, I can cast the blame onto another star. Indeed, I must, because one of them is now trying to evade her deed.

Ha! What am I talking about?! Am I serious now?! Casting blame won't solve any problems. I must mend the threads, not cut them further. I don't want us to part ways—not me, not her, not any of the others—not in circumstances like these. I took a deep breath before saying: "You are my older sister, and my dear friend. Bearing this blame for you is my way of thanking you for all you've done for me; you were always by my side, unlike the rest of the Stars. Although I was a little annoyed at being chosen for your adventure tonight, I truly felt happy when I was chosen again, and when you didn't stop as soon as I took your hand to return. I had a wonderful time near the Legislative Center."

That's enough. I can end the conversation with this gentle phrase, and I'll be perfectly satisfied. I stood up quietly, ready to leave, my destination clear before me now: that tall shadow hiding behind the tree could only belong to Star One. Since she witnessed everything that happened, I know she won't be stingy with her answers to me; she will be my ideal savior at this moment. But before I could move, her voice came again, quiet yet cutting: "Where are you going? If you're thinking of talking to Star One now, it won't do you any good. She's in shock, barely able to distinguish her surroundings while muttering prayers. If you have questions about what happened tonight, it would be better to talk to Star Four. You know her habit when she gets angry; she always runs away from us, so you'll find her in the destroyed lab at the front of the ship."

Then she added, in a lower voice: "Can I also accompany you there?"

What am I looking at in what I'm doing? My goal wasn't to turn these pages into a dramatic mystery story. But I felt something different tonight—resolve and determination. Was this one of the effects of this book I'm holding? Or was it the effect of a wound I only now realized, a wound suddenly created by my imagination? Was this a desire for separation, to solve things alone? Perhaps. But when I heard her request, when I heard she wanted to accompany me, a faint smile broke across my face involuntarily, as if it dusted me off.

I am not alone. She was always by my side. I said that before, so why was I trying to distance myself from her? She sees the shore, and I see the wave, and together we create a complete scene. I am the one who writes, and she is the one who reads what I weave for her.

"We can get through this together, like we did before. Remember? Your first day in the sky, when you hid in the library? I imagined you were me back then. Because from my first day, I was alone. I used to look outside, at the schoolyard, where they played and their laughter rose, and I blamed myself because I didn't have enough courage to go out and interact with them, because I felt the whole thing was scary and complicated."

She paused for a moment, looked at me, then continued in a warmer voice: "And when I saw you, I told myself: I must help her get out, because perhaps I refused inwardly for another star to live through the feeling I had lived through. And without realizing it, because of you, I found myself stepping onto the garden grass for the first time. Helping you then pushed me, made me forget that fear, blinded me completely. And because I'm not one of the stars who show their feelings easily, like kind Four, you saw me follow you without apparent interest, but in reality, I was afraid of leaving you, and I followed you without uttering a word."

I couldn't hold back my tears at all, nor stop my hands from reaching back and hugging her tightly. I had told myself moments ago, but hearing her say it with her own tongue, confirming that the relationship connecting us isn't just a fleeting friendship, that she refuses for it to be so, gave my heart new desires: a desire to survive together, until the end of this tale, and a desire to explore every detail of this world, before our inevitable end arrives.

(4)
(Excerpt from the book Seven was reading before Star Two interrupted her.)

Persistence doesn't create corruption, but it reveals it. The continuation of any illicit action, like jumping over the wall for example, makes it easy to discover over time. And as I mentioned in the previous chapter about the importance of the Uprising as a necessity for change, there is a dangerous matter that you shouldn't overlook before you join an opposing party, or join hands with activists calling for change:

most of them carry a hidden interest behind a mask of principles and postulates. They will call for freedom, a better future, more jobs, liberation or war—something that makes you believe in the soundness of the doctrine they follow. But, have you asked yourself about their past? About their hidden goals? About their followers and their sponsors?

You might find yourself following a party that does what is right and says what is right, but carries hidden intentions within it. And when the decisive moment comes, when it realizes it grasps the absolute truth, that might push it to do something crazy, unexpected. And you don't want to fall into the nets of the unknown. Therefore, don't follow them blindly; don't surrender your mind to any banner waved by the crowds. Understand, analyze, think, then choose. Follow your heart, and rise up as you wish, but don't forget to always ask yourself: To whom do I truly belong? And why?

(5)

The shooting stars that fall from the sky and collide with the earth leave behind a tale worth telling, a trace that beings sing of as long as they live. But for the sky, they are nothing but a loss and disappearance, the vanishing of one of its landmarks. Perhaps that rock was featureless, just a stone without an identity, nothing distinguishing it. Yet, that rock which seems worthless today might one day become a unique planet, or a world teeming with life. The sky lost a chance, a slight possibility, but an indispensable hope. And I, like the sky, lost a story, lost a chance whose value I only realized after it was gone. Oh, my luck and my misery!

The school bell rings, and everyone runs outside immediately upon hearing it—everyone except me. I remained silently in my place until the Sun approached me, gently took my hand, and led me to the yard where the Stars were playing. Then, I saw for the first time the wide schoolyard, a vast green garden, filled with laughing Stars, full of life. How did the Sun expect me to join them, when the Stars formed a closed circle with no place for me in it?

And in a far corner, there was one star, sitting silently, watching calmly from afar. It was Star One. I felt in that moment that I had found the only place I could sit that day. I approached her shyly. She smiled at me and said: "Is that you, Star Seven? Why are you sitting here? Don't you want to play with them?"

"I don't know how I can join them. All this noise and movement, I don't know if it really suits me. I don't want to insert myself among them without an identity."

Her smile widened slightly, then she said calmly: "Although you were granted the number seven, you are still young. I forgot that. Actually, it's not necessary for you to play with them. The break period exists for us to do what we truly desire. I, for example, use this time to draw what I find attractive to the eye. If playing doesn't suit you, you can simply look for something that suits you better."

It sounded easy when she told me, but when you yourself begin an endless adventure searching for a hobby, you realize the matter is harder than it seems. After hours of searching and experimenting, I realized I had been lying to myself; I never had enough courage to move beyond the observation stage. In the end, my path led me to the library. There I found quiet and solitude, found the perfect place for a quick nap, to rest myself and my nerves from the exhaustion of trying to integrate.

Her presence was quiet and shy, without any expression showing on her face. She stood behind me for a moment as if thinking of the ideal way to wake me without startling me, then approached step by step, gently extended her finger, lightly touched my cheek, whispering my name until I woke from my reverie. I slowly opened my eyes to see her standing behind me, quiet, shy, observing me with her eyes that never settled on one state. I don't know how she recognized me even though we hadn't spoken before, but I didn't feel anxious around her; her gaze was warm and calm despite the mystery of her presence. I tilted my head slightly and saw her face partially hiding behind me. It was Star Two. She said in her delicate voice, though it carried a firm tone: "Presence here is forbidden! Okay, not entirely forbidden, you can stay for a while, but you can't spend the whole break alone here. You have to play with them outside. Being alone isn't good;

calmness, if prolonged, becomes terrifying. Come on! I will accompany you there."

What a greedy star, did she want to seize this little paradise of isolation for herself? But because of her, I got a companion for the first time. Perhaps, together, I could find something to make me enjoy these long days.

"I haven't seen you before, are you new here?"

"That's right, this is my first day at the school. I received the number seven."

Her eyes widened slightly, as if the number sparked some memory in her, then she smiled and said enthusiastically: "Seven?! That's wonderful for a new star! It seems the Sun expects much from you." She paused for a moment, seeming to think before adding in a low voice, as if recounting an old story: "Do you know the story of the previous Star who carried the number seven? She was nicknamed the White Chrysanthemum. She led the Engineering Squad previously, and it's said the ship hanging outside is one of her masterpieces. No one helped her design it; she laid out its plans herself, worked on it alone, from beginning to end. It's even rumored she designed the Celestial Color Wall."

All this? I had never heard of such a great star before. I myself had never imagined being in a position to hear such stories. I whispered to myself, before uttering it in a barely audible voice: "I don't think I can become like her, with such greatness..."

Star Two didn't smile this time; instead, her voice took on a serious tone as she said: "The life of Stars is extremely long, and you are still in your early days. Countless nights await you, during which you might surpass that star, you might even leave a greater legacy than hers. It all depends on your determination, and on the strength of the flame of your passion."

Can I truly become like her, O Sun? To be something the Stars talk about one day? Then, I will exert all my effort to surpass your expectations!

(6)

The flagstones of the corridor end just as the conversation finishes. I look at her, and she offers me the reins of initiative. All I have to do now is finally pack my bags to leave. I close my fingers on the handle without moving it. Then her hand touches mine gently, holding it in place. I raise my eyes to hers, and an ancient, deep, and proud smile forms on her lips; it was the first and last time I saw her smile. She said nothing, but she didn't need to; that smile alone equaled for me thousands of encouraging phrases.

I pushed the door, and with it, I pushed my fears. I had found one of the two lost ones, and I would continue with her until

I found the other. Before the end of this evening, I would be a complete star.

As we crossed the threshold, the garden's bright light blinds our eyes for moments, and its noise drowns us so we can barely hear the calls of the other Stars. But they were there, close by. As soon as I regained my sight, I found myself surrounded by them, holding onto me as if I were a missing element that had finally returned. It was a large group. They carried me with them deep into the heart of the garden, while Star Two followed behind, silently, unnoticed by me, and with no one paying attention to her presence.

"Where were you?! We've been looking for you since morning!"

"We need one last player to join us. You'll play with us, right?"

I couldn't refuse, nor did I want to. Unlike all previous times, I was eager to participate. I followed them from one game to another, the smile never leaving my face, completely forgetting what had previously prevented me from delving into their relationships. It no longer required thought; I became part of them.

My eyes were closed; I had been chosen to search for the Stars hiding in the garden. A simple game. I finish counting, open my eyes while kneeling, but instead of finding them scattered and hidden, I see them all around me, gazing at me with bright smiles. "Come on!! It's hide-and-seek, not chase!" I said it laughing, before falling onto the grass, stretching my head towards the sky. It had been an unbelievably fun day, and now, after my strength had completely failed me, I wanted nothing more than a single moment to catch my breath. Then she appeared.

"Star Five. that's clear, right?"

I raised my head to her, and she continued steadily: "Actually, we grant one star, at the end of each day, the decision to choose the game we end with. And today we decided it's your turn! So, what do you want us to do?"

"A game I choose for everyone?"

"It doesn't have to be a game; it could be a competition."

I fell silent for a moment, then an idea sparked in my mind: "I want to see our school from a clearer angle. There's a hill not far from here, we could..."

"Adventure far away to the hill!" She interrupted me enthusiastically, before turning to the others and shouting: "I'm sure the Stars will like it. So, you got it!"

This seems perfect, but where is Star Two? I completely forgot about her as soon as I got immersed in playing. It didn't take long to find her. She was conspicuous, sitting alone atop the school gate wall, as if she had been there from the start, watching silently. I called her, waving my hand: "What are you doing up there, Star Two? I thought you were playing with us the whole time!"

She didn't turn her head immediately, merely staring at the horizon for a moment before replying in her usual monotonous voice: "I felt tired from the first game. Running, clinging, searching—all things my body rejects, as a reclusive library star, I mean. But I wasn't alone; I was sitting with Star Six and Thirteen. They explained entirely new ways of tying knots to me; this will help me later in reassembling worn-out volumes."

Then she looked at me, her eyes pulsing with something hidden, perhaps curiosity, perhaps boredom: "Is there anything new?"

"We want to go out together on an adventure to the hill. Do you want to accompany me?"

She didn't answer immediately. She jumped from the top of the wall to the ground with agility, without any preamble. After she landed, her gaze shifted towards me. No expression graced her face, as was always the case. Then, without another word, she began walking, leaving me behind this time.

"Alright! Star Five is a little busy, so I, Star Four, will lead this adventure. O Sun! We haven't been on an adventure in a long time." Her tone was full of vitality, as if this trip alone was enough to reignite the spark of adventure they had missed. "Are all Stars present and ready?"

Cheers of enthusiasm were the answer. We moved from the yard towards the hill together, the flame of excitement never leaving us the whole way. Star Four was amazing in her ability to create a cheerful atmosphere, making us forget the length of the distance. Even Star Six joined her in that, making the journey seem shorter than it was. When we finally arrived, we each dispersed towards our own destinations. I stood there, satiating my eyes with the view of the small school gleaming with marble and glass below. The scene looked magical under the glow of the sunset, where the golden color reflected on the grass, making it appear yellow, and the sky turned into a mixture of red and orange, as if we were in a living painting.

And so, my body decided to betray me, dropping me again onto the grass, leaving my head to the sky. I wanted a short nap, hoping to wake up alone before everyone returned, but that didn't happen. When I opened my eyes, calmness had filled the place. For a moment, I thought everyone had left without noticing my disappearance amidst the grass, so I stood up terrified, until I saw her. She was sitting there, under a tree. Darkness had fallen, and everyone had left, but she hadn't. She was alone, accompanied by her book, which she closed as soon as our eyes met. She was waiting for me, alone. This was the beginning of our story, and it will continue until the end of this tale, no matter what happens.

In the quiet room, where there was only the lamp's dim light casting shadows on the walls, we were lying beside each other, each lost in her thoughts. Star Two was slowly turning the pages of her book, while I stared at the ceiling, hearing the sound of my breathing harmonizing with the night's stillness. Then I suddenly broke the silence, in a hesitant voice: "Star Two, I was thinking on our way to the hill, how the method of immortalizing experiences and days by drawing them, as Star One does, is wonderful, and I want to do something similar, to immortalize this day I spent with you. But I don't think I'm good at drawing."

She fell silent for a moment, then answered quietly: "What do you think about writing?" I looked at her with surprise, so she continued: "A picture may be worth a thousand words, but describing something as your eyes see it, conveying it accompanied by your feelings, with a gap for the reader to see the story from their perspective and imagination—this is much more beautiful to me. And I will help you with that. Perhaps I haven't written before, but as a reader, I can correct what you write."

"Yes, I'll try to do that tomorrow. As for now, I will sleep for centuries; I feel tired."

She closed her book, placed it aside, then looked at me as I sank into a deep sleep. Finally, she smiled and lowered her head onto her own pillow. Thus, I wrote the end of this long day for us, a special day for her, as it was for me, a day I almost forgot, even though its effects are what made the Star Seven who speaks to you today. What irony.

(7)

We immediately set off for the next stage, bravely passing the crowd of watchful eyes together, and then descended into the crater the ship had left when it struck the earth. I followed her silently, but my eyes were fixed on the ground, carefully watching the darkness so that one of my feet wouldn't get trapped under a tree trunk buried deep below. Then, I saw the wreckage, and saw how the light of a candle on the white wood highlighted the traces of tears brilliantly, as if they were part of a hidden architectural art that only appears during disasters.

At the end of the path, I stopped for a moment and didn't find her. How did she not notice I had strayed from her? How did she not notice my absence, even though I had the lamp? I took a deep breath, then advanced alone. With every step forward, I saw the ship sinking into the dirt, fading into the darkness as if being slowly swallowed. The scene was strange; when you move at a relatively constant speed amidst similar surroundings, the mind starts to deceive you, making you feel you are stationary while the world is moving away from you. And at this specific time, the night crafted the scene perfectly for me. A strange feeling began to creep inside me, an unjustified fear, but real. This advance would only end when the ship completely vanished from my sight; then, I would have reached my destination.

(8)

The quietness brought my memory back ten pages, where something mentioned in the book had briefly stuck in my mind before disappearing due to the reader overpowering the writer. The title was: *Freedom Makes War.* If inhibitors have meanings, one must be peace. It isn't always linked to stability; rather, it can be synonymous with powerlessness and submission, as a quiet life is merely a restricted, routine life, granting you the illusion of contentment while you are, in reality, just a being adapting to a fluctuating reality, deceiving its mind to close the valve of truth upon its heart. Many see opportunity gleaming before them, but their fear prevents them from leaving their comfort zone. Governments understand this well and exploit it cleverly, by planting the fear of failure in souls until success seems unattainable, or by cementing the idea that any attempt to change the system is doomed to fail, even if the change is for the better. This isn't a lesson in economics, so let's take a closer example: the American Return Revolution. Everyone today believes that taking to the streets could mean their end; they might be imprisoned, punished, or hunted down. But can they crush everyone? No. If we unite together, this might make breaking the system possible. Breaking the system isn't impossible as you might imagine; on the contrary, it might be closer than we think. Let's bring back democracy, let's bring back freedom.

"I don't really share his opinion. In fact, what was said here is just to encourage the revolutionaries. Let me clarify something for you, Seven, with which we conclude our discussion about the Uprising book. When there are two main opponents in a game, both using the pawns available to them on the table, we can then say they are two armies, and it's an evenly matched war. But when you find yourself without any pieces on the board, then you have no choice but to try and gain control over the pieces discarded off the board, because they are the only ones who might share your goal. And if you can't even do that? You will play yourself. And then, just imagine how the white king alone will face the entire black."

She fell silent for a moment while I tried to absorb her words, but she continued in a low voice, as if stating the truth many refuses to hear: "He sees that revolution might solve his country's problems, and it might indeed be the right way to expel the deep-rooted corruption in the government. But it's also the fastest way to plunge the country into the mire, and this is what some are ignorant of. Revolution, simply put, directs a blow at the government by pressuring it, whether peacefully or aggressively. But the strike's fragments scatter randomly in three directions: Security by destabilizing it, the economy by weakening it, and the law by marginalizing it. How can any rational human being think the repercussions of revolution are easily fixed? When a tree burns randomly, it needs years to rebuild itself, unless the fire kills it completely."

"He wasn't successful in leading the revolution either; the whole thing was a deception. It seems humans really weren't that intelligent. Their randomness, their hastiness, and their chaotic way of doing things—all lead you to that assumption, don't they?"

She looked at me. I didn't know if she shared my conclusion or was just giving me space to think, before whispering with a faint smile: "And they are indeed." She laughed lightly, then added: "I won't spoil our adventure for you. Let's explore their story together."

"I'm sure it will be an extremely enjoyable adventure if this is its beginning..."

I said it while adjusting the lamp's position in my hand, but suddenly, I realized I was talking to the void. I stepped back slightly, my eyes searching for her in the darkness, but I found no trace of her. Where could she have gone, when the light is in my possession?

(9)

It seems she reached the destination before me. I saw her there, as soon as I approached, standing beside the black, shattered facade, covered in dirt. Next to her, another shadow stretched from inside; it must belong to Star Four, standing opposite her inside the ship. They were talking, but I couldn't hear what was being discussed between them, only their intertwined, incomprehensible voices sneaking towards me with every step. I can't believe she couldn't wait for me!

When I got closer, and the lamplight became prominent, Star Two raised her hand, gesturing for me to approach. She was continuing a conversation that had started before I arrived, then turned to Four and said: "Regarding this matter, Seven and I have come because we wish to get some answers about what happened tonight. Can you help us with that?"

Four lowered her head slightly, before sighing in frustration and muttering: "But you know my way! I don't like talking about past misfortunes. I believe repeating their events attracts more disasters, and the dead then rise to curse you until the day you die."

I didn't expect this response from her. But Star Two didn't seem surprised, replying with her usual calmness: "You know I don't believe in this type of superstition. And although I can always go along with you in it, I beg you, not today." Then she added, her voice more serious, heavier: "If Seven doesn't find a suitable justification to present by sunrise, I would prefer then for the dead to curse me over the living."

Four raised her eyebrow slightly, as if her words astonished her. She fell silent for moments, before whispering in a hesitant tone: "Their opinion and their word, does this matter truly concern you, Seven?"

"Yes. I don't want the Stars to look at me that way someday. I want to clarify the misunderstanding that occurred and get past the morning's ordeal. A disaster has happened, and its results are fixed. Whoever died, has died. What lessons remain for us; we must learn from them before tomorrow."

Her eyes fell into confusion, and she couldn't stop shifting them right and left. Sweat began to form on her forehead, revealing her overthinking, as if she were drowning in doubt. And this was somewhat funny; Star Four makes no effort to hide her feelings. She's like a cat moving its tail and ears with every slight change in mood, and the dilation of her pupils reveals everything. She didn't remain like this for long, until Two tilted her head with a faint smile that barely showed, and this alone was enough to make Four take a deep breath, raise her head again, then say in a wary tone, while gesturing with her hand towards the ship: "We can't talk standing out in the open. Let's sit inside, under the light."

(10)

Did she really invite us to sit inside? I thought it was a joke, but... if only she were joking. Star Four and Two jumped through the opening in the destroyed wall at her invitation, which compelled me to enter as well. Beneath our feet lay piles of crushed wood, shattered glass, charred parts of some equipment, and many dark stains that were once fresh blood. The place was drowned in ruin. She walked ahead of us, then suddenly, extended her hand and swept all the chaos that was on the table onto the ground, without the slightest concern. I couldn't hide a small tremor that appeared in my fingertips; that action wasn't merely clearing the table, but seemed like a desperate attempt to vent anger, or perhaps pain. No doubt the shards of glass and wood injured her hand, but I didn't have the courage to point it out. She was trying to hold herself together, presenting herself as if she were still strong, but she chose the worst possible way to do it. Afterwards, she began pulling two chairs from among the debris, dusting them off violently as she lifted them, filling the place with clouds of suffocating dust that made breathing harder, but she didn't care. She finally sat down *on* the table, wearing a strained, pained smile, hiding her arms behind her back, then gestured for us towards the seats, as if preparing for a bitter interrogation session.

"What part do you two want to talk about? Knowing the cause of the explosion, right?"

I hesitated slightly, before intervening to clarify what we really wanted: "Actually, the matter goes a little further than that... much further."

Here Two interjected, seeming precise and logical in her speech as usual: "The wolves smelled the food even though it was stored at the bottom of the ship, most likely because it was eaten up above during dinner. But there's something else; apparently, some of you were not sleeping at the time of the attack, specifically the three squad leaders, and perhaps you too, and of course Seven and I. Why did that happen? What were you doing?"

I found myself adding quickly as I watched her reaction: "Five was already in the corridors when things unfolded. As soon as she heard about the wolves, she likely rushed to protect the

Stars. So, who was behind the idea of detonating the fuel? Was it your idea or hers?"

She took a deep breath before starting to recount the details, as if pulling them from her heart with difficulty: "There was an urgent call from Five to hold a special meeting at night, prepared by Star One for the squad leaders only. Through it, she wanted to discuss the true situation of this planet and the chances of survival from it, without alarming the rest of the Stars, because of what the report *you yourself* presented this morning contained. When we gathered in the hall, Five told us she couldn't find you two, so One asked us to search for you inside the ship and in its vicinity, but at that exact moment, the wolves attacked us."

Two interrupted her, asking: "Were you inside then?"

"Yes, I never left the meeting hall; I stayed there with One and Three."

At that point, I found myself quickly asking a question to confirm what I understood: "So Five was only in the corridors because she was looking for us? She didn't leave the ship after the wolves entered?"

She sighed audibly, as if the question brought back a painful memory: "That's partially correct. Actually, Five was outside the ship with Thirteen, specifically near the ramp. She was the one who saw the wolves entering through this chamber where we are sitting now. She immediately rushed inside towards the sleeping quarters, but unfortunately, she only found the bodies of the Stars who were in the corridors. The wolves had surprised them unawares and didn't give them the slightest chance to escape. Luckily for us, she reached the sleeping quarters just in time and managed to save at least some of them."

A short silence fell before Two asked her next question, trying to maintain her usual calmness despite the tension that filled the place: "If that's all that really happened, then why did the explosion occur?"

Four's expression changed suddenly, as if she had received a direct insult. Her forehead contracted sharply, and she replied with anger she couldn't hide: "I can't believe how cold-hearted you are to say it like that! Those who died there were dear sisters to me, and companions of no lesser standing than any other star! And what do I expect from you? It's *you*, of course. I even doubt my anger will have any meaning to you."

She paused for moments, as if catching her breath which had become very short, before resuming her speech with some bitterness: "After securing the lives of the remaining Stars in the sleeping quarters, we had to get the wolves out by any means possible. After a quick discussion, we decided the best way was to cause an explosion that scares them and forces them out of the ship, while simultaneously opening an exit for them far from the sleeping quarters. This was my plan, and I decided to execute it using the fast-igniting red liquid we found this morning, by exploding the sides of the gear regulation room and the wall leading to the storage area, without damaging the external fin. It was a perfect plan when I devised it."

Here I interjected, in a tone I tried to make as gentle as possible: "It seems it really was a perfect plan, but it didn't go as you expected."

She shook her head slowly and confessed in a low voice, as if the memory pained her more than she showed: "The explosion did succeed, and drove out the wolves as planned, but perhaps the blast was stronger than I anticipated, as it reached what was above the gear room: the engine room. The flames continued to consume the floor rapidly, and within moments reached the fuel stored there. It in turn exploded with tremendous force, setting fire to everything and bringing down most of the ship's lower structure."

Four continued, but she seemed weaker this time: "That's why I realize part of the blame falls on me too. Forgetting about the fuel in the engine room wasn't a simple matter. I thought superficially and ignorantly, and that's unforgivable for the leader of the Engineering Squad."

She didn't really care about showing her remorse; it was clear from her way of speaking that she wasn't trying to apologize so much as trying to place the greater blame on us. She wants us to admit that our sudden and irresponsible departure from the ship is what caused this entire chain of events, which suddenly made me feel the weight of guilt upon my chest. Two intervened at that moment with strict seriousness, directing her words straight at me: "So, now that things are completely clear, can you let me bear this issue alone? I made the mistake, and as an older sister, it's my duty to bear responsibility for what happened before everyone."

I looked at her deeply and firmly, and found myself replying with a confidence previously unknown in my voice: "Our departure might be one reason for the catastrophe, but it wasn't the main reason. The wolves would have entered anyway, and perhaps another disaster would have happened even with our presence. Therefore, I will not leave you alone before their anger. I will stand by your side, and defend you and myself, and we will close this case together."

And here, Four smiled with obvious sarcasm, saying with some cruelty: "I don't want to discourage you, but we discussed the matter previously, and your friend knows very well what she has to do before sunrise."

(11)

Truly, I began to realize the real face of this adventure before its first day was over. Remember when I asked her if this journey would become a beautiful adventure? When the sun was setting, making a mind-intoxicating mix of the clouds in the sky, rosy, orange-eyed, alluring to illusions. Was I naive enough to listen to the whispers of the birds passing over my head telling me so? Back then, I was confident that this adventure might hold some hope or light for us, but today I know the answer clearly, and I can write it down here, on this page before the next: No, this journey is the beginning of a nightmare—likely a gentle one compared to others, but the Stars will never be able to adapt to the winds of its misery, however weak their force. Were we really this fragile, such that merely thinking about survival becomes difficult for us? If that were the case, then why did the Mother decide to send us on this journey in the first place? Perhaps death was lurking for us even before we arrived, whispering a harsh truth into our hearts. Or perhaps it crept into my soul ever since I put my pen to the first paper, and its ink began to bleed. No, it wasn't really the birds who suggested that question to me; it was death itself, or perhaps some demon who chose to mock us in its own way. And now you will ask me, laughing sarcastically: And did you think falling into the depths of Jupiter, for example, would have held a better experience for you?

My mind was completely scattered, and I could no longer determine the destination of this journey. Should I sail right, leaving the homeland for which my entire cargo sank, and for whose sake I lost my dearest companions? Or left, leaving my entire boat behind, setting off towards lands the sun was about to bid farewell as we lost hope of returning? I could also choose not to choose at all, thus remaining stuck behind the huge block of ice threatening to split my soul in two: the first cursing me for my forced choice, and the other cursing me for my cowardice and refusal to choose. This thought brought me back slightly, to an old question: Freedom or Homeland? The same two paths life granted them previously. But, after I lived that story and they explained its implications and effects well to me, I could now choose between them without hesitation.

(12)

Here, a testimony declaring my failure as a writer is inserted, because I simply don't know how to describe this specific scene. How can I put words to a scene my eyes couldn't even see in the first place? I wept bitterly below until I thought I had gone blind as I ran away, aimlessly, unconsciously, after none of Two's and Four's attempts to console me succeeded in easing my pain. I felt for a moment that my heart would shatter; only a second separated me from death. Even breathing became a heavy burden, and my hand was still clenched, trembling, feeling through it every pulse pumped outside my body, as if my soul were tearing itself away from me. And the pain resulting from all the collisions in my path was unbearable pain. It seemed to me that hiding the matter from me until the last moment was nothing but a stab in the back, a blatant betrayal. She knew very well I would strongly oppose her action, that I would never accept her choice, indeed I would fight anyone to change the verdict. Yet, she ignored me with a cold, unbearable cruelty. Who does she think she is to decide her fate while ignoring my existence? Does she truly think I am capable of continuing life in her absence?!

My breath caught suddenly; I felt suffocated as if life were leaking out from within me. I rolled on the ground, searching for air between my intermittent sobs. I sneezed and felt a taste in my mouth, perhaps it was blood, but I couldn't even see it amidst my tears. The pain wasn't just physical; it was something deeper, something gnawing at me from the inside without mercy. After moments that felt like eons, I slowly began to regain consciousness. The first thing I felt was the sound of footsteps; someone was passing beside me, ignoring me as if I were just a shadow cast upon the ground. At that moment, the disregard was harsher than the pain itself. I struck the ground with my fist, hard enough to feel something other than helplessness, until the physical pain completely vanished before the weight of the deep wound inside me. My screams meant nothing to anyone; no one turned to look at me.

But when I finally opened my eyes, my voice suddenly died down, leaving space for my turbulent breaths to settle. There, before me, a scene unfolded that made the whole world fall silent for a moment. The sky mingled with shades of gray and red, a sea of clouds began to form with the first threads of sunlight sneaking slowly from the horizon. And between them, the stars still twinkled, as if trying to cling to the last darkness of night, suspended in a void between death and rebirth. How could this journey carry all these contradictory meanings? How could I, in one moment, be on the verge of death, and then in the next, desire life so intensely? This question occupied my mind for a moment, before I closed my eyes again.

But they didn't stay closed for long. It was that instinctive sense of danger, like the one animal possess when they feel an unseen threat, that suddenly woke me. I sat up hastily, caring only about looking out onto the plain. And indeed, I saw them there, as if I had sensed their departure even before seeing them with my own eyes. I took two steps back, slowly, then took off running again. I no longer cared about the walls I collided with time after time, and perhaps I knocked down a star in my path without giving it a thought; there was no time to stop. I grabbed my bag from the sleeping quarters and rushed back to the destroyed lab again, as I still couldn't believe what my eyes had seen and wanted to make sure they had truly left. I had no time to waste returning via the usual path. I threw the bag directly from the gap onto the surface, pushed the table until it pressed against the glass-covered mud wall, and jumped across it without hesitation. I picked up my bag and took off running with all my might, head held high, my feet barely touching the ground from my momentum. I didn't allow myself to stop or slow down no matter the cost, until I reached them.

Is this the farewell? Will this be the last time I see the ship, my last encounter with the Stars? Must I forget everything we lived through, all the memories that brought us together, as I run now, away from everything? Must I be reborn as a writer star who knows only how to write stories for Star Two, the one who will read my words and mock them as she always used to, even if it means leaving everything else behind, content just to stay with her alone? Our days, our lessons, our ranks we carried proudly for so long—will they all truly be consigned to oblivion now?

(13)

I reached them with great difficulty after minutes. I was barely able to stand, but my arrival at that moment saved me a lot of argument. I knew very well what they would say, and I had prepared my answer in advance. So before either of them could open her mouth, I interrupted sharply, still catching my breath: "Were you two really thinking of leaving and abandoning me back there?! You've really lost your minds!"

Four addressed me first, her tone worried: "What are you doing here?! You have to go back; someone must lead the Engineering Squad, and you would be great at it, Seven. I trust your abilities!"

Two added in a quiet voice, which seemed to be trying to suppress sadness: "You can be the new White Chrysanthemum and create your first masterpieces to return them home. I want to depend on you for this. The Sun herself depends on you for this!"

But I didn't hesitate for a single moment in my answer. I looked directly at her with eyes full of determination and said firmly: "You know what? I prefer to die exploring this world with you, rather than trying to escape it. I thought about it for a long time: this world is too wondrous and doesn't deserve to be left by us easily. That's why I won't leave this place before I live at least one day with every story in it. Our fall here was a miracle that shouldn't be wasted!"

I paused to catch my breath again, then added as tears began to fill my eyes: "I want to stay with you. I am afraid of returning there. If I don't leave with you, I will have no future. But if I stay by your side, perhaps I'll live an exciting tale written and immortalized someday in a book exceeding three hundred pages!"

Two looked at me with a reproachful tone, saying: "But the Stars need you! Indeed, every individual who can help!"

I shook my head, rejecting her words insistently: "We could have changed this fate if you hadn't ignored me. I lost trust in you after you decided for me without my permission, so I won't grant you the right to choose whether I stay with you or not, and I will never forgive you for what you did!"

Four suddenly smiled sympathetically, then looked at Two and said with gentle firmness: "Didn't I tell you your plan would never succeed? She would have insisted on accompanying us from the start. As for you, Seven, you will never change your decision, right? Then let's go, a long day awaits the three of us!"

But we didn't move immediately. We sat for a little while where we were, as I felt for a moment that I was on the verge of death from exhaustion.

Chapter Three:
Featherless Birds Bring Down Dreams

But I know little about dreams; I had never even heard the word except from the world outside, from you.

(1)

That was the first time we had seen rain. It came with sudden violence, without prelude or warning. It seemed like one of the reasons humanity might have gone extinct, and moments later, I was certain of it, as its drops were followed by massive explosions in the sky, like celestial bombs cascading down relentlessly. Soon after, the world darkened. Dense clouds formed, obscuring the light of the Great One, and the rain-laden winds turned into raging waves that nearly tore us from our spots. Walking became impossible.

We had no choice but to take shelter beneath a large metal sheet we found along the way. Underneath it, we lit a small fire, hoping it might grant us some warmth amidst the madness. We sat there, waiting for the rain to subside, listening to the rhythm of the drops falling on the metal, and to Two's incessant stories, which were already becoming tedious. Thus, I found no escape but to try and drift away, even just a little, hoping to reclaim the peace that had been stolen from me earlier.

Two was speaking with enthusiasm, her eyes gleaming in the fire's reflections on the metal: "... And that's when Eight realized the Stars would have no way to survive except by arming themselves. It was the first time in history that Stars were recorded carrying solar weapons. Their goal was to protect the universe from the Black Light. More than two thousand stars set off aboard the Polar Ship, heading towards an unknown fate outside our galaxy, the Milky Way, in an attempt to save the world."

Four interjected, her voice contemplative: "And then Seven and those who remained with her at the school designed the Sky Angel Ship after contact was lost with the previous group. The Sun told us that story in the early days."

Silence fell for a few seconds before Two continued in a lower voice, as if afraid to admit it: "Seven and Fifteen were chosen to pave the way for the next generation—us. The Sun also chose them to prepare our ship, the greatest ship ever built. They said that those who came next deserved a masterpiece to distinguish them."

Then she sighed heavily, lowering her head: "I feel sorrow for our destroying it."

Our destroying it?! That phrase was enough to ignite a spark of anger within me. I could no longer remain silent. Provoked,

I cut short my moment of repose, broke my silence without fully emerging from my torpor, and burst out with clear indignation: "Come on! I don't think the fall was our fault at all! Three's piloting and Four's command observation are unparalleled. The previous Seven should have checked the ship properly before putting it into service, and taken it on at least one test run! The predicament we're in now, and all the disasters we've faced, are because of her stupid, broken ship. A masterpiece?"

Two gave me a stern look, then replied in a serious tone: "If you have issues with our predecessors, at least speak respectfully. And sit down!"

Four intervened, though her tone wasn't as sharp as usual, rather somewhat understanding: "It's not because she praised me, but I agree with Seven. If the ship had gone out on a prior test run, the malfunction would certainly have appeared. Crashing before even crossing a single galaxy shows it wasn't fit for sailing from the start. The first day ended with us trying to grasp our hopeless state, exploring our surroundings fruitlessly, and wading through troubles. We weren't given enough time to discuss the fall and its causes like we are now."

I raised my eyebrows sarcastically, glancing at Two out of the corner of my eye. *Someone* ran off in the evening to gather some stories, tirelessly doing her enthusiastic job of chronicling, and now *she* wants to sleep. I sat down heavily, betting that Two shared my feeling, but she didn't back down from her point. Instead, she continued, her gaze shifting between me and

Four: "You were both in the observation chamber when the incident occurred, and there was no malfunction in the indicators, as you claimed. So where could the fault possibly be, according to your expertise?"

Four sighed, crossing her arms: "It's not like we have extensive, practical experience in shipbuilding. Only the Wise Sun could state the cause with certainty. But if you want me to guess, the initial fault wasn't in the piloting equipment, or Three would have noticed immediately, and she wouldn't have been able to control it as she did during the fall. Nor was it in the sensors or the engine, because any malfunction there we would have seen instantly on the indicators. The ship's hull design is meticulous, and it launched perfectly, no doubt about that. So... there's really no room for guessing here."

I didn't like her answer, so I cut in sharply: "But it's impossible for it to fall without a malfunction! What if the sensors were frozen on a normal reading, while the ship was sinking without us realizing?"

Four's eyes widened for a moment, then she gave me a puzzled look: "How could it sink without us realizing? And frozen sensors?"

She suddenly fell silent. I saw her link her fingertips together and tap her index fingers on her knees while staring quietly at the ground. She was thinking, which meant she was starting to take my possibility seriously. Moments of anticipation passed. Suddenly, she raised her head, her eyes widening as she stared directly at me. She couldn't hide her expression, and I knew exactly what it meant: she had solved it. "The administrative gear chamber at the bottom of the ship! The flooding must have impeded it without us noticing, freezing parts of the main computer due to insufficient power reaching them. And who would care about something like that at the start of the journey if the readings were normal? Seven! You're a genius!"

But Two didn't share her enthusiasm. She raised an eyebrow, saying skeptically: "Shouldn't Three have realized it then, from the ship's sudden heaviness?"

Four waved her hand dismissively, as if rejecting the idea: "It was a small leak initially, barely noticeable in the handling. You know how the mind adapts to minor environmental changes? It's hard to notice something creeping up slowly, just like if you were in a room whose temperature was gradually rising — you wouldn't feel it until it exceeded your tolerance level."

I continued her train of thought enthusiastically, but she wasn't the only one connecting the dots. I finished for her, thinking aloud: "It started with a tiny leak from the bottom. The extra weight wasn't an issue at the start of the journey, but undoubtedly the leak widened over time. As we approached Earth's strong gravity field, we fell due to the sudden weight. Maybe Three tried to lift the ship, but she wasn't prepared to handle it without prior warning from the observation chamber."

But then I sighed with weariness, realizing this was all just pointless debate. True, the possibility was logical, but it was an assumption we could never confirm. The ship was now buried in the dirt, and what evidence remained was obliterated when we blew up the gear and engine rooms. Even if we knew the cause, what then? What's the use of discovering why we fell when we're already stuck here?! I felt the need to end this futile discussion, so I feigned interest in something else and suddenly asked, deliberately changing the subject with a question utterly devoid of significance, a meaningless question: "Two! I have a silly question. Where do animals hide in this weather, I wonder?"

(2)

I was wrong! That question opened a Pandora's box, turning the matter into a lecture so long that Four couldn't bear to listen anymore and got up to prepare something for breakfast. Meanwhile, I sat there, unable to even blink throughout Two's talk, because I knew if she stopped now, she would never answer another question from me, and I would lose the greatest encyclopedia of knowledge the universe had ever known. The weather outside was still stormy, and the cold continued to gnaw at my words slowly despite my proximity to the fire, making me truly wonder what the others were doing out there at this very moment. Despite all the positivity I tried to maintain, the negative thoughts relentlessly plagued me. Then Four finally broke her silence, saying: "May I interrupt your conversation for a moment?"

I looked at her eagerly. Finally, a chance to escape! "Of course!! Do you have any comments?! Two will definitely have an answer!!"

But she didn't have a comment, rather a question. She looked up at me, then at Two, and asked in a calm tone: "I was thinking, what will we do later, when the rain stops?"

Two answered after a moment of reflection: "When Seven and I went out at dawn today, we spotted several large structures north of the city, west of our current location. It's possible we might find some necessary equipment inside them that could help us repair the ship."

Four frowned slightly and said doubtfully: "So, you want to return there despite what happened…"

Two nodded confidently, as if she hadn't hesitated at all in her decision, before adding in a firm tone: "I am one of the Older Sisters, and I absolutely refuse to abandon them, no matter what I might have done. As leader of the Exploration Squad, I will fulfill my mandatory duty and find what we need to survive and return."

I sighed as I looked at her. Still thinking only of returning after they threw us out of there. Is that all that matters to her? Before I could open my mouth to object, Four spoke up: "Ha! How selfish of me! Absolutely… My apologies. I too, as leader of the Engineering Squad, will assist you in your mission. I will select what we need to complete the maintenance campaign, and we *will* return!"

I lifted my head and stared at them with displeasure: "All you think about is returning! I'm not going back until I get an exciting story."

Four laughed and patted my shoulder, saying: "I'm sure we'll find one for you. Ah! What a cute little sister you are!"

I immediately objected, waving my hand in mock anger: "I'm not *that* little, like insisting on buying a doll or else I'll cry on the pavement."

In truth, the conversation wasn't just about the ship, the adventure, and the animals; it was more like an indirect attempt to ease the tense atmosphere. I watched the rain pouring onto the metal sheets above us, the water gathering in small puddles reflecting the dancing glow of the fire. It seemed as though the black sky was stretching beyond its dimensions, swallowing the horizon endlessly, and its stillness overhead for hours made me feel as if we were trapped in a place not belonging to reality. In the end, I felt this moment was suitable for making my gentle offer, so I turned to them, smiling: "Why don't we rest a bit and sleep while we wait? Then we can continue our adventure in the evening. That way, we gain safety, and also energy."

(3)

Even after I woke up, the storm hadn't completely passed, but the rain had calmed noticeably, and the winds were less frantic, meaning we could now walk without worrying about being swept away by another gust. I looked around; Four wasn't there, as if she hadn't slept at all. She must have left as soon as the weather calmed down a bit. It was hard to tell the time amidst the thick clouds, but fortunately, a ray of sunlight pierced the veil of the sky for a moment. A short shadow revealed that the sun hadn't passed its midpoint by much, meaning we had long hours ahead to explore the vicinity.

I tried to get up enthusiastically, but immediately realized how steeped in aches I was. I didn't think I could ever stand long on these worthless, trembling feet. So, a little extra lying down wouldn't hurt, until I could regain control over my joints. For some reason, this didn't sit well with my lazy companion, who was barely opening her eyes beside me. She mumbled in an exhausted tone, eyes closed: "I don't know where you get this energy right after waking up. You're really annoying…"

I laughed and pulled the cover off her mercilessly: "Come on, lazybones! The rain has subsided, we need to continue our journey!"

She answered grumpily, covering her eyes with her arm, trying to avoid the faint, intruding light: "But I haven't slept in two days. I was so excited about the trip I had no idea it started at dawn."

"That's funny. I don't even know how The Mother finally convinced you to leave the library."

She sighed, turning onto her side to ignore me, then said in a low voice: "She didn't convince me; she simply used her authority over me."

Even I had considered staying when I first heard about the journey. But the mere idea of an adventure spanning multiple planets, where I could write a story and have a genuine experience, was enough for my excitement to overcome my hesitation. From there, I started pressing Two, persuading her, pursuing her in the library, presenting arguments, and tempting her with the idea of exploring the unknown. But she met me with cold refusal every time, insisting the journey would be boring and tiring, and that she preferred gaining lessons from books rather than undergoing experiences herself.

She interrupted my thoughts with her quiet voice, scanning me with her tired eyes: "You were whimpering just now, weren't you? Did something harm you? Or a chill?"

"It's nothing important. My feet are kind of tired, and my right-hand aches a little too."

She looked at me with a subtle smile that barely touched her impassive features, but I felt it. After her gaze lingered, she quietly turned her back, opened her bag, and rummaged inside for a bit as if looking for something specific. Then she pulled out a torn book, barely worthy of the name; its pages were worn out, and some were completely erased. But it was undoubtedly a treasure to her; she must have brought it with her from yesterday's adventure. She placed it on the ground in front of me and said in a gentle tone: "I haven't had a chance to read it yet, but I noticed the name of the hero of the uprising in it, so it might complete some part of the story. What do you say we read it together while your feet get better? And you forgive me?"

I looked at her suspiciously, certain she was trying to manipulate me, and gasped with exaggerated theatricality: "A trap! I expected this! I will never forgive you, never ever, absolutely not, not even for a bribe like this."

She shrugged nonchalantly, tilting her head slightly as she sighed with theatrical flair: "That's unfortunate. In that case, we'll continue our discussion about the lives of animals until Four returns!"

My eyes widened in horror, and the words tumbled out of my mouth before I could think: "I forgive you! I really forgive you!! Anything but talking about the life cycle of animals!"

She smiled, but this time it wasn't that usual, sarcastic, sideways smile. It was a wide, soft smile, as if she had finally allowed herself to feel for a moment. Then she laughed, a clear, genuine laugh I had never heard before. A laugh that rose until it drowned out the sound of the rain, filled the space around us. Then suddenly, it wavered, as if transforming into something more fragile, more pained, until her tears began to fall.

At first, I didn't understand; I couldn't even process the scene. I was still astonished to see Two in a state other than drowsy or enthusiastic. I had never thought she could move beyond those into a complex state like pain or regret.

She was crying for the first time, not loudly, but as if trying to stifle her sobs, as if everything inside her had suddenly collapsed without her being able to stop it. I cast a fleeting glance at the tattered book before us, then it vanished completely from my mind, as if it had never existed. I didn't think, didn't hesitate; I leaped towards her and hugged her tightly, without saying a word. I felt her cling to me, as if she needed that embrace more than anything else, as if she were trying to hold onto something to stop her from falling into a dark abyss. She continued to cry nonstop, while I just held her tightly, unwilling to let go, even though I still didn't understand everything going on inside her. Then amidst her cries, she began to repeat, whispering in a choked voice: "Believe me! I didn't mean for that to happen! I never imagined things would end up like this! I don't care about anyone but you! And I don't care about anything on this journey except staying by your side, finding stories with you! I would never have left without you! I don't even have the courage to do that! I'm afraid of a future without you in it! And my biggest nightmare was that you would one day stop visiting my library!"

I found no words to answer her, feeling a sharp pang of guilt for all the feelings I had harbored against her before. How had I forgotten all those days we spent together? How had I chosen to wound my own heart and drown it in pain, ignoring all that her presence beside me meant? How ungrateful I am, what a hateful star I am, undeserving of spending more days with her. But no, I would never leave her, I wouldn't let this rift grow between us. Even if she stabbed me in the back multiple times, I would ignore it, just as I know she would do the same if I ever wronged her.

Gradually, her breathing calmed, and her crying stopped. She finally released my shoulders but stayed close, her eyes red, her features tired and strained, marked by the tears that had streamed down her cheeks. She lifted her head slightly, and with a rare, warm smile that made me feel I deserved blame, she patted my head and began to play with my short, silver hair with her fingers. Then she said, her voice thick with tenderness: "I lied to Four. I just want to bring us back to our old days and leave this nightmare as soon as possible. I want to sit with you in the library, explain to you over and over why you shouldn't write novels without underlying ideas, read a dusty book with you just so we can learn a new word or two, then explain the lesson on elemental density that you didn't understand from the Sun for tomorrow's test. And finally, we sleep alone in the evening, while you write and I watch quietly from behind under the pretext of arranging books. Do you forgive me now?"

I lifted my head and looked directly at her, but I didn't answer her question immediately. Instead, I smiled slyly and said: "Not before we read that tattered book together. Then I will definitely and forever forgive you."

She paused for a moment, as if considering an appropriate response, then suddenly moved evasively, pulling herself back lightly, causing me to lose my balance and fall flat on my face. I let out an annoyed sigh, then turned my head towards her, only to find her long hair dangling above me as she smiled mischievously, looking down at me with a look of mock disdain, and said: "What a greedy star you are!"

Then, as if forgetting everything else, she adjusted her sitting position, picked up the book, and began flipping through its pages, while I remained lying on the ground, laughing quietly. Two was back to the way I knew her.

(4)

It's not just a headache that makes you sensitive to every sound around you. It's something that seeps deeper, like a constant tense feeling that never leaves you, as if your heart pumps adrenaline against your will, pushing you slowly towards madness. But it's not random madness; it's an evolved sensation, like sensing danger before it happens, only more harmful, more lethal. And when it intertwines with latent anger and a loss of control over one's nerves, it produces nothing but an unleashed beast in the eyes of some, and a legend in the eyes of others. This is what we're talking about here. This is what I will soon encounter.

"Air Squadron Shark-8-S! This is Top Sergeant, Lieutenant Brad. You will return to base immediately upon confirmation of target hits. Until then, you are not there to conduct any strikes. I repeat! You are not there to conduct any strikes outside your orders!"

His voice faded after that, while I sat beside him in complete silence, wondering when this madness will end. My thoughts were still scattering in every direction, but I didn't dare speak. Sitting before a man like Lieutenant Brad, rumored to be a cold, cruel beast, made conversation a risk whose consequences I cannot bear. The least that might happen to me later is being killed under his knees while he screams in my face. The irony was that, so far, he had shown me nothing but terrifying calm and wisdom, or perhaps it was just a mask hiding a brutality I hadn't yet seen. Minutes passed like this, then he gathered his papers from the table and walked out. I followed him.

"Are you sure you served in the army before?"

"Yes, Sir!"

"You have a strange record… It says you were one of the key elements in Operation Drown Earth."

"Yes, Sir! I was responsible, in a way, for smuggling the core of the nuclear bomb used, and safeguarding it. I worked with my group to achieve that goal."

"And sentenced to life imprisonment for military incitement against the government… Tell me, were you planning to detonate it in the White House or what?"

"No, Sir! I didn't know about it amidst those events until I was informed later."

He looked at me sarcastically – I was behind him – as if he'd suddenly lost interest. Then he returned to his usual silence until we reached the hill overlooking the enemy city. The sound of sirens tore through the sky, accompanied by the echo of screams, while warning shots were fired above us, demanding civilians move away from military installations to a safe distance of no less than half a mile. Suddenly, a voice cut through the radio—sharp, dry, carrying an air of readiness: "Shark-8-S to Sergeant Brad! Sir, radar has detected several enemy warplanes looming on the horizon. The crew is preparing for aerial combat. What are the orders? Over."

He grabbed the radio, and with clear tension beneath his steady voice, he replied: "Top Sergeant, Lieutenant Brad speaking. Your job requires only confirming the targets. The strike will be initiated at any moment. Avoid any engagement with enemy elements until you receive orders to withdraw. Over."

The sky rained fire, and the sound was like a force compelling you to cover your ears, but I couldn't. I was beside the Lieutenant, frozen amidst the inferno blazing before me. Tongues of fire surged up to touch the clouds, while daylight vanished completely, leaving behind red shadows, as if the sun had been replaced by the light of hell itself. The strikes didn't stop for minutes, and with each explosion, clouds of black smoke expanded anew on the horizon, swallowing everything. I couldn't imagine any survivors there, so why were the warning sirens even sounding? What was happening wasn't a battle; it was annihilation.

"Shark-8-S to Sergeant Brad. Confirmation received: all targets hit, either directly or within proximity, resulting in their complete destruction. Air force will commence turning and withdrawal maneuver now. Over."

So, the show was over, or so I thought. In reality, I didn't even know why I had been brought here in the first place; this place seemed more like an exile for soldiers than a prison where I'd spend the rest of my life. No, it wasn't over yet. A sudden explosion erupted in the middle of the city, lighting the sky again with a brighter red, pushing the clouds of smoke towards us. It was followed by another explosion, larger, and fiercer, forcing everyone to hit the ground and pray.

I was surprised when I learned that Shark-8-S was participating in this campaign, and perhaps some would disagree with me on that. Anyone hearing the name for the first time might think it's just an aerial reconnaissance support unit, but the truth is entirely different: Shark-8-S is nothing less than the backbone of the US Air Force, a squadron composed of 112 F-35 fighters, used only for special operations deep within enemy territory, under the command of one of the most reckless and insane officers in the government: Sergeant Scott. That's how I knew the attack wasn't random, and this wasn't just a conventional military operation. What's happening here is a major secret operation, surpassing anything we've known from previous wars.

"Lieutenant Brad speaking. What happened there?! Please confirm. Over."

"Shark-8-S to Sergeant Brad. There were no elements in the area at the time of the explosion, but we can now confirm a massive crater, and possibly a tunnel network, beneath the site of Residential Complex Five, which was completely destroyed. Over."

A huge secret weapons cache, whose existence no one could have imagined in this specific location. I never expected the Chinese would reach this level of audacity, hiding lethal weapons beneath a residential complex packed with innocents. I was now unable to determine which was worse: the army launching a sudden genocidal operation, or an enemy using civilians as human shields to hide its arsenal? Suddenly, Lieutenant Brad stood up hastily and started running away, but he stopped to turn towards me with extreme surprise, saying in a sharp tone: "We are in the heart of the enemy empire! We won't be able to hide anymore, especially after this catastrophic attack. The area will be completely wiped out in minutes, and if you don't want to die here, you must leave immediately!"

"By planes or artillery?"

"You'll die by both!"

We re-entered the hidden camp beneath the hill, and chaos reigned. All the soldiers were ready to flee; it was clear they were accustomed to operations like this. I alone was completely out of context. I'm not really a soldier, and I still don't know why I was brought to this death party. Before the unit moved out, a sharp voice came from Sergeant Brad's receiver:

"Sergeant Scott from Operations Command Room to Sergeant Brad. An urgent operation has been approved in the Chinese city of Shanghai, following detection of a severe disturbance in the communications network due to our previous strike. Leaked information so far confirms the presence of a sensitive enemy command center and extremely dangerous lethal weapons. Within the next few minutes, the Air Force will begin bombing the entire city, and immediately afterward, you and your unit will enter to reconnoiter the target site. Squadrons Shark-3-S and Shark-8-S will provide air cover for you for only two hours. After that, we will withdraw the cover. Understood?"

"Understood!"

Let's pause here a moment, while I explain some things to you, dear readers: There are fundamental problems with this plan. The enemy now knows exactly where we are, and if the site is truly important, they will muster all the force they have to secure it against us. The other problem, and the more dangerous one in my view, is that Sergeant Brad's unit is fundamentally small, equipped for reconnaissance and infiltration, not for direct combat or storming cities. Sending them there is nothing but a suicide mission from corrupt command. But I understand it now! Yes, I finally understand why I am here: Perhaps God intended for me to be executed alongside my comrades, the protectors of the homeland – these soldiers who chose death on the battlefields seeking a peace that will never come – instead of dying alone in a dark, narrow cell. What a great end, and what a high station.

(5)

The rain outside has stopped, the sky has begun to gradually regain its blue, and warmth returned to the earth with its rays. Peace be upon the green grass that endured the torment; it is now rewarded with flourishing verdure. But something worried Two throughout her reading: the absence of Four, who hadn't yet returned to the shelter. Yet, there was nothing we could do but wait; if we moved away, we'd fall into a spiral of searching for each other. We sat again around the fire, and I added two logs to keep it burning, then we returned to reading.

Everyone in the camp was re-packing for the final migration, waiting for the birds to carve us a path through the waves, destination: the heart of the destructive hurricane. And if you think hurricanes are man-made, then consider it a devastating flood basin, and don't tell me that again! Do you really think the weather is a game they control? You're surpassing madness now; rather, they are the soldiers of the Lord. Finally, I gathered my courage and called to him, somewhat hesitant: "Sir! Apologies for the disturbance, but you haven't told me yet, why am I here?"

He gave me a fleeting glance, then said, tying his belongings with annoyance: "I read your Uprising book. I actually liked it, unexpectedly. If I were a poor young man, I might have decided to mobilize because of you, and I'd probably have blown myself up at a police headquarters too."

I stared at him silently, before murmuring: "I still don't understand what my book has to do with my being here."

"You were supposed to be smuggled to the Chinese capital to lead a league of secret recruits. The government trusts that you believe in peace and seek good for our country. And because you are a hero in the hearts of many, this was your atonement. But you'll likely die with us before evening."

I sighed, before raising my head to say with bitter sarcasm: "Well, at least I'll fight alongside Sergeant Brad. I could never stand Sergeant Scott."

Sergeant Brad chuckled under his breath as he placed the bag on the table before him, then said: "You mentioned him in your book, didn't you? Called him a rabid pig. I remember that well. I showed him the book once, laughed hard then. He would have killed you instantly if he'd met you!"

A shiver ran down my spine imagining that. I prayed three times, and in each, thanked the Lord thrice for not meeting him. Honestly, I don't know if I'm lucky to be with this calm old man, or if I've just been postponed from one inevitable death to a slower one. Brad has changed, or perhaps this is his other face, the one untold in the stories. In the books, he was a feverish beast, leader of assault teams, a man who drank blood before sleep. But now, he's just a hoopoe bird, fluttering his eyes afar, watching the coming storm, as if he knows none of us will make it out.

Minutes passed slowly as I sat in the chapel—which was nothing but a burnt-out Chinese tank, someone had sarcastically drawn a Nazi flag and a cross on it, as if trying to summarize the irony of war in a single visual glance. But there was no time for contemplation, as urgent orders soon reached us from Sergeant Brad to hide and take cover far from the camp. Under the shade of the trees, I saw Chinese army planes flying in the sky. They weren't much interested in us, focusing instead on bombing any supplies that might reach us, launching heavy shells that shook the ground violently, their shrapnel reaping everything around. It seemed then that the camp's location atop the cliff wasn't a random choice, but a calculated strategic plan. The hill provided natural protection against the bombing and allowed us to shelter in its crevices, also giving us the upper hand if we were forced to flee.

And in the sky, a fierce battle raged while we hid. Shark-3-S squadron entered the fray like eager ghosts, their jets weaving between the swarms of Chinese aircraft that tried various ways to repel them. Then they executed a smooth flanking attack, lowering the noses of their planes at a sharp angle, flying like that for a mile before the decisive moment of firing. They opened fire on their opponents from above while regaining balance, then vanished amidst tongues of flame, only to emerge afterwards as they were, continuing their mission: clearing the path for us through the targeted city, as if the Chinese planes never existed for them.

Amidst this chaos, we began to move, leaving the camp, crossing the edges of craters that had become the new feature of the land. Wherever we advanced, repeated airstrikes targeted the surrounding buildings. It was said this was to secure our movement and prevent the enemy from advancing towards us, but it seemed to work against us more than protect us. Every explosion obscured vision, every collapsing building blocked our winding path. For a moment, I thought they were working for the Chinese; if we hadn't had armor and helmets, we'd be corpses amidst this destruction now.

On our way, landmarks told the story of the battle before our arrival: burning tanks, remnants of destroyed military vehicles, scattered pieces of unexploded rockets and shells, piles of empty bullet casings covering the streets like rusty autumn leaves. All this without any ground invasion of the city yet! And here I realized something terrifying: we were in a city the US army hadn't reached yet, a city supposedly still far from the direct front lines, yet it had been nearly wiped off the map. What annihilation! As we continued walking over soil where corpses had blended until they were mere shadows on the ground, I found myself thinking: How will I write this story? What title could describe what's happening here? And will I even stay alive to write it?

"Shark-8-S to Sergeant Brad. Informing you that the aircraft have departed the city's airspace within the last minute. Also, something important was observed, and command has requested we pass it to you now: Eastern Union forces are evacuating positions near the city and withdrawing their soldiers, instead of launching a counter-attack. Have they really lost hope? Sergeant Scott advises you take extreme caution when advancing. Over."

This was strange. No, *suspicious* is the right word. If the site we were heading to was this important to the Eastern Union, there were two possibilities, no third: First, they were about to self-destruct it as soon as we entered, which is expected from a government that doesn't mind sacrificing humans to keep its secrets. Second, they had completely lost hope and were trying to secure their important positions before falling into our grasp. But this possibility was impossible; the Eastern Union's power was still immense, and abandoning a strategic location this easily made no sense. We advanced with extreme caution, moving in a tight defensive formation, watching every shadow, every movement, anticipating the trap we might have already fallen into without realizing. Until we reached the main entrance: a deep pit plunging us towards the earth's heart, exceeding thirty meters in depth, with narrow tunnels extending into the darkness, equipped with a rapid transit rail, and dim lighting flickering intermittently, as if dying. Empty control screens, and sensors mounted on the metallic-cement walls, giving us the feeling that someone was watching us, even if no one was there. Then at the bottom, we found the surprise. Remnants of missiles, but not ordinary ones. They were Russian-made "Father of All Bombs" type, easily distinguishable as the largest non-nuclear bombs, designed to wipe out everything within a radius of kilometers upon detonation, specifically a tunnel network of this size. We immediately realized they were the cause of the huge explosions we saw earlier; nothing else could have created such destruction. This was all we found. No secret weapons, no advanced equipment, nothing but sealed tunnels and bomb remnants. There were no signs of a real strategic target here, nor any indication the Eastern Union used the site as an important military base. I felt then my heart sink in my chest. We had fallen into the trap.

(6)

To better understand what happened earlier, let's leave Chinese territory for a moment and relay the next event from inside the famous war submarine "Ohio W. N." or as known among navy men: Nightmare Without a Trace. Inside the command room, the observer's voice rose sharply as he announced: "Captain! We're tracking an unknown vessel bearing identifier Eater4, not registered in any of our previous documents. It's approaching at an angle of 140 degrees. No doubt it's Union-made!"

The captain didn't need to hear more. In a steady tone, he ordered: "Ordnance and Observation officers, proceed to your stations immediately and give me a report on our current status."

"Submarine depth forty meters, bottom at sixty-five meters. Deep water three kilometers away, estimated time to safety point is four minutes!"

"Good. Helmsman, turn left twenty degrees, and ascend gradually."

But only moments passed before the radar sounded again, this time laden with more anxiety: "Sir, the tracking device indicates the target is ten kilometers away, but the sonar is emitting an extremely loud noise. I suspect the actual distance is much closer!"

The captain's eyes narrowed; this wasn't normal. He turned towards the helm and issued another quick order: "Turn right two hundred forty degrees. I don't want any surprises."

Seconds passed, charged with tension, before the weapons officer called out: "Launch station ready, torpedoes fully loaded!"

"Open tubes, enter launch settings, and remain on standby."

But before any weapon could move, a sudden alert came from the radar: "Captain! Enemy torpedo approaching fast! Angle 120, distance one thousand meters!"

Eyes in the room darted nervously; there was no time to think. The captain shouted immediately: "Evade! Launch countermeasures! And launch torpedo three to intercept!"

But before execution was complete, a cry came from the observation station: "Captain! Enemy submarine... it's vanished!"

That wasn't possible; nothing disappears that quickly in the ocean depths. The captain growled, staring at the screens that had lost any sign of the mysterious target: "This isn't normal... Are all systems operational?"

"No, sir! Helm control is unresponsive!"

"Ordnance system too!"

Silence filled the room, then faint whispers arose, but everyone understood: The submarine had been completely hacked. This wasn't just an ordinary attack; control of the sub had been seized without a single shot fired. The captain breathed slowly, trying to maintain calm, before giving his final order in a firm voice: "Send an urgent message to Sergeant Scott and Secretary of Defense Kendrick. Explain the situation fully, then await instructions."

He looked around at the officers frozen in their places and murmured, barely audible: "Eater4. What a fitting name for a demon capable of swallowing us alive."

(7)

We stopped outside under the sun, catching our breath while the Sergeant tried to contact command. There wasn't the slightest sense of danger, just a heavy feeling of failure, as if defeat besieged us from all sides. I, specifically, felt it more than anyone else; I had been part of two consecutive traps, and now I didn't know what I would say in my career after all this?!

Lieutenant Brad still held the receiver, his tone unchanged as he spoke: "Lieutenant Brad to Command. We are at the location now. It is completely empty. Over."

He didn't move the receiver from his ear, just waited, angry, but in a calm, terrifying way. I tried to break that grim silence, speaking cautiously: "Sir, may I ask you something while we wait?"

"We're leaving soon, if that's your question."

"No, I'm not interested in returning, as you know my fate there is prison. But I want to ask about you, about your personality. You were never like this, so what changed you to this degree?"

He looked at me for a moment before answering, his tone different this time, as if part of his past had crept into his words: "Age is harsh, like a wind carving you as it pleases. Don't you wish now for the war to end so you can return to your wife and children? Whereas previously, I wanted nothing more than to see the entrails of my enemies."

Age? What an answer! Aren't your wife and children supposed to be the reason? I've heard often about this transformation, how having a companion you're bound to can take away some of your strength as a human, at least temporarily, forcing you to change your way of thinking, even your habits and beliefs. After a while, their unique influence appears, one of two effects, no third: either your heart ignites with a flame leading you to change, or the fire that burned in your mind for years is extinguished. Before I could process his words, a voice came over the radio, rough and cold, carrying an omen of ill-fortune:

"Sergeant Scott speaking. Sergeant Brad, it seems we've fallen into the enemy's net somehow. Within the last few minutes, the Eastern Union army exploited our focus on bombing the center and seized control of the nuclear submarine 'Ohio WN' using a sophisticated hacking system called Eater. The submarine is now located near the southwestern Malaysian coast. Be assured, whatever happens next, it is the beginning of the era of eternal chaos. Anyway, your mission is over. You will be evacuated from the area soon. Over."

A cold shiver ran through my body. What did I just hear?! Am I dreaming?! Damn it! This means war is no longer just a possibility; it's now inevitable.

Sergeant Brad turned his head towards me, his tone stern but carrying something else, something unexpected: "Officer Gordon, Special Missions Unit, what are you still doing here?"

I froze in place, not fully understanding his meaning, and stammered in reply: "Apologies, I don't understand, Sir! What do you mean?"

"The mission is over. Since you don't wish to return home with us, why don't you leave?"

My fingers trembled; I couldn't believe what I was hearing: "But... won't you stop me if I try to escape?"

He laughed a little, not sarcastic, more like a tacit admission that what was happening was no longer bearable: "Today's news was unfortunate enough that I closed my eyes for a minute, and didn't see you escape."

One minute! That's all he gave me, one minute to save my life. What generosity! I didn't waste a single moment. Instantly, I leaped forward and ran with all the speed I possessed, my feet almost collapsing, but it wasn't the time for pain. I closed my eyes, seeing only the sky before me without landmarks, one hand clenched on my chest as if praying, the other pushing me forward, as if escaping fate itself. I raced the wind until my heart pounded past endurance, until I lost feeling in everything except running. I don't know how much time passed, but when the minute ended, the bell rang, and bullets began to rain down from behind me. The firing didn't stop until the army helicopter appeared, at which point I hid among the rubble of houses, catching my breath and blood while listening to them search for me. But they found no trace, and luckily, the helicopter couldn't stay long and left quickly.

I survived that day. Finally, I was free, possessed my life anew, possessed my words anew, to write for you the facade of the final era in this book: the Era of Eternal Chaos. Two schemes, and the war began. This is the title of my story. And the coming world war won't be just a cold war like now, but a devastating fiery war, a nuclear ballistic war crushing the environment, a war for what remains of drinking water and clean air, a war that will define right and wrong for generations, a war that determines which humans will survive, a war for survival.

(8)

Ah! What pain! My back definitely arched from that long sitting session. I can't believe we wasted the entire day reading, and now, with the sunset, I can't even think about our next step, considering the danger of night and the storm. There's something else, something nagging at me, but it disappears instantly before I grasp it.

Star Two was stretching as she walked outside to get some air, yawning even though she had already slept hours ago. The long reading must have exhausted her. As for me, I preferred staying inside looking for something to eat, rummaging through bags hoping to find leftover food, until a sudden scream from Star Two cut through my thoughts. I turned quickly to find her fallen on the ground at the entrance. "Is something wrong?! What happened?!"

I didn't wait for her answer, rushing out to see for myself. And there sat Star Four outside, her hands stained with blood, and between them, a skinned rabbit. This must be the scene that made Two scream, and I couldn't blame her; even I felt a shiver run through my body. Four said calmly, continuing her work without looking up: "Apologies if I frightened you, Star Two. I wanted to prepare something special for dinner and kill some time. I assume you two finished reading, right?"

I couldn't stop myself from trembling slightly; the cold air intensified the harshness of the scene before me. I stared at her, astonished, then asked her with extreme annoyance while hugging my arms trying to warm them: "But it's cold! How long have you been sitting out here?"

She replied, shrugging nonchalantly: "I don't know exactly. I wandered the area for hours chasing this rabbit, and when I returned, you two were engrossed in reading, so I didn't want to interrupt. So, I sat here."

At that moment, Two regained her composure slightly, but still looked at the rabbit as if not fully comprehending the scene. She said in a low voice, as if still trying to push the idea from her mind: "You really didn't have to do that. Nothing can capture my attention and break my concentration."

I said laughing, trying to lighten the charged atmosphere: "I can confirm that information! When it comes to reading, she leaves the world entirely. You said you wandered the area for hours; did you find anything interesting?"

Four finally raised her head, glanced at me sideways, then smiled a small, mysterious smile before saying: "Isn't spending hours outside sufficient proof that I found something interesting? Or do you think I'm foolish enough to chase a rabbit for that long?"

She paused for a moment before continuing, her voice calmer and heavier: "Rather, we are now sitting in the special place the fog hid from us earlier."

(9)

Two and I took a few steps back, trying to see exactly what Four was talking about. And then, the truth emerged before us. We had been sitting the whole time under the structure of a fallen aircraft, embedded in the ground, greyish-green. Its shattered wing, parallel to the ground, had formed an open-sided pyramid inside which we had sheltered from the rain. I had greatly wronged it earlier by describing it merely as a large metal sheet. I stared at the aircraft for moments, trying to grasp its true size, then asked hesitantly: "Is this the plane described in the book? Shark-S?"

Two stepped forward slightly, examining the structure's details, then shook her head slowly before answering: "I don't think so. It's too huge; its size would make maneuvering difficult during evasions."

A few steps away, Four watched the scene silently, her eyes fixed on the aircraft as if seeing more than we did. After a moment, she whispered as if revealing a hidden secret: "Ever since I came out and saw it, I've been wondering if it could take us back home."

My eyes widened slightly; I stared at her, disbelieving what she was saying. With this junk? I looked again at the battered aircraft and scoffed at the idea, then said realistically: "But it's broken junk."

Two didn't turn to me but continued thinking aloud, as if trying to piece together the missing parts of a huge puzzle: "She probably means the engine."

Only then did it start to seem logical. Impulsively, I raised my head and said enthusiastically: "If the engine still works, it might help us fly up a bit, but we could never break through the atmosphere with it." I paused briefly, then added quickly: "There's something else described in the book, jet engines! Maybe a set of engines from those F-35s could do the trick."

Two didn't respond immediately, just kept staring at the aircraft as if thinking deeply. After moments, she let out a short sigh then replied in a calm tone: "But from what the book also mentioned, their purpose wasn't to penetrate the atmosphere. We need space rocket engines. We cannot risk the lives of the remaining Stars, or what's left of the ship's wrecked hull."

Four was quick to agree, shifting her gaze between us and the aircraft, as if trying to connect the possibilities.

From the inside, it wasn't just a large metal sheet; rather, it held hidden secrets and unique elements within its folds, giving it a value we hadn't expected. Apart from the scattered manuals and various devices contained in the passenger cabins, which included varied information from maps to technical manuscripts, something more interesting fell into our hands: an old disc player. It wasn't eye-catching at first, looking like any neglected piece of electronics amidst the rubble, until it landed specifically in my hands. Then, the memory of the morning's adventure flowed into my mind, and I remembered the discs I had kept in my bag. Among all those discs, one specifically caught my attention, made my eyes sparkle with a brilliance they hadn't experienced before. The idea of listening to its contents via the player was tempting to the point of madness.

I rushed blindly, ran at top speed without looking back, not even stopped by the sudden slip that threw me between the seats. The pain in my feet doubled, but I didn't care. I straightened up immediately and continued running towards the camp where I had left my bag. Barely two seconds passed before Star Two caught up with me, her features overflowing with concern about what had happened to me. Then Four followed moments later, both watching me silently as I frantically rummaged through the bag, scattering its contents without the slightest care, grabbing and throwing, turning over and tearing papers and damaged equipment, until I found it.

I held it high, like a revered treasure discovered after a long search. The setting sun's light reflected off its metallic surface, granting it an aura of sanctity. It was clearly the chosen one among all, the one I had kept carefully and diligently, while the rest of the discs were piled up carelessly. Two picked up the case, held it between her hands, stared at its title written in bold script on an adhesive strip surrounding it: International Escalation - Are We Approaching World War III? She couldn't hide her astonishment before finally uttering in a voice full of amazement: "My God! Is this what you rushed off for?!"

Then Four contemplated the title written on the case in her hands, raised an eyebrow with a slight smile before saying, in a tone revealing a mixture of realization and sarcasm: "I can definitely tell it's related to your previous story, just from the title. This must be the reason for your unjustified excitement, little one, right?"

I jumped up from my spot, clutching the discs as if they were a precious treasure I had finally found, and exclaimed with irrepressible enthusiasm: "I finally got the chance! Come on! Let's listen to it now without delay!"

Two couldn't hide her displeasure. She frowned and pointed to my bag filled with scattered belongings, before commenting sarcastically, crossing her arms: "As if it's going to escape from those foundling hands of yours?! And what are all these things you have?! Now I know the reason for your quick fatigue and aching feet."

I smiled slyly, ignoring her remark, before replying with provoking playfulness: "You won't hide your enthusiasm under that mask! I know you're eager to listen to it now too."

Two didn't comment, but I clearly saw how she blinked quickly, how her eyes gleamed for a fleeting moment, confirming to me that I had hit the mark exactly. As for Four, she contented herself with a calm smile as she put aside my discarded notes, then looked at me and spoke in a more practical tone: "I think inspecting the aircraft from the inside will require much more time than I expected to understand it properly. I'll prepare dinner now, so we can focus on work at night without any distractions. During this time, we can listen to those discs and continue your story."

Two let out a long sigh, as if expecting this decision, but didn't give up without another try. She turned to Four, saying in a half-grumbling, half-pleading tone: "Stop giving Seven everything she wants, you doting mother! We need to work hard to return soon to the ship before other disasters happen there, and inform them of what we found."

Four shook her head slowly, her smile never leaving her lips, then replied quietly, leaving no room for argument: "I'll prepare dinner anyway. It's your decision whether to sit or go back to work alone."

In the end, Two could only let out another sigh, more resigned this time, before sitting down, reconciled with her fate. I didn't waste a second. I stuck close to her, the fire, and the smell of food that began to fill the air, while I prepared the player and wiped the discs with extreme care, as if handling a precious artifact. With the first pulses of sound emitted from the device, the fire flared strongly, and as the echo amplified, I felt for a moment as if we were no longer here, but immersed within that tense session, as if attending it with our own eyes and ears, not just distant listeners.

(10)

Welcome to our evening newscast. I'm Matthew Blake, and I'll be covering today's top global events. Headlines dominated in bold red, with an unprecedented event shifting the geopolitical landscape: The United States directs a decisive nuclear strike against advanced strategic industries. In a complex military operation, Washington succeeded in preventing China from accessing prohibited technology in Taiwan, amidst concerns of limited fallout on the ground and urgent moves to ensure regional stability. We bring you the details. In a dangerous development, the US Department of Defense confirmed its success in executing a precise strategic strike targeting vital industrial facilities in Taiwan. These facilities, which were threatened with falling under Chinese forces' control following their invasion of Hsinchu city in recent days, prompted the United States to take decisive action to prevent the exploitation of sensitive technology. A senior Pentagon official stated that this operation was necessary to protect global technological superiority and prevent these resources from falling into the wrong hands. He added that the precise nuclear strike was carried out with extreme caution to limit collateral damage and ensure the safety of allies in the region. Despite the scale of the operation, the White House spokesperson confirmed that the greatest threat has been neutralized, stressing that China is now unable to access the technologies it sought to control.

"We have proven to the world today that the United States is prepared to make the toughest decisions to protect its national security."

But the strike's effects were not without domestic repercussions. Initial reports indicate widespread destruction in Hsinchu city, affecting civilian infrastructure, while radiation from the strike caused limited contamination in some areas. However, experts assert that the regional impacts will be temporary and that humanitarian operations have already begun to aid those affected and stabilize the situation. In contrast, some neighboring countries expressed concerns about potential environmental consequences, but the US State Department affirmed that measures to address these risks are underway to ensure containment of any negative effects. Regarding international responses, positions varied clearly. US allies in the region, led by the Republic of Korea, were quick to welcome the operation, considering it a decisive step to curb Chinese expansion, affirming that this action enhances stability in the Asia-Pacific region. On the other hand, the Chinese reaction was angry and sharp. Beijing strongly condemned the strike, describing it as an unjustified aggression and a blatant violation of international sovereignty. It also intensified its diplomatic rhetoric, warning of serious repercussions for the future of relations between the major powers. Amidst these escalating tensions, Washington continues to monitor the situation closely, prepared to take additional measures if necessary. However, the world remains witness to a pivotal historical moment, where the United States has once again demonstrated its readiness to do what is necessary to preserve its national security and that of the free world. Thank you for joining us. Follow us on the midnight newscast for more analysis and updates. Goodbye.

Welcome to this special discussion where we analyze one of the biggest events the world witnessed this week: the US nuclear strike targeting strategic facilities in Taiwan, and its repercussions on the international stage. Joining us today: Professor Jonathan Harris, expert in nuclear and environmental affairs, and retired Colonel Richard MacKenzie, prominent military analyst. Thank you both for joining us this evening. Let's begin with the question most pressing for the public: Professor Harris, how do you describe what happened today from an environmental and humanitarian perspective?

"Simply put, we are facing an unprecedented humanitarian and environmental catastrophe in the modern era. The nuclear strike destroyed a densely populated city and caused the release of radiation that will linger for decades. Millions of people are now exposed to the risk of death or chronic diseases and deformities, and there is a threat of a transboundary environmental disaster, especially with radiation leaking into the ocean, which could affect neighboring countries."

"With all due respect, Professor, focusing on environmental damage distracts from the real issue. This wasn't just a city; it was the center of the most dangerous technological threat that could shift the balance of power in China's favor. Decisive military action was necessary, and the losses, however grievous, are part of the price for protecting American superiority."

So, Colonel MacKenzie, you see this action as fully justified?

"Absolutely. The United States sent a clear message: there is no room for leniency with China or any party attempting to threaten our national security. Furthermore, there were Chinese forces in the city at the moment of the strike; therefore, they bear the consequence of their military intervention. If China doesn't want losses, it should think twice before making such hostile moves."

"But you ignore that this escalation could lead to an all-out world war! China will not let the killing of its soldiers and officers pass without response, and Russia, its closest ally, might see this as an opportunity to expand its military and economic influence. What happened isn't just a military strike, but a dangerous gamble with the world's future."

Professor Harris, what kind of response can we expect from China and Russia?

"The response could come in more ways than one: large-scale cyberattacks on American infrastructure, military strikes on US bases in the Pacific, or even the use of tactical nuclear weapons in strategic areas. More dangerously, the response won't just be direct; it could lead to igniting regional conflicts that draw the United States into multiple confrontations, draining it in the long run."

"China and Russia realize that nuclear escalation would not be in their interest. Any reckless move will be met with a stronger response, and the United States proved this week it is prepared to use maximum force to protect its interests. The message is clear: there is no room for compromise."

Colonel MacKenzie, don't you think the killing of important Chinese leaders and soldiers inside Taiwan might push Beijing towards a violent reaction?

"Undoubtedly, there will be a response, but I believe it will be limited and calculated. China does not possess the capability to confront the United States militarily directly. As for Russia, it knows that any confrontation with the West means mutual destruction. They will not risk an all-out war."

"That's a dangerous oversimplification of the situation. China and Russia don't need direct military confrontation. Instead, they might choose to drain the United States through proxy wars, isolate it economically, and foster new alliances that shift the global balance of power. This isn't just a military crisis, but a moment that could completely reshape the world order."

What about the international stance? How do other countries view this escalation?

"I believe most countries will feel terrified. Traditional allies like Japan and the Republic of Korea will rethink their reliance on American protection, while neutral countries will demand a swift diplomatic solution to prevent the crisis from worsening. As for America's rivals, they might see this as an opportunity to rebalance the world."

"On the contrary, allies will cling more tightly to the United States. This operation proved that America is capable of protecting its interests and those of its partners. The world needs strong leadership, and the United States showed today it is up to the responsibility."

We conclude with a question for you both: What is the next step you expect? Professor Harris?

"There must be urgent diplomatic action. If the major powers don't move to find political solutions, we will see more escalation and retaliatory strikes, which could lead to an uncontainable global catastrophe."

"The next step is clear: The United States must reinforce its superiority and prepare for any possible scenario. Diplomacy is an option, but it must come from a position of strength."

Thank you both, Professor Jonathan Harris and Colonel Richard MacKenzie, for this insightful discussion. It seems the world stands on a dangerous precipice, and it remains to be seen how events will unfold in the coming days. Thank you for watching, stay with us for more exclusive coverage.

12

...The company provides potable water at competitive prices starting from three dollars per liter, varying by quantity. Drop of Life, available now in __ [static] __ Ladies and gentlemen, we apologize for interrupting the current program, but we have just received urgent reports of a serious event that could change the course of the current global escalation. Following circulating leaks that appeared on unofficial Russian screens, we now have confirmed information from reliable sources in the US Department of Defense. According to these sources, a joint Chinese-Russian force managed to seize control of an American Ohio-class nuclear submarine while it was near the western Malaysian coast. The submarine, carrying top-tier strategic offensive capabilities, including long-range nuclear missiles, fell into the grip of Chinese-Russian forces after a complex naval encounter. Initial reports indicate the use of sophisticated electronic techniques to disable the submarine's systems and gain control during combat, forcing it to surface where it was detained by military vessels belonging to the Sino-Russian alliance. Meanwhile, the US National Security Council is meeting in an emergency session inside the White House. Our sources indicate the US President will deliver an address to the nation within the coming hours, where he is expected to announce Washington's official position on this unprecedented escalation. Initial reactions within Washington reflect a state of anger and shock. A high-ranking Pentagon official described the seizure of the submarine as an explicit declaration of war, asserting that the American response will be decisive and swift. We now go to our correspondent in front of the Pentagon. What details do you have?

"Yes, we are here in front the Department of Defense, where an atmosphere of unprecedented tension prevails. Currently, information remains scarce, but our sources inside the Pentagon confirm that the military leadership is considering all possible response options, including direct and unconventional military options. The main concern here relates not only to the nuclear capabilities the submarine carries but also to the presence of sensitive intelligence information aboard. If China and Russia succeed in breaching this data, this incident could become not just a direct military threat, but also an intelligence catastrophe, placing Washington in an extremely dangerous position. There are unconfirmed reports that the Pentagon has ordered Sixth Fleet units to move towards the Pacific Ocean, which could indicate preparations for an imminent military response!"

The world today stands before a pivotal moment that could reshape the international order. Will we witness an escalation leading to open confrontation between the superpowers? Or will diplomatic channels manage to contain this explosive tension? We will stay with you around the clock to cover any new developments. Stay with us.

Path of Goodness, we bring you this breaking news reflecting the strength of Sino-Russian will in confronting continuous American provocations. A few hours ago, joint Chinese-Russian forces succeeded in executing a precise and unprecedented naval operation, during which they managed to seize control of an advanced American nuclear submarine that was illegally present near the Malaysian coast. This submarine, carrying targeted nuclear missiles threatening Chinese national security, was disabled and brought under control using the latest artificial intelligence technologies, forcing it to surface, where it came under the complete control of the joint forces. This decisive military operation confirms beyond doubt China's and Russia's capability to counter any external threat or aggression. The American submarine, which represented a direct danger to regional stability, is now fully in our possession, with its crew and weapons transferred to secure locations to assess the situation and take appropriate measures. Mr. Li Wang, strategic relations expert, what message are China and Russia sending through this achievement?

"This operation is a strong and clear warning: American aggression will not go unanswered. China and Russia are capable of breaking American military arrogance, and whoever threatens our national security will face dire consequences. What happened today is the initial response to the blatant American aggression the world witnessed against Taiwan. The United States, which chose to use nuclear weapons to destroy an entire city, revealed its true face as a source of threat to global stability, and now, the time for response has come. Seizing the nuclear submarine represents a strategic opportunity to understand the weaknesses of American military technology and enhance deterrence against any future attack. Meanwhile, senior Chinese and Russian military leaders are meeting to determine the next steps."

The message is clear: the era of American hegemony is over. The world today witnesses the emergence of a new alliance capable of facing any threat, an alliance putting an end to decades of American arrogance. The United States, which chose to destroy Taiwan mercilessly, will face the consequences, and American crimes will not pass without response. Stay tuned for more exclusive coverage as soon as updates arrive. We are here to bring you the truth, without distortion, and without falsification. Stay with us.

(14)

Welcome back. We continue with you in this discussion about the escalating international developments, especially the expected Chinese response after the US nuclear strike on Taiwan, and the seizure of an American nuclear submarine by joint Chinese-Russian forces. Professor Harris, let's start with you. What do you expect now from China? Will the response be diplomatic or military?

"I don't think there's room for diplomacy anymore. The nuclear strike on Taiwan was a direct insult to China, especially after the killing of prominent military leaders there. If we add the submarine incident, we find that China and Russia now feel strong and confident. The coming response will be military, but it won't be conventional. We might witness comprehensive cyberattacks, or precision strikes on American bases in the Pacific."

"Let me clarify something. Any direct military response from China or Russia would be tantamount to suicide. The United States is prepared, and we have the necessary military and technological superiority to contain any threat. The submarine? An unfortunate incident, yes, but we know how to regain control."

"You underestimate China and Russia, and that's a grave strategic error! Their seizure of the nuclear submarine is more than just an incident; it's a show of force and a clear message to the world that the United States is no longer in a position of absolute control."

"With all due respect, Professor, messages don't change facts, and the facts say Washington is still capable of crushing any direct threat. China might try escalation, but it will quickly realize this path is not in its favor."

Ladies and gentlemen, I see we have an extremely urgent development. Both Iran and Japan have just announced in an official joint statement their joining the Sino-Russian alliance against the United States. Iran confirmed it will provide comprehensive military and logistical support, while Japan dropped a bombshell by siding with China, citing its disappointment with American policy in Asia. At the same time, reports confirm Washington has begun forming an international military coalition including European nations, other Asian allies, and some Arab states, in an attempt to counter the new alliance. It seems we are witnessing the first moments of a Third World War. What are your thoughts on this? Colonel MacKenzie?

"This is clear betrayal by Japan, and a strategic shock! But it won't change reality. The United States, with its allies in Europe, Asia, and the Arab world, remains the number one superpower. We have the military, technological, and economic superiority necessary to crush any rival coalition. This escalation is dangerous, yes, but it doesn't mean China, Russia, and their allies can win this confrontation."

"This announcement means we have passed the point of no return. Alliances are forming rapidly, and the coming confrontation won't be just military, but also economic, political, and environmental. But what frightens me more is that this escalation will inevitably lead to wider use of nuclear weapons. Each side is now mustering its strength, and the victims will be in the millions."

"Professor, enough with this catastrophic tone! We are in a position of strength, and the new coalition lacks the resources and sufficient military capability to confront our alliance."

"Strength alone isn't the solution, Colonel MacKenzie. We are heading towards humanity's total destruction. This is not the time for military displays, but time to think about the future of the entire planet."

Dear viewers, apologies again for the interruption, but we have a second extremely serious development. Minutes ago, at the exact moment the previous statement was issued, Sino-Russian alliance forces launched an extremely intense strike on the US naval base in Guam, one of the largest and most important American military bases in the Pacific. Initial sources confirm partial destruction occurred, and numerous strategic facilities were hit, including air defense systems, logistical facilities, and command rooms. Meanwhile, China issued an official statement, which read: 'This operation is a direct response to American provocations in Shanghai. Any future American strike on Sino-Russian alliance territories will be met with even greater force. We are prepared to wage nuclear war if the United States desires it, but we refuse to be the direct cause of the planet's destruction.' And the final sentence was surprising: 'Although we possess the American nuclear submarine, we chose not to use it against the United States, because we fear for the safety of humanity.' Let's now return to our esteemed guests for their opinions on this unprecedented escalation. Professor Harris, how do you view this move by China and its message indicating refusal to use the nuclear submarine despite having the capability?

"I see that China, despite everything that has happened, is acting rationally amidst this crisis. The strike on Guam is a major escalation, yes, but it's a natural response to clear American provocation and intervention. As for their refusal to use the nuclear submarine, this shows they recognize the dangers of entering an all-out nuclear war. This is a clear message: China wants to send a strong warning, but it doesn't seek to destroy humanity, according to their claim."

"Rationality?! A clear message?! Do you hear yourself?! They destroyed an American base! This isn't a defensive act; it's another explicit declaration of war! And how dare you describe China as rational? These are the same people who detained our submarine and its crew, and threatened nuclear war!"

"And what about the American nuclear strike on Taiwan?! How do you justify this brutal act? China didn't nuke Taiwan, nor did it do what the United States did! They are only responding to unprovoked aggression!"

"This is nonsense! You speak as if defending them! The United States did what it had to do to protect its national security. China is the one who ignited the crisis with its political moves in Taiwan and its pursuit of controlling technology there."

"And you defend the killing of millions of innocent civilians for no reason! Nuclear war is not a solution, and every escalatory step takes us closer to total destruction! China, at least, shows restraint in some aspects!"

"Restraint?! Are you blind or a Chinese agent?! This talk is treasonous! You defend those who killed our soldiers and destroyed our base!"

"And you, with your narrow military mentality, are pushing the world towards the abyss! Do you think responding in kind is the solution? The world needs dialogue, not continuous escalation!"

"You understand nothing about reality! This world isn't run by idealistic speeches, but by power! And with this talk, you betray your country!"

"And you betray humanity and the entire planet!"

Ladies and gentlemen, please, let's maintain our composure...

"I am trying to preserve my country, indeed save it from the madness led by mentalities like yours!"

"You are a disgrace to this studio, and to all of America!"

That's enough! Dear viewers, we apologize for this unprofessional scene. We will return shortly to follow more developments.

(15)

Welcome back to our ongoing special coverage of this escalating global crisis. Developments continue to unfold, and the international scene grows more complex. To discuss potential scenarios, joining us now is political analyst Dr. Jonathan Collins, expert in international relations and geopolitics. Dr. Collins, thank you for being with us. Let's begin directly: After the intense Chinese strike on the American base in Guam, and the message from Chinese leaders affirming their readiness for nuclear war while simultaneously avoiding excessive escalation, how do you see the shape of the upcoming American response?

"Thank you for having me. This is a difficult time for all of us to understand the major repercussions of what is happening. The American response will not be simple. Guam isn't just a military base; it's a vital part of the United States' ability to conduct its military operations in the Pacific. Washington will certainly respond, but how it responds depends on several factors: Will there be direct military strikes on Chinese facilities? Or will the United States try to use economic and diplomatic pressure to expand the isolation of the Sino-Russian Union? Considering the current administration, I believe the response will be multi-faceted and strongly worded. We might see a rapid movement of additional forces to the conflict zone, imposition of broad economic sanctions, and perhaps greater support for Taiwan and supporting forces as a clear message."

But can Washington risk a direct military response against China, especially after its threat of readiness for nuclear war?

"This is a sensitive point. The United States realizes China is not a country that can be easily weakened. Direct military response means the possibility of unprecedented escalation that could end in nuclear catastrophe. For this reason, I believe Washington might initially focus on building a strong international coalition that puts China under multilateral pressure."

Speaking of alliances, China now surprisingly has support from Russia, Iran, and Japan. On the other hand, the United States is working to rally Europe, some Asian and Arab countries, and currently relies on Korea, NATO, the Gulf states, and its forces operating in East China. How do these alliances affect the world order, in your opinion?

"These alliances reshape the world order in a way we haven't witnessed since World War II. The Sino-Russian alliance is militarily and economically strong, and the presence of Iran and Japan adds strategic weight. In contrast, the coalition being built by the United States primarily relies on the economic and diplomatic power of NATO and EU countries, in addition to support from the Middle East and some Asian nations that still view China as a threat."

How will this affect the world, especially countries not involved in this conflict?

"Neutral countries will face immense pressure. The major powers will use all available means to recruit support from as many countries as possible. Small and developing nations might be forced to take a stance, either through economic incentives or military threats. But the most prominent impact will be economic. The world will witness tremendous economic turmoil due to mutual sanctions and disruption of global supply chains. Uninvolved countries will be significantly affected by rising energy and food prices, and might find themselves in internal political crises as a result of external economic pressures."

Considering the current escalation, do you believe we are truly on the cusp of a Third World War?

"Unfortunately, all indicators suggest we are at the beginning of what could be a world war. Military escalations, fiery threats, reshaping of international alliances—all are elements present before the previous two world wars. But what distinguishes this conflict is the presence of modern technology, like cyber warfare and drones, which could make the conflict less conventional and more complex. However, if any party slips into using nuclear weapons, there will be no return."

And is there a way out of this escalation?

"The only way out is to return to the negotiation table. Both sides need strong international mediators capable of talking to all parties. The United Nations, despite its current weakness, could play a role here, alongside countries like India and Brazil which might be acceptable as mediators. But amidst the inflamed nationalistic feelings on all sides, achieving this might be very difficult. The world must realize we are facing a defining moment in human history, and escalation will only lead to an unprecedented catastrophe. Leaders must exercise wisdom and humanity, or everyone will pay the price."

Is this the final distress call to save humanity? Is our fate now hanging on the decision of several madmen who managed to reach power with our support and despite our opposition? Rather, what everyone must constantly ask, the question that must receive the greatest concern from now on, is: Will we actually survive?

(16)

That was the last disc in the long package, and when its words ended, it cast a lengthy thread stretching meters forward, seen by no one but me. Its beginning was arrogant, swollen with pride and charged with foolishness. The United States reigned with the illusion of absolute superiority, standing atop a world it tried to shape according to its iron will, preventing any other party from achieving power or influence. The decision to strike Taiwan with a nuclear bomb wasn't just a military step, but a terrible declaration carrying a clear message in its essence: *We will not allow anyone to surpass us.* Pride was fuel for madness, a moment they imagined everything could be settled with a single explosion. With all pride comes recklessness, and there was no time to think about consequences. Cries of warning were lost in the political noise and strategic interests, and fears drowned in the intoxication of the euphoria of control: Striking Taiwan wasn't just an attack on a city, but an attack on an idea, on a connected world, on a shared human mind.

What began as a preemptive act ignited the flames of conflict, and its tongues continued to spread until the final curtain fell, revealing the background clearly: China and Russia, then Japan and Iran, gathered in a vortex of overwhelming rage. The strike on the Guam base wasn't just a military response, but the cry of a deep wound, a cry of war, uttered by leaders with aggressive, grim faces. Anger was additional fuel in the blazing fire, widening its path, drawing the lines of alliances, uniting old enemies in shared hatred.

Then came fear, and after it regret, and then silence. Silence came late, but it was closer than anyone imagined, as only ashes finally remained. In deserted meeting rooms, where political debates once raged over decisions and fates, only terrified whispers remained, echoing the final question: How did we get here? Regret was bitter, but it saved no one from the inevitable end.

The world they knew had ended, and ruin became a permanent color under a sky that witnessed only its final agony. And perhaps we, who coincidentally remained to witness such unique stories, were just faint shadows of endings that should not have happened.

But the thread didn't end; rather, it extended additional meters beyond the metal sheet, invisible to those not searching for it.

Its first of three pieces carried the symbol of struggle, for life refused to be extinguished easily. Deep in the rubble, in the forgotten corners of the world, the first sparks pulsed with resistance: green algae clinging to black stones, insects settling in the ruins, new water flowing over the devastation. Nature was resisting as it always had. As for the middle piece, there was healing. A hundred years passed, and the planet began to mend slowly, but it was definitely mending. New trees rose from the heart of the dead earth, small animals that resisted radiation appeared and returned to roam silent expanses, and the oceans, once empty even of waves, teemed with life again. Healing was slow, but it wasn't an option; it was law. Earth didn't need humans to continue. Yet, this wasn't the final victory for nature as it might seem. Poisonous dust carried by the wind reached the newborn buds, and soon another law, harsher than extinction itself, was revealed: everything born here, until it adapts to the scene, will not live more than four days.

Then came the final part, the part I couldn't look at without my eyes tearing up until they reddened: oblivion. All the wars, pride, anger, perhaps love in a lost phase of memory—all dissolved into time. Nothing remained of them but buried dust and non-decaying scrap, just like the metal sheet that protects us. What remained before us wasn't a shattered world, but a world that no longer held any memory of humans, just a blank page waiting for a new story to be written on it. Perhaps our story.

Two snatched the disc player from the ground in front of me. She stood up, her lips tightly drawn horizontally without any other features allowing me to understand what she was trying to do. Perhaps she was angry. I was sure of it when she slammed the player onto the ground with all her might, along with the pack of discs, then kicked them far away with her foot. Her breath hitched, she rushed forward, then returned and sat beside me. I didn't feel sad at all, nor did I pay any attention to those discs. The message they contained was nothing but a catastrophic tale that must be erased, not remembered and repeated with every new creature that comes here. This useless past is just additional torment for your heart. She said to me, staring at the shattered discs with eyes burning with anger: "Don't cry over them! Whoever sets his house ablaze with his own hands, then stands afar watching it burn, smiling boastfully, doesn't deserve prayers recited for him. War isn't a sudden event nor a departure from human nature; rather, it's the direct result of an accumulation of wrong choices over long centuries. Humans, in their constant pursuit of hegemony and control, created imbalanced political and economic systems that fed and sustained conflicts. History proves, and recordings testify, that major wars aren't just fleeting mistakes, but mechanisms for reshaping powers that had already reached the breaking point."

I interrupted her, feeling some anger stir within me: "You're holding humans fully responsible for what happened, and that's not fair at all!"

She looked directly at me with a stern gaze, as if I had wronged a clear truth beyond debate, then said with unnatural calmness: "And why shouldn't I hold them fully responsible? Not only because they irresponsibly developed their technical and military capabilities to unprecedented levels, but because they always lacked the collective will to prevent disaster. They let national selfishness control their decisions and define their narrow interests, ignored the clear lessons of history that punished them on every page for what they did. Everyone failed to think long-term and about the major consequences, whether political leaders, military figures, academics and researchers, or even ordinary citizens."

She fell silent for a moment and caught her breath, as if gathering her thoughts or perhaps her emotions, then continued in a slightly quieter voice, but still sharp as a blade: "At some stage, they could have begun gradual comprehensive disarmament of all nations, under strict supervision by a supreme peaceful institution. They could have built a balanced world order preventing unilateral decisions leading to wars. They could have directed the global economy towards infrastructure, education, and environmental preservation instead of military spending. They could have promoted moral and philosophical education, absorbed history as a means to avoid mistakes, and enacted firm penalties against any violations. But if we look closely at human history, we realize these changes were nearly impossible, not because of the complexity of solutions, but because of deep-seated human resistance to change. Leaders won't give up their power, nations won't relinquish their sovereignty. And herein lies the true human tragedy: humans possessed the ability to see their fate clearly, but were utterly incapable of changing it."

We fell silent after her words for moments, while our eyes remained fixed on the discs scattered broken on the ground before us, like remnants of a bygone world, a world from which nothing remained but bitter memories and the trace of irreversible wrong human choices. I stretched out my legs and pushed my body forward until I was lying on the ground. I had no answer to give her, bewildered in choosing decisive words to refute her appalling argument, until Four spoke suddenly: "You say this now, pointlessly, after everything has ended. No one is left outside to comprehend your words, and they wouldn't hear you even if hearing sound were possible. Those who built the towering buildings, turned deserts into green gardens, ultimately chose to crush themselves under the weight of their pride. It wasn't nuclear bombs that killed them, but the arrogance, selfishness, and fear that nested in all their hearts. And now, green will cover their cities, and the earth will not mourn their absence. They could never realize how generous it was with them."

She fell silent, accompanied by a tear she tried to hide. After moments, she returned to muttering in a faint, trembling voice: "If only you had given mercy a chance... if only you had paused a little... perhaps, perhaps..."

Then she broke down crying before finishing. I hated humans so much that if I had been there then, I would have wished for the war to continue until they went extinct as actually happened, and wouldn't have stopped it as Two wanted. I saw now, and understood clearly, how the extinction of humanity was the optimal choice to solve all their problems. Two's firm words cut through the sound of crying when she said in a dry tone: "Have you two rested? We need to get back to work before the day ends."

I answered her in an annoyed, grumbling voice: "What a hasty, persistent nag you are! What good will rushing do you?!"

But she completely ignored my words, just stood up slowly and steadily, then stared at me with strange calmness. Her face was devoid of any features as usual, and to be honest, her calmness at that moment became truly frightening. She conveyed to me with her gaze a terrifying message that seeped deep into all parts of my heart, until I almost felt she would pounce on me, killing me, if I didn't stand up now willingly to follow her. How pitiful I am, she directs me however she wishes with a single glance.

(18)

I never thought inspecting the doomed aircraft from the inside would require all the effort we expended without realizing it. We sank deep into it, accompanied by a silent desire to avoid conversation, and it continued for long hours of hard work, lasting even until sunrise. The advanced technology we found in our hands at that moment was greater than Two and Four, or even I, imagined finding, but this didn't simplify the work;

rather, it complicated it further. When you research something completely removed from your scientific background, you quickly reach a futile conclusion: studying it is pointless. And so, we stopped. We had to find a simpler clue to understand the construction method of that massive metal engine, which looked more like a cube of internal chambers alternately opening and closing, full of delicate, sensitive gears. All this, for a single desire we placed amidst those lost hours: trying to improve and develop the engine to be capable of penetrating Earth's atmosphere and saving what remained of the ship. But without an engine, insisting on surviving here forever is more absurd than trying to understand this thing itself.

I was the last to leave the warm inner chamber, dripping with sweat, after a final moment contemplating the immensity of the central core, and the ingenious connection method between the front parts and those under the wings. There was an amazing coordination between the elements, working with superior integration without needing a separate large body. Every space was utilized to achieve a perfect form that didn't interfere with the aircraft's mechanism but enhanced it. Unlike our ship, the aircraft didn't keep elements separate in independent chambers but integrated them in an interconnected loop, like a single connected piece inside a monolithic chamber of random shape. I named it the central core, as mentioned at the beginning. It's controlled from a single cockpit, directly connected to the main computer, which is actually the mind responsible for checking and controlling everything.

In the end, I left, compelled. And as I was leaving, it seemed as if wires floated around me, trying to pull me to stay, as if I might get stuck there forever. If I had the choice, perhaps I would have. I would have enjoyed spending years drawing diagrams for this engineering marvel, instead of burning the entire experience searching for a ridiculous clue. My philosophy sees the writer, who invents words to describe a complex scene like a ship falling from space, as a great engineer capable of building an aircraft from nothing.

I jumped down onto the grassy ground, forcing the wires to leave my world, only to find a hand extending towards me, real this time, bringing me back to my world. It was Four's hand, her gaze burning with the same passion I had possessed moments ago, as if she saw something in my eyes she had already realized: "How wondrous it was inside. Did you love it?"

Then she continued, her voice dreamy: "I am eager to build one with you, and fly it far away, high, in the sky, among the stars."

But the aircraft was more like a nightmare to me, its weight surpassing mere description as wondrous. I don't deny it's a true engineering marvel, and how I wished to stay beside it. But in the end, it's nothing but a rusty metal sheet that won't get us off this planet, and I don't even know if we are capable of developing it to achieve that impossible dream. The problem isn't our ability to modify, but the limits of the vehicle itself. It's a single idea that crossed my mind since we first saw it and Four spoke of leaving: If its makers, humans, left it here to be buried in despair, then invented space rockets to travel off-planet, why should we waste our time trying to develop it, instead of starting to build a space rocket from scratch?

We left the metal tomb as the sun rose. And what we left behind, that entity which surpassed the mere symbolism of an inhabited home, wasn't a banner raised calling for freedom with every tour, but a featherless bird, whose function was confined to bringing dreams down to earth, without any regard for their owners. It was a killing machine made to participate in the catastrophe that led to human extinction. We delved deeper into the tale than necessary, forgetting to ask ourselves the most important question: Were humans even able to travel off-planet in the first place? We still don't have an answer. Consequently, asserting whether relying on their technology is a sound idea or not remains purely a mystery that swallows time, leading us towards more unanswerable questions.

Chapter Four:
A Flame Whose Color Marks the Sail of Tragedy

And never mind the title. In reality, there is no tragedy greater than what has become of people's lost humanity today.

(1)

The scene from afar as we advanced on foot was more beautiful than you can imagine when you hear the word "facilities." With the reflection of the morning sun's rays, the view before us transformed into a majestic painting, especially when the light refracted on the wreckage of gleaming metal in the huge plaza. But this beauty was only a deception hiding the reality of destruction in its depths. Most of these facilities were destroyed, and what seemed peaceful from a distance soon revealed its dark face as we drew closer. The enormous aircraft that were lined up like perched steel birds now looked like mere dismantled skeletons, or meaningless scattered parts, as not even this place, isolated from the city, was spared from the fierce attacks of the Eastern Alliance. Besides the giant armored chambers, we had aimed for from the start, the remains of a huge building clearly appeared before us. Nothing was left of it but faint signs suggesting its former greatness: broken stones, twisted iron rebars intertwining chaotically, and pieces of thick walls scattered here and there. Next to it, shattered glass wreckage reflected light in a way that hurt the eye. As we got closer, we noticed more clearly that the ground around it had turned into something resembling a cemetery for that lost civilization. Even the huge building was no longer standing; it had fallen and surrendered to the earth, and algae and grass had begun to slowly creep over it, as if trying to hide the traces of past sins. And while we were crossing that cracked road, we discovered a huge fence, so hidden in the grass that we didn't realize its existence until we stepped on it with our feet.

We set up our camp beside the concrete plaza to rest a little before continuing the search, and to have a lunch meal from the remains of the provisions we had. This was likely the last time we would eat our authentic food; afterwards, we would be forced to hunt and harvest to provide food. Four would certainly be happy with such a job, unlike Two, who would not accept the idea easily. But a worrying thought soon crossed my mind: there wasn't much food on the ship when we left. They must have reached this stage long ago over there. This thought only increased my fear of what might await us, the punished ones, upon our return.

The battle of gathering the remains was not yet over when the sky suddenly flashed. I immediately returned to reality, not paying attention to the other two, and came out clinging to the rope of our small tent, looking at the sky from afar. Dark clouds were accumulating beyond the horizon, as if threatening the arrival of something greater than just a storm.

I brought my head back inside, then sighed, saying miserably: "It's a strong storm!!"

At that moment, we had no choice but to leave the calm aside and start working. Quickly, I dismantled the tent and folded it, while Four took care of arranging and organizing the luggage. During that, Two left to check the warehouses, searching for a place where we could shelter and work until the storm passed.

(2)

The sky poured with unexpected intensity, and the wind raged with a violence that tore tree branches and carried them with it instead of leaves; at times, it even tried to uproot entire trees. What an incredibly greedy element! Then the temperatures dropped until sitting far from the fire became impossible. It went beyond that, as we sat clinging to each other, hoping for a little warmth. We spread the bed linens beneath and above us in an attempt to trap the heat, but to no avail; we were freezing in the literal sense of the word. I was in the middle. To my right was Two, who had somehow managed to cover her clasped hands up to her fingertips with the sleeves of her shirt, raising them close to her mouth to warm herself with the heat of her breath—perhaps because she was the least accustomed to the cold, given she spent most of her time in the warm library in the sky. To my left was Four, the most experienced in roaming through different seasons. She emerged from under the cover more than once, sometimes to feed the fire, other times to move her joints, thereby forming the source of heat that renewed itself now and then. Despite our urgency, we found no alternative but to wait for the storm to pass, thinking it would dissipate quickly just as it came suddenly. We even decided to sleep a little, hoping time would pass. When we awoke, there was no sign suggesting its imminent end. It seemed to be a long-term storm, insisting on clinging to the earth until the last breath. Therefore, we had no choice but to be brave, leave the fire behind, and set about to work now, without waiting for what might not come soon.

(3)

There wasn't a corner in the darkness where Four's eyes didn't gleam with enthusiasm during our exploratory journey, nor mine. This vast, dark place was nothing but a treasure of ancient technologies, and its remaining in good condition to this day, despite the constant strikes and storms, was only further proof of the solidity of its foundations. And the two Stars and I weren't the only ones who thought so; there were dozens of other animals we encountered during our exploration, who had made this place their home for decades before our arrival, we the intruders. At that, we raised our rifles without mercy, as any human setting foot on a new continent for the first time would have done. When we threw the torch in the air, most of them left, while the lightning consumed millions of birds exiting immediately.

The beginning of the adventure of separation was at the bookshelf that caught Two's attention. She sat silently beside it, picked up a book from one of its collections, and began to read it in a low voice, ignoring our presence. She let us advance alone, justifying it by saying she came here to search for knowledge, not for exploration—although both lead to the other. In reality, we didn't insist on bringing her with us anyway. The second part was at a power generator; a small engine connected to a huge box of switches. This is what caught Four's attention. She sat beside it quietly, examining its components and tampering with it without the slightest caution. She left me with the excuse that understanding a simple engine like this might help us understand larger ones, oblivious that we came to understand it together, step by step, not each one individually. And once again, I didn't insist on bringing her either. As for my end in this journey, it was with that strange, armored, tightly sealed door. I knew this after minutes of failed attempts to open it without giving up. It seems I was the only one who wasted her time arguing with an inanimate object, searching for that special element that always appears at the end of stories, not at their beginning.

Finally, I dropped my head to the ground in admission of defeat and disappointment. From this low position, I saw black dust descending slowly, falling from an endless ceiling, like snow on a dark new moon night. Amidst the dilapidated decorations of time up above, an image appeared of a figure holding a torch, exiting its cave full of engravings and drawings to feed, to live, before its exit transformed into a revolution and a renaissance—a renaissance destined for annihilation in the end. It began slow, accelerated, then fell forever. The moment the story ended, Four suddenly appeared, as if my torch was what had attracted her, interrupting my rest period with an unexpected question: "Have you seen any fuel around?"

We went out again then to search, and as expected, we found a lot of it in one of the warehouse's corners, and next to it, bundles of canned food and light equipment. It wasn't the main corner, considering the huge size of the place compared to the quantity of items left behind, but it was useful enough to continue the journey. I returned with Four to the engine, which had somehow transformed in a few short minutes into small scattered pieces. I didn't know Four was this skilled at reverse engineering, but I sat beside her and watched. When she felt I was ready to absorb, she began to explain: "This small fuel engine consists of several parts you see before you: a cylinder, a piston, a crankshaft, and heating plugs. This housing contains the cylinder, and the piston moves inside it in a reciprocating motion, allowing the crankshaft to rotate. Next to it is a precisely calibrated system for injecting fuel into the cylinder in specific quantities, which ignites due to high pressure and the heat of the plugs."

We assembled it together according to her diagram, but it didn't work. I initially thought it was broken, until Four put her hand inside and began fiddling with the internal flow valves, trying to start it again, but nothing happened. She tries a second time. This time, the engine emits a loud noise that pulls Two from her world to sit beside me and watch. She repeats the attempt over and over, until the engine begins to vibrate violently, as if resisting death. Then suddenly, it didn't die. The place exploded with thick, foul-smelling black smoke, but after moments, it gradually cleared, accompanied by the receding darkness. The engine wasn't just a piece of old junk; it had illuminated the entire warehouse, revealing its great truth to us for the first time: this wasn't just a treasure of ancient technologies, but an integrated base for creating miracles.

Before us stretched a vast space lit with a harsh whiteness, where rays of light struck the huge metal structure extending to the high ceiling, revealing a world from which we had only seen fragments in the darkness. On the right side, shelves piled high with gleaming spare parts as if they were new, arranged as if waiting for Four's touch. Next to them, compressed vehicles ready for assembly stood as if preparing for service again. And in the middle, a shelter appeared, buried deep within the warehouse. The only thing that prevented us from finding it was that stubborn door, which remained closed until power became available. It even had a spare key hanging beside it, which I hadn't noticed before, to open it immediately upon power loss. When we stepped inside, the scene looked like something from a movie about the end of the world, and indeed it was: reinforced steel walls, huge, tightly sealed doors, small rooms equipped with metal beds, simple tables, and monitoring screens watching every corner outside. And on the left side, where we had found the fuel and food earlier, it wasn't just a secondary corner as I had thought, but the beginning of a maze of storage shelves and huge boxes, lined up like a wall hiding another world behind it.

The metallic smell mixed with the coldness of the place, until I felt as if time stops inside it, as if everything within was prepared to withstand countless disasters, but it failed to protect humans from their annihilation in the end. When I presented my viewpoint to Two, as expected, she disagreed with me as usual, replying in a quiet but cutting voice: "As I read in the documents, this warehouse and others were part of a huge military logistics project, dedicated only to transporting goods and weapons and temporarily securing units in emergencies. It was designed to be capable of building vehicles when needed, and it's also equipped to withstand the worst consequences of nuclear war. Its survival to this day is clear proof of that."

But I didn't need documents to know the truth I saw with my own eyes: "It wasn't designed to protect anyone from the end, only to postpone it."

(4)

Next, we entered the administrative room, the largest by a vast margin compared to the other rooms, filled with complex equipment, buttons, and mirrors. In the center of its ceiling, a red light blinked continuously. Below it, a wide table occupied the floor. On one of the screens, the only one still working, was a broad warning: Maximum power-saving mode is active due to loss of connection to the main generator. This mode prevents people from having full control over the facility and reduces energy consumption, which made the room somewhat useless. But we didn't reach this conclusion without tampering and attempts. In fact, all the device covers were exposed, as if someone had previously tried to activate them by bypassing the protection system, leaving behind a large collection of parts and tools scattered on the floor and walls. Four, for her part, tried to manipulate the systems, but what we saw before us wasn't just traditional computers and devices; it was more like a showcase in the complexity of building microcontrollers, where they were separated into huge groups of distributed circuits, connected by millions of identically colored wires, all with the aim of misleading any potential hacker. And the designer had succeeded perfectly in that; even the greatest engineer I know failed to activate it.

We stopped there to take a break before starting the study session. Four and I began by cleaning the lower facility, as if it only needed someone to bring it back to life. Then we scattered the food boxes in the warehouse to examine their contents: dried meat, nutritional supplements, fibers, sugars, and proteins—meals designed for front-line fighters, and they weren't bad-tasting at all as you might expect after all those years of storage. They were delicious, and also available in huge quantities sufficient for us and the rest of the Stars for months, if we economized in our consumption, and we had no other choice anyway. When we returned to the administrative room again, we spread the canned food over the table, except for the square occupied by Two's book, which had already changed three or four times since we went out. After we sat down, Four spoke with fiery enthusiasm, as if trying to make us imagine what she saw in her mind: "This place contains everything, and is built to rebuild anything—a place one step away from perfection. If I can get it running, it will just take some time, then it will be indescribably perfect. Imagine with me: an underground base, fortified, full of food, warm, protected, containing all the required equipment, close to the forest. We can return with these resources in just one month if we cooperate! This place is so perfect you feel like life can't possibly go this way, so perfect you walk around trying to find a problem with it to criticize but you never find anything!"

This was the second time I had seen Four this excited; her enthusiasm even surpassed the moment we first entered the ship. And how could she not be excited, when she was now in her own paradise? This place gives her all the means to innovate without limits: all the equipment at her fingertips, all the resources, everything she needs to redesign and rebuild the ship. But there is one thing we lack: a super engine capable of penetrating the atmosphere, to return us to the Sun.

She looked at me, then gave a sideways smile and said with worried sarcasm: "I didn't expect you to be so quiet, Seven. I thought this would ignite your curiosity too."

I shrugged mockingly and replied: "I'm just trying to hold back my laughter while I see your ears pricked up like a cat's!"

But inside, that deep feeling of unease hadn't left me; my heart was still beating strongly since we entered here, at a speed I had never experienced before. Two closed her book after a moment, perhaps she had just finished it, then said in a quiet voice that carried a hidden warning: "One of us will have to bring the rest of the Stars here as soon as the storm ends, otherwise everyone outside will perish. I just hope we weren't too late in finding this place for them, and that the storm hasn't struck them with a catastrophe or loss."

Four said immediately: "I'll go."

"Rather, I think I'm the one who should go. You will have to stay to operate the facility and build the engine with Seven. As for me, my presence is of no expected use."

I didn't like what she said, so I quickly replied: "Don't say words like that! I'm sure you've already figured out how to build the engine from those books, or at least part of it."

Two lifted her gaze from the last book, then tilted her head slightly, as if weighing my words before answering coldly: "Rather, they were books explaining the automation system that humans relied on in their final days—integrated systems connecting human to machine through a common language, which later evolved into an artificial intelligence that can converse with humans and guide them in their tasks."

She placed her hand on the tabletop and drew a faint line with her fingers, as if preparing a hidden concept, before continuing in a more serious tone: "Let's say Three's job was to pilot the ship, but with a dedicated system like this running, her job could become just to intervene during emergencies, while the ship itself would pilot itself according to the set path, and with utmost precision, surpassing any human error we might commit due to the slowness of our response."

Four looked at her with interest and said: "An automated piloting system, connected to satellites, like the one that was on the sunken aircraft?"

Two shook her head and said: "A slightly more complex system. This time, it might contain an artificial intelligence that thinks, makes personal modifications to the default plan, corrects the flight path to avoid danger, or modifies the ideal values based on certain sensor readings or..."

Four and Two continued talking about that system nonstop, exchanging ideas about its capabilities, its mechanism, its complexity, and the precision of its parameters. I could hear the excitement in their voices, that enthusiasm which stems from seeing a much bigger picture than others see, from noticing interconnected threads in the chaos that might seem like just dead data to others. As for me, despite my love for engineering and design, this type of talk seemed to me like discussing Earth's biology again. It's not that it's complicated, but it's something that pulses with a life I don't understand, something that hides dark and terrifying secrets within it. And in the end, the matter seems simple from the outside; you just need hours to teach the machine what you want it to do exactly via the controller. But inside lies that mysterious void you cannot control.

(5)

Two left to search for other important documents and papers on the shelves outside, after nearly an hour of long talk about software systems far beyond our reach—or rather, summarizing books she had read before and sharing their essence with us. This was despite her always being the most insistent on utilizing every minute for hard work. As for Four, she sat as she wished, on the floor, trying to break the central device's protection again and again. Even if it required dismantling the entire device, there was no hesitation in her resolve nor retreat in her decision. Both of them were serious about taking over this place, whatever the cost. As for me, I remained as I was, sitting on the wide table without doing anything different, not because I was the youngest, but because I still didn't understand what I should do alone, without one of them sharing it with me.

Four suddenly raised her head, then said in an inquisitive tone, though not without precise observation: "You are certainly quieter than usual! Is a complex issue occupying your thoughts?"

What is this? She repeated it. Quiet. But I'm sure I was always quiet.

154

Yes! I understood it now. Since we arrived here, I haven't uttered any strange desire.

She definitely meant that. I am now less enthusiastic, less weepy, and less needy.

I rose from my chair and sat beside her; it was the least I could do out of respect for conversing with her. Then I said, as I contemplated the internal space of the device before us: "The journey to get here is like an adventure we undertake behind the school wall—the ruins, the trees, the submerged legends, the danger of darkness, and the awe of space and clouds. The Sun always warned us against doing it, but the soul's yearning for freedom always forced us to disobey her word."

She smiled a little and added in a quiet voice, but laden with some sadness: "And we would return to meet each other after parting before the gate at the end of the day to receive a scolding from her. Whereas now, everyone we've lost will never return to life. I thank the Sun every hour for your survival from the fall, and I thank her for my survival too. We specifically lost the largest number in the incident."

Her eyes truly teared up, and reddened. I hadn't meant to open the same topic for the tenth time, but they just turn the course of any conversation to that point, and stay there, talking about it and crying nonstop. I can still hear the sound of the laugh with which I ended my words, and for which she paid the price with tragedy. I tried to lighten the atmosphere a little, so I said, joking: "Did you know that the first adventure I went on, you were the one leading it, not Three or Five? For me, it was the most wonderful adventure I had ever experienced, to the point that I wrote two stories about it."

She laughed, but it seemed as if she was trying to hide a different feeling beneath that laugh.

Unfeeling hypocrite! That's the first thing I threw at myself to laugh in front of her again.

And shallow! I followed it up in my mind, as if disciplining myself for trying to make light of the matter.

I continued, as she watched me with warm eyes: "And that's probably why you and Two were the ones I connected with most during my days at the school."

She raised her eyebrows in surprise, then said: "But I thought you wanted to join my team because of your love for mathematics and engineering!"

I shook my head slowly, then replied in a sarcastic tone: "Not really. If there was a special team for library-goers, Two and I would have joined it."

"So, you have no desire to build a new ship like the previous Seven did?"

"Not at all!"

She looked at me for a bit, then asked, trying to delve deeper into my thoughts: "And do you remember anything of what we used to learn in the engineering hall?"

"No! Nothing at all."

She stopped and turned her head towards me, with surprise and disdain, her eyes narrowing as if she were seriously considering strangling me with the cable in her hands. I felt real danger approaching, so I quickly raised my hands in surrender, then said in a rushed tone full of pleading: "I was joking! Believe me! I loved the design; it's like writing, but instead of weaving and knitting words, we weave elements and give them meaning. And I loved the practical building sessions; it's like finding a knot and solving it, and leaving a door for mystery called the development aspect."

She looked at me for a moment, then sighed quietly, as if deciding to postpone her revenge for a later time, and said with a faint smile: "And that's why I hope to ride a ship of your design. You are the one who had the honor of finding the previous ship's problem, and as a brilliant writer, it won't be difficult for one who creates a story from nothing to build a ship, right? Perhaps I'm good at connecting and estimating, but I'm bad at inventing."

I shook my head smiling, then replied in a calm tone: "You're just exaggerating my worth, and diminishing your own out of modesty by comparing yourself to me."

What am I saying?! Everyone knows that Four is the most direct star, who neither flatters nor puts on airs. Nevertheless, she smiled, then laughed, a short but genuine laugh, before raising her eyes to me seriously and saying: "Not at all! Even the Sun knew your worth and gave you the number seven so suddenly. Haven't you thought about this before? Among the first twenty Stars, you are the youngest. Then you earned the title of deputy leader of the Engineering Squad suddenly as well. You just insist on hiding your true mettle from yourself by constantly putting the excuses of writing and your youth before you. And that's why I will keep pushing you forward until you overcome that fixation and show what you can do—for your sake, for my sake, and for the sake of the lost Stars on this planet."

My eyes widened amidst unexpected astonishment. Although this wasn't the first time I had heard such words, when they come from Four, you know it's the truth that cannot be denied. My lips hesitated, wanting to speak, but they found no words. They paused with a slight movement, ultimately unable to produce any response. Then a shy smile I couldn't hide broke out on my face, later transforming into a smile of growing confidence as I nodded my head, acknowledging the absolute correctness of her opinion. Four pulled her hands out of the cluttered chamber, stood up, dusted them off, then raised her finger, pointing to the device in front of me, and said firmly: "You can try your hand at it until I return. Remember the most important lesson we learned in engineering: when we face a problem, it doesn't matter how many mistakes we make as long as we find the solution in the end. For we make possibilities from mistakes that build us the lost ladder of salvation. Without mistakes, there would be no way out of the problem. And never surrender yourself to fear, for all mistakes are correctable no matter their cost, and surrendering is the only loss."

I felt then a mixture of fear and challenge, but with her standing behind me, she gave me a stronger feeling, pushing me to grab the hem of my shirt and, in one motion, lift it upwards, letting my arm be gradually revealed until it bunched up above my elbow, gathered around the upper arm. My skin, which had long been hidden, shook hands with the air for the first time. I adjusted my seating position, as if preparing for a battle. Indeed, it wasn't just a confrontation; it was the beginning of a story of strength and suppressed patience. What was before me was like a fearsome beast, just unleashed. Seeing it this way, occupying my entire field of vision, gave me a completely different sensation than seeing it from afar. It looked more like paintings crowded with elements like small cities, topped by towers of various delicate components, surrounded by intertwined black wires like nests of snakes. The sound of silence then rose, broken only by a faint electrical hum, as if the device were whispering its own secret to me. Up close, everything pulsed with chaos and infinite possibilities, challenging, awaiting my first bold touch, where it might be, and what it would reveal of its secrets. I tilted my head slightly and took a deep breath, perhaps so I would be ready to dive into the depths of its maze.

I slowly extended my hand inside, feeling the cold surfaces, and carefully ran my fingers over the lines and edges, trying to comprehend the expanse of this hidden metallic city. I was looking for a pattern, a way to understand this chaotic tangle that seemed random, but certainly wasn't. I began to untangle some of the intertwined wires, trying to organize a small part of the chaos, like someone rearranging the pieces of an incomplete puzzle. But, while I was working, something strange caught my attention; one of the wires was unnaturally soft, as if it were hollow. I felt that something was wrong. I followed it with my fingers to its end, and there it seemed cut, although outwardly it was perfectly connected. I froze in place. This was not a natural method of disconnection. I stopped my hand and focused my eyes with all their power on the cut, trying to understand what I was seeing. Then I followed another adjacent wire to discover the same surprise: the wires were connected, but they were originally cut. What an ingenious way to hide a disconnection!

My mind began to work in a different way, like a detective perhaps, trying to form a logical explanation for this incident. This wasn't random tampering, but a deliberate act. Who did it? Was it the device's designer, or the expert who tampered with it later? And why? I looked at the rest of the device, my eyes following the threads of extending wires. There was a specific system to the chaos, as if the person who cut the wires was trying to deliver a message, or perhaps lead us into an impossible situation. I felt a tension run through my veins, but it quickly turned into sharp focus. I looked around, searching for other clues. There were small pieces of wire remnants strewn near the device, and fine, scattered copper strands. The person who did this didn't try to hide their trace; on the contrary, they left clear signs indicating their intervention, as if leaving us a clue, like a challenger offering a thread to the one trying to fix it. I ended up muttering in a low voice: "This is not a child's tampering at all. This person knows very well what they're doing. They're an expert."

I closed my eyes for a moment, trying to recall the details and organize them in my head. Who could access the device? And who had the motive to disable it? There was no clear answer, but the only thing I realized was that what was before me was not just a broken device, but a case carrying hidden intentions behind it. I looked back at the device, this time with different eyes. I no longer saw it as just a piece of technology needing repair, but as an explicit challenge, a puzzle intended for us to solve. I went back to examining the cut wires, inspecting their edges carefully, searching for an answer to two questions that had occurred to me: How were these wires hollowed out and connected in this way? And what, specifically, do these hollow wires connect? The process wasn't easy; every step required careful thought and hundreds of different possibilities. But I wouldn't give up. The feeling of challenge that Four had given me was stronger than any frustration that might creep in, especially since I was sure she would return with the answer. And for that, I will push my mind to its utmost to find at least one plausible scenario.

(7)

I was sitting on the floor, clinging to the last atom of patience I had, as the tangled and cut wires before me seemed like a puzzle impossible to solve. Amidst my futile attempts carrying the banner of non-surrender, and after a deep breath, my hand moved randomly among the hollow wires, pulling one of them, disconnecting it, and reconnecting another with a similar core in its place. It was like a final move in a mind game with a device designed to thwart it. Then suddenly, without any warning, a faint sound emanated from the device, an electrical hum that vibrated in the air, followed by dim lights gradually glowing on the screens and control panels. I stared at it in amazement, disbelieving that something had changed with a ridiculous move like this. I paused for a moment, trying to comprehend what had happened.

The device had started to work. A small screen on its surface lit up with the power sign and emitted a familiar sound indicating it was ready for operation. I screamed, involuntarily, then let out a short laugh, full of astonishment and victory.

"I did it!!"

I said it out loud, addressing the great entity of the device.

And I stared at it, declaring my small, overwhelming victory in the challenge.

Then I wiped my forehead with my palm, leaving a trace of exhaustion and joy.

But before I could finish my celebration, a quiet voice came from behind me: "I don't want to interrupt your moment of triumph, but you didn't actually do anything that caused it to turn on."

I turned around quickly to see Four standing at the door of the room, leaning lazily against the frame. She was looking at me with a faint smile that held a mixture of admiration and amusement. I then raised my eyebrows in surprise and asked her: "What do you mean?! I fixed the problem of the hollow wires and rearranged the chaos!"

She approached me slowly, cast a quick glance at the device that was now working smoothly, then pointed with her finger towards the outside, towards a main cable connected to the wall.

"The problem was never in here, and the device wasn't tampered with. The problem was with the main cable's plug. It seems it wasn't plugged in properly."

I froze in my place. I looked where she pointed, then looked back at the device. I felt a wave of embarrassment rush to my face, but I couldn't help but laugh. My laugh was light at first, but it quickly turned into pure, loud laughter. I asked her between my laughs: "So everything I did was useless?!"

She shook her head lightly and said in a reassuring tone: "On the contrary. That kind of out-of-the-box thinking is what you do just before you're about to give up. At least, you learned what the device looks like inside."

I went back to looking at the device again, then sighed, this time with a satisfied smile: "Well, maybe I wasn't the reason it turned on, but I was here when it came back to life, so I'll consider it my own personal victory in the end."

"Deal!"

She said it, patting my shoulder lightly, then added jokingly: "But next time, don't forget to check the external cables first."

I stood up from my place, feeling a strange weight in my chest. Perhaps I wasn't the one who fixed the device, but I learned a valuable lesson. The device was working now. It was time to prepare for what comes next.

(8)

I hate pages that have three identical numbers, and I hate the moment when the three of us are gathered in the same room for a long time without a specific topic to talk about. Jumping from one point to another is like a train moving on a track without a specific destination; sometimes it moves forward, and sometimes it retraces its steps backward. The meeting ended, and its substance contained only one single important point that I had stated from the beginning, after which I paid no attention to the content of the rest of the conversation: The device is working now, almost. And how, "almost"? By fixing the main plug, we bypassed the maximum power-saving mode and were granted partial control over the device. This is what we concluded from the number of lit screens and the alarm light turning off. But despite the colors emanating from the control panel, it wouldn't accept any commands. Pressing and fiddling with its buttons, switches, and wheels randomly was completely ineffective, which immediately put us on to another possibility: perhaps the control panel was broken and needed replacement. The device isn't reading any inputs.

I was at the forefront as usual, due to Four's desire to push me forward, sitting on the floor. I wasn't studying the depths of the device so much as diving internally into possibilities not previously considered. I had already wasted a fair amount of time examining the device and touching its components, and only two possibilities came to mind: the hollow wires are what connect the control panel to the partitioned mainboard, or perhaps the panel is just old and broken and needs replacement. Four sat on the floor beside me after I explained my two theories, then she began to scrutinize the wires, examining them in a way that if you saw her from afar, you would immediately say it was the hand of a retired engineer.

"The idea of hollow wires never crossed my mind, because it's impossible to hollow them out without leaving clear marks. These are wires without scratches on the outside or signs of customization, as if they were designed this way. Perhaps they are thin pipes designed to transport some substance, like oil maybe, and they're somewhat flexible, so it's likely they're also intended for cooling."

I hadn't thought of that at all. Her belief made me realize the clear difference between an engineer and a writer: We don't reach scientific and practical truths through plot-driven imagination and ridiculous conspiracy theories, but with sound, realistic, logical thinking. A sigh from Two interrupted us. It came from amidst the piles of dusty equipment and the rust-spotted metal walls outside, even though she was sitting there on the metal table, next to hundreds of documents that brought that smell here. She took a deep breath as she ran her fingers over the surface of one of the documents; she was likely scanning its contents instantly with her eyes. She captured my full attention, putting me in a state of full readiness, because I was sure of the importance of those words to our situation. Meanwhile, Four seemed preoccupied with trying to detach the control panel from the device, ignoring her sigh, unlike me. It was a minute of waiting, then she uttered: "Yes. I think I finally understand the composition of this place."

That phrase made Four stop, looking then at Two with wandering eyes, but she was interested: "What do you mean?"

"This warehouse, and the shelter inside it, isn't just a storehouse or an ordinary military logistics base; it's also designed to repel enemies if it's exploited or seized. One of the reports I found here mentioned an old incident. There was a similar facility whose defensive system was tampered with, which led to its deactivation. But instead of that being the end, it was just a trick."

Four tilted her head, and said slowly, as if the word had astonished her: "A trick?"

"Yes. The system gave the impression that it was partially working, which encouraged the group that had taken over the place to stay in it. But after that, the worst happened. The doors locked automatically, and the ventilation system was disabled. The result? They all died within minutes."

Silence filled the room, and only the sound of heavy breathing and the echo of the receding storm outside could be heard. Four tightened her grip on the screwdriver in her hand, as if trying to absorb the information: "This means tampering with this device could be more dangerous than we thought."

"Exactly. If this place is designed in the same way, it's likely that this device isn't just an ordinary control system. It might be programmed to retaliate against any hacking attempt."

And before Four could reply, we all noticed a change in the lighting inside the room. Faint sunbeams infiltrated through the small cracks in the warehouse's upper windows, sending golden threads of light into the shelter where we were staying. The scene then looked like a sign from nature that the storm had ended. She then continued: "We can't back down now. We need this place, so we have no choice but to take the risk. If any indications appear that things are deviating towards danger, we will withdraw immediately. But until then, I will be careful, and I won't allow a single mistake to put us in the same trap you warned us about."

I was the only one sitting without a role in the conversation, and as the discussion between them continued without needing my participation, I felt my presence had become marginal. I stood up quietly, heading towards the exit, leaving them immersed in their thoughts. There, outside the room, the cold air saturated with the smell of old metal and lingering dust after the storm greeted me. I raised my head upwards, towards the ceiling where the faint sunbeams had infiltrated through the small cracks and flowed softly onto the concrete floor. The color of the sky seemed lighter than before, and the wind no longer howled as before, but had turned into light breezes caressing the surfaces of the deserted metal structures. I took a deep breath, as if inhaling the first dose of clarity after a long night of chaos, and whispered to myself as I watched the light seep inside: "The storm is over."

I didn't realize I wasn't alone until I heard Four's voice come from behind me, in a calm tone, as she approached with Two, who was still holding some documents in her hands: "But our battle with this place has just begun. I'll give the control panel one last try, cautiously this time, while you start designing the ship's model so we can work on it together later."

Perhaps the storm was over, but I preferred, if only for a moment, to enjoy the calm of this brief period before facing what awaits us.

(9)

The sun had infiltrated through the remaining scattered clouds, casting long, winding shadows on the rain-saturated ground. The air was unusually clean after the storm, but it still carried a coldness that lashed the faces, as if reminding us that winter had not yet departed but was standing on the horizon, watching. I stood beside the warehouse, a step away from the door, staring at Two who had stepped ahead of me, looking as if she were a part of this new scene, familiar in the midst of this strange world. When we went back inside, there was no time for talk. I didn't wait, but I saw her lift her dilapidated bag onto her shoulder, while her gaze moved between the provision boxes, adjusting the quantities she was carrying with her several times, silently second-guessing herself. Her face was expressionless as I was used to, but there was something in her posture that held a mixture of determination and melancholy, as if she realized her next step would be long and desolate. We didn't speak before she left; Four had returned to the administrative room, trying to utilize every available second, while I, the least busy and the most absent-minded, remained by her side until the last moment.

As soon as she had packed her belongings and stood up straight to read some prayers to inaugurate her journey, I began to realize that her actions suggested a deep sense of anxiety, an anxiety she couldn't dispel despite the appearance of the sun which had promised us a temporary respite. When she finished chanting, she turned her face towards me, her eyes staring directly into mine. There was no need for words; I read her decision clearly and knew what she intended to do. She didn't need to tell me verbally. Nevertheless, as if my saying it could change her mind, I tried: "I'll accompany you!"

I said it in a steady voice, with a tone that carried a stubbornness I didn't feel internally, because I knew the attempt would be futile. She shook her head gently, as if she were expecting this objection, then replied in a quiet voice that carried a firmness that made me step back: "No. You must stay here until I return. Work on the ship's schematic, and help Four."

She lifted the bag onto her shoulders, as if trying to escape the weight of the conversation, but she added in a low voice, this time carrying a real anxiety she couldn't hide: "I must get there quickly, not out of fear of the road or the darkness, but because for every day we spend on the surface of this planet, we lose several stars in return. That's why we need you two here, to work together and quickly on the map of survival without wasting any time in useless wandering. I am the only one who can venture out now as the leader of the Exploration Squad. This is my job, and this is my specialty, just as you two are the only ones capable of accomplishing what is necessary to get out of here."

I looked at her with concern. I knew she was right, but I didn't want to let her go alone. I tried again, as if searching for any flaw in her logic to keep her here: "You know we need you here in this place too. Everything seems like an impossible puzzle, and no one understands it the way you do. You know this place better than all of us. Who will explain the systems to us later? Who will warn us from making mistakes?"

Her expression changed slightly, but she didn't hesitate, as if she had already decided her fate: "My staying with you here will waste time we don't have. Look at Four, working nonstop to maintain the device. And you, despite your constant complaints, sometimes do the same. You two at least provide something tangible. As for me? Just words and notes from some books that anyone can find, to the point that I sometimes feel I'm more of a hindrance than a help."

I felt her words pierce me, but she didn't give me a chance to reply. She continued her speech, and this time it seemed as if she were talking to herself more than addressing me: "This place, and these systems, they are just tools. And you two will decide how to use them. Four knows how to build, and you know how to connect the threads together. I have no place in this equation."

I wanted to say something, anything to convince her that her staying with us would be useful, but I found nothing. I tried to search for words, any words to convince her that her staying with us wasn't useless, but she didn't give me the chance. Before I could speak, before I could find anything, I felt her hand pat my head gently, a touch that reminded me of the days we spent together in the library. Then she said with a faint smile: "My biggest fear is leaving you two here alone, but I'm depending on you to keep this place safe, and to rein in Four until I return. You can do it, right?"

I couldn't reply, but I knew she was right, completely right, and that she was the only one who understood things properly, the only one who saw the world as if it were an open book. She knew where the road was leading us, she knew who was at fault, and she knew how to prevent disaster, and escalate the uprising as well. And for that, I felt weak before her, unable to refuse her claim.

"If it weren't for you..."

She didn't give me a chance to finish my sentence. I saw her turn, and her steps were slowly moving away. Then the words rushed from my lips before I could think, as if they were suffocating inside me and now finally came out: "If it weren't for you, I wouldn't have understood what happened to humans. If you're the one who always leaves, abandoning me here to work until we find a way out, how will I understand the rest of the stories I brought with me about Earth? I need you more than any other star. I want you, with all selfishness, to stay by my side, to ignore their tasks, for us to stay together until we return to the library again!"

She stopped for a moment, her back still turned to me. For a short moment, I imagined she might have changed her mind, that perhaps I had finally touched something inside her. But she didn't turn around, said nothing, just continued walking, her steps moving farther and farther away, until the shadows among the dense trees swallowed her.

(10)

My feet were heavy, and every step towards the shelter carried with it an additional weight of disappointment. I could see her shadow disappearing among the trees, and something inside me was screaming, but I remained silent, as if a part of me already realized that nothing I could say would have changed her decision. In the end, I didn't say everything that should have been said; I didn't find the right words to convince her that her presence with us was more important than any other exploration. But, would it have really helped? I know she sometimes tends to make her decisions out of the impulse of that innocent child who still resides within her, but at the same time, she never forgot her role as an older sister and her responsibility towards the Stars when it was time to make firm decisions.

I returned inside, burdened with worries. I couldn't even look into Four's eyes when I passed her. She, in turn, seemed absorbed in her concentration on the device, as if the world outside didn't concern her. I stopped in front of the wide table where papers and documents still filled the surface—chaos here, and another chaos of thoughts not yet complete in my head. Should I start immediately? Could I move forward on my own? I thought for a moment about asking Four for advice, but my feet didn't move, as if the heavy thoughts had completely paralyzed me.

Then it happened.

The first catastrophe I am a part of.

There was no warning as we had expected, just a sudden and violent explosion that tore the silence of the room. I felt the whole world shaking around me, then I found myself flying through the air. It was a brief moment, but it seemed to stretch into forever. The heat of the explosion lashed my face, then the powerful shockwave came to push me forward, throwing me like a weightless doll, carrying with me metal fragments and torn panels, until I ended up on the metal fence hidden under the grass.

I fell to the ground hard, my body slamming against the damp rocks. A sharp ringing filled my ears, like an echo of a world collapsing from within. I tried to open my eyes, but they were heavy; everything was blurred and hazy. What I saw through them looked like a distorted dream. Raindrops began to fall slowly again on my face, not heavily, but they carried a harsh coldness on my burnt skin. I tried to move too, but my limbs seemed as if they were frozen. I could barely breathe; every breath pained my chest as if I were sinking deep.

Then I saw her, and she was the only thing that broke this cold scene.

Her face was distorted with horror. She rushed towards me with quick steps, seeming to move in silence, although I knew she was screaming. I couldn't hear her voice, as if the world around me had completely lost its sound. I didn't need to hear her; her face alone was enough to tell me everything. Her eyes were gleaming with a fear I had never seen in them before, a fear her expressionless face couldn't hide. She was crying.

I tried to say something, anything to reassure her, but my voice was stuck somewhere inside my chest. All I could do was look at her, at her trembling, close face, at her hand that reached towards me, holding onto me as if trying to pull me from this darkness, until the blackness swept over me. The cold rain was the last thing I felt, and the warmth of Two's hand, and her tears falling upon my face were the last things I perceived before it swallowed me. I didn't know what had happened, nor how we ended up like this, but I knew that something there had changed forever.

(11)

(Let's return to those days that preceded the journey.)

I always used to wonder before the lights were turned off about the meaning of this day and what distinguished it from its predecessors, before I reached a conclusion that wasn't unique, but found its way through a lazy loophole I wasn't accustomed to: Does a day have to be special to be a good day? No, what I really mean is… because, whatever was going through my head on those nights, I would reach the same conclusion: a wide smile. And that was before I covered my eyes with one hand, shielding them from the light, and then that smile would widen until it turned into a laugh for no apparent reason. Perhaps this was what made every day special, that I was able to sleep with this joy never having left me for a single night.

"I don't know how you always keep this cheerful look on your face, even during your sleep. What a cute sister I have!"

I didn't have to concentrate to know whose voice this was. I would see them as soon as I opened my eyes, as usual, after they had drawn the curtains to flood the room with light.

"It's not fair that you say this to her every morning when you have a perfect angel like me!"

"That's impossible, you look so much older than me! Imagine how I'd look saying that to you? The other Stars would surely laugh at me!"

The usual argument, happening every morning between Star Six and Thirteen. The same scene, the same voices, the same tone, and yet, I never felt bored of it for a single day. I would tilt my head slightly as the warmth of their relationship floated around me, then I would slowly lift my body, leaving the warmth of the bed which had turned into stagnant energy at that moment. Although I could barely manage to sway beside them, that wasn't going to stop their continuous argument. Nothing stops it. Nothing stops this morning.

She suddenly encircles me from behind. That didn't give me any time to process it before my whole body shivered. I raise my shoulders and clasp my hands together as if I were a flower closing in on itself amidst the cold, then I slowly turn my head backward, my eyes half-closed as if I were a miserable cat about to cry.

"Come on! Don't you like your older sister playing with you a little?"

I tried to slip out from between her arms, but her grip was stronger than I expected.

"Your body is extremely cold. Could you please move away from me."

She tightened her arms around me more firmly, clinging as if trying to keep me with her forever, then she laughed, saying in a sly, childish voice: "That's impossible. It's the first time I've caught you before you left, and I must take advantage of it."

I sighed in frustration as I tried to free my arms from her grip to no avail, then I remembered something that made me raise my head quickly: "But... Two must be waiting for me in the library now. I have to go there quickly."

At the mention of Two's name, a strange smile lit up her face. She then suddenly turned to the door, as if she had been waiting for this specific moment. I didn't understand the message she conveyed to Thirteen through her eyes, but suddenly, as if receiving an unspoken order, she left the room with incredible speed, leaving me alone with Six, who had no intention of letting me go so easily. I sat on the bed after futile attempts to outmaneuver her, one dodge after another ending in failure. She was incredibly stubborn, as if preparing for a discussion of great importance that couldn't be missed. I finally asked her as I sighed in surrender: "Is there something you want to talk about?"

She paused her tight grip for a moment, then gave me a sly sideways glance, as if planning something else.

"Why do you make it seem strange for me to stay with my cute little sister?"

"Excuse me?! You are imprisoning me now, of course this is strange!"

She raised her eyebrow defiantly, as if trying to give me a false sense that I was overreacting, then said coldly: "Unfortunately, this is the only way I know to make you two leave the library."

"How can we leave the library when we haven't even entered it yet? Are you aware of what you're saying?"

I paused at her last word, make you two? I didn't notice it at first, but now, I began to realize there was something unusual in her way of speaking. Not much time passed before the door opened again, and Thirteen returned to the room, but right behind her was Two. My eyes widened as soon as I saw her.

She wasn't fully awake yet; she was swaying as if her body were still attached to her previous dream. She sat right beside me and began to examine my features with that slow gaze, heavy with sleepiness, which made me feel a slight anxiety. Then, without any expression on her face, she uttered in a low voice: "Are you really hurt? If you hit the door, wouldn't the site of the collision swell?"

"What are you talking about? Are you still asleep? I didn't hit any door!"

I understood now. This was the trick Thirteen had used to bring Two here despite her heavy sleep. How did she manage to deceive her so easily? She must have woken up startled and rushed to me without giving her mind a chance to think. Why would Thirteen need someone else if I was hurt, when she is the school doctor herself? But instead of looking angry or embarrassed, Two smiled, a small smile different from the usual that isn't obvious to others. Then she quietly rested her head on my shoulder and closed her eyes again, that smile never leaving her face, saying: "That's good. I can sleep now then. Don't forget to finish your latest story before classes begin."

"You're definitely still asleep. What story are you talking about?!"

I watched her silently as she slowly slipped into her slumber, my eyes not leaving her relaxed features for a moment. I wondered then, since when had our relationship become this close? When did Two start worrying about me this much, to leave her sleep—one of the things she cherishes most—and rush to me just to check on me? I found no clear answer, but I felt an unfamiliar warmth surrounding me, making me lean my body unconsciously towards her, as if searching for some comfort in her presence. But of course, we weren't going to be allowed to remain in this scene for long.

"See? I told you it was worth the trouble."

"How mean of you, Six. I didn't know you were trying to steal the cute Seven from Two."

"But you're here, aren't you? You're actually all I need, my dear."

I thought it was a nice flirtatious phrase, but I knew very well that Thirteen wasn't the type to accept this kind of talk easily. My intuition didn't fail me. In a flash, she immediately dropped her to the ground and knelt on her back, pinning her with a stern, superior look, before it turned into a laugh from her, then from me, then from Six, then from everyone. During that, I put my hand behind Two's back, then began to push my body slightly to the side until she fell gently onto the bed. I then pulled the cover over her and rearranged her sleeping position as if she had never moved. I was absolutely sure that when she woke up, she would be amazed and wonder how she suddenly got to my bed. Just imagining the expression on her face then was enough to make me laugh continuously.

All I could see then was darkness. My palms were covering my eyes completely as they lay on my face, and my breath would spread across them, giving me a temporary warmth that vanished in a moment. Then I felt a movement beside me. Six sat down quietly, as if waiting for the right moment to join in. At that, I clasped my palms together in the middle, making way for my eyes to see her as she spoke, while I was wrestling with myself over a completely different matter: whether I should have given Two a goodnight kiss or not. At that moment, Thirteen left our room. She's responsible for the Stars' health, and therefore, always busy. I felt she sometimes needed some warmth and rest, just as we all do. Six interrupted my thoughts when she said, contemplating me with curiosity: "The matter of your friendship has occupied my thoughts for a long time. Given that Two is one of the stars who has been less open to others since her birth, and a bit scary, how did you manage to get to know her?"

I thought for a little before answering, recalling my first memories with her: "It might be somewhat surprising, but she was the one who took the lead then and made the first move. I figured her out later, and I don't really know why. When she first took my hand to play with me outside, she squeezed it firmly and pulled me behind her. I felt she was just trying to push me away, but she stayed there by my side. She even agreed to go on an adventure with me later. It was then I was sure I had been wrong: she wasn't trying to push me away at all; she was asking me to stay by her side."

She tilted her head slightly, lost in my words, then murmured as if talking to herself: "So that's what it's about..."

Her tone wasn't entirely convinced; I felt she wasn't as persuaded by my answer as I thought. Perhaps because I myself wasn't sure of the real reason Two had approached me in that way, or perhaps because my words were just the delusions of a shy girl who one day found herself holding the number seven, lost amidst a vast universe of different activities. She didn't give me more of a chance to think. She smiled her usual smile, then declared with arrogant confidence: "I was sure no one could resist your cuteness, Seven! And because I am Six, the most elegant and cute star in this galaxy, fate must have chosen to bring us together in this room. It was no coincidence at all."

Hearing that foolish phrase with such excessive confidence made me stifle a laugh, but I choked amidst a sneeze I couldn't get out at the last second. Luckily, I didn't have to search for words to respond to that false claim, because Star Five suddenly entered the room, interrupting her with a sarcastic tone as she stood at the door: "What are you talking about? If it weren't for your repeated argument with Star Four over the desk in the room, the Sun wouldn't have kicked you out of there. Then luck smiled upon you strangely in that your friend Thirteen's room had an empty spot. Otherwise, no star would have agreed to share her room with you because of your arrogance and possessiveness."

Six gasped as if she had been insulted, then exclaimed defensively: "My arrogance and possessiveness?! I needed it for sewing costumes, but she always insisted on putting her tools and equipment on it. Come on! What's the importance of putting them on the desk anyway, instead of spreading them on the floor wherever she works? They're made of metal, not fabric!"

Five sighed audibly, her features grumbling, yet her stubborn, haughty posture never left her, just as Six's expression of calm and composure never left her; she always cares more about her appearance than refuting the claims.

"And I stood by your side then, just as I stood by Four's side to reach a compromise between you two, but you refused all solutions, remember that? We're not going to discuss this topic anymore; it's ridiculous and funny at the same time."

Then, in a less sharp tone, she directed her words straight to me: "Grumbling first thing in the morning! Forgive me, Seven, for this noise. It's impossible for this girl to accept any idea other than the one in her head, no matter how we explain it to her."

"But she really is elegant and cute, and her costumes are beautiful too. You didn't have to criticize her so harshly."

Five raised her eyebrow before admitting, reluctantly: "Yes, she is cute and elegant, I can't deny that, but her personality ruins it completely."

Six straightened her posture, feigning calmness, and said, while waving her hand dismissively: "I'll take it from any star but you, you blind monster! Shoo! Shoo!"

Five placed her hand on her forehead, sighing theatrically before announcing with exasperation: "See?! This is exactly what I'm talking about! Arrogant! I can't take it anymore, I'm leaving now."

But despite her angry words, she left with clear joy on her face; she wasn't really saying it seriously. Then I looked at Six, who was about to scream and complain in a waterfall of words because of Five, but she suddenly returned, which made her swallow her words, letting them explode internally with all calmness.

"I can't believe I forgot why I came after hearing Six's words. I saw Two rushing here, and later heard a crashing sound. Is everyone okay?"

"Two is sleeping here, and the crash was because of a friendly fight between Six and Thirteen."

"That's reassuring. Don't forget the morning class in a bit, and wake Two up so she can attend too."

We have to go to class, that's right. Before leaving, I looked at Two one last time. I didn't have it in me to wake that flower shrunken under the cover. She wouldn't have attended class anyway; she would definitely go to the library. So, I let her continue her nap, thus disobeying Five's word. I was thinking about that as I stepped outside, not noticing that Six had closed the door right after she left. I collided with it forcefully and fell to the ground. It was a truly painful injury, one worthy of having people around you rush to check on it.

***

"Six, I know it's a strange coincidence, but can you stop laughing? This isn't really funny."

"But don't you see how weird it is? What started as a trick in the morning has somehow become reality. It's so cute that whenever I think about it, I can't stop laughing!"

"You're exaggerating. It was just a simple accident."

"A simple accident?! She hit the door exactly as you claimed this morning! Even if we had planned this, it wouldn't have happened with such precision. Could it be that I have the power of prediction?"

"Oh, please, don't start boasting about this now."

"I'm not boasting, but you must admit it's a funny coincidence, or at least a strange one! Come on, Thirteen, don't be boring."

"It's not that I'm boring, but there's a difference between laughing and mockery."

"No mockery, just enjoying the absurdity of fate. Now, let's hurry before we're late for class."

Thirteen hummed grumpily, but she couldn't suppress a faint smile as she followed Star Six, who was still laughing to herself as if she had discovered a new cosmic law.

Chapter Five:
The Glow of Disappointment at the Banquet of Silence

This time, Star Thirteen writes the story for you — we take you back a little to the distant past, the early school days.

(1)

I was more excited to enter the school than any other star, but that enthusiasm vanished completely before the first week was over. Back then, there were only five adult stars, all of them around the Sun, surrounding her all the time, which made the school empty and quiet for me, terrifyingly hollow throughout the day, where you could see nothing but her bright light. Each one of them already occupied a place in assisting her, so I was left alone in the garden without any of them having the time to extend a hand to me so I could harmonize with them in that circle. This is what my innocent right eye saw. The other, however, saw something entirely different: each one of them never stopped working for that Sun who, in the end, is just another star. They revolved around her without stopping, as if they were part of her system. This is because her light is the only thing that grants a feeling of safety in this place. If you move a little away from her, you see the darkness extending inward with all contempt and arrogance, crawling mercilessly.

And when you see it, only then, you realize that staying by her side is bliss. But I refused to exploit the rare safety as long as I was unable to advance, as long as I had no clear role, as long as my existence was no different from my non-existence at all.

On that day, the morning lesson ended, and everyone left the hall with her, while I remained alone. I didn't move from my place at all, as I had grown utterly bored of the garden. And then, for the first time, I surrendered myself to the darkness. I wanted to know what it meant to belong to the gloom in a world like this. I felt something extinguish within me, I lost my enthusiasm completely, and I no longer believed in the light as if it were life. Then I heard them, whispering around me, laughing as they watched me fall, as if waiting for my disappearance. But I was alone in the vast garden; the school no longer had any existence, only empty spaces extending endlessly. And if I looked closely, I would have seen myself sitting there, alone somewhere, as I always had been. But, in the end, I wasn't alone. There was one who created light for my sake. She sparkled just like the Sun, and despite the inadequacy of her gleam, she kept the darkness away from my heart. I still remember how innocent my expression was then, my eyes filling with tears, my heart about to scream. But she paid it no mind, just sat beside me, then extended her hands to reach mine, holding them gently as if pulling me out of that dark depth. My tears didn't give me a chance to see her features, but I saw her smile, a sincere smile, glowing like a small light in the middle of a pitch-dark storm. I also saw her dazzling, strange double ponytail hairstyle, and then I heard her voice when she said those words with unparalleled

spontaneity: "I didn't know I had a colleague this cute, but...
are you really okay?"

No, I'm not okay at all.

I could barely say it before my eyes closed and I fell to the
ground. I wished then that I could have finished my sentence
and told her: You don't have to lie by saying I'm cute; I'm the
furthest thing from cute. I didn't realize it then, but that was
the first time a star had been afflicted with the curse of the
shadow—the illness that makes Stars gradually lose their
sparkle until they turn into a black shard. It comes with despair
and stillness, and grows when a star isolates herself from
others, just as happened with me.

The Sun was beside me when I woke up, with no one else.
Her light was as brilliant as ever, her beauty beyond words to
describe. Her hand enveloped my small hand with all
tenderness as I lay on the bed. Her presence surrounded me
like a protective shield, a feeling I didn't know I needed until
that moment. I found myself asking a question I hadn't
thought of before, but it slipped to my lips before I could stop
it: "What does it mean to be a star in this world?"

The Sun smiled, as if she expected this question, then
answered in her quiet, warm voice: "Being a star is not just a
title or a name; it is a special destiny we were born to live, and
we exist to illuminate the sky like our souls, no matter how
intense its darkness becomes. To be a star means to carry a
constant torch of hope for the world, to be a guide for the

lost, and a pillar to rely on when others crumble. It's not necessary then for us to be the brightest; it's enough that we create a balanced, harmonious sky filled with beauty. To be a star means to sacrifice a part of yourself for the warmth of those around you, to bear the weight of responsibility, and to transform from a mere individual into an inseparable part of a larger entity, of the universe itself. Therefore, no matter what happens, never forget: Stars do not belong to themselves, but to the sky, and the end of their journey is to leave new life behind them, in countless galaxies, worlds, and planets."

I took a deep breath, still trying to process her words, until my fears surfaced, fears I could no longer suppress: "But what if I'm not brave enough? What if my light is extinguished again?"

The Sun patted my hand gently, as if trying to reassure me before she answered: "When you think you're about to be extinguished, remember: Stars are never alone. Look at the other stars around you; each one of you possesses something unique that makes her an indispensable part of the whole. The leader needs an explorer, the captain needs an engineer, and the protector needs a doctor. All of you exist to light the way for each other, for the light begins from you, no matter how dark the path before you is."

"If that's the case, then I want to be a star like the others. I want them to rely on me to show their path, and I want to protect them from the darkness I fell into today, whatever the cost. And I want them to turn to me whenever they feel distress, despair, or loneliness."

I saw her smile widen with pride, as if she saw something in me that I hadn't yet seen in myself. She patted my head for a while before saying: "Since you arrived here, I've been thinking of a suitable number for you, and I think I've chosen one. You are now Thirteen, the star who fought the darkness so her sparkle would be destined for eternity. And you will be the leader of the Health Squad in the school."

It's a decimal number, ordinary, easy to forget, even though she could have given me a vacant single-digit number. But she didn't, because she believed I could bring honor to my number myself, not for the number to bring honor to my character. This was my beginning at the school, the place where Stars' beginnings are born.

I was still lost in my thoughts then when a familiar, mischievous voice interrupted me: "Star Thirteen, I heard there's a lonely star in the library. Want to go bother her?"

I looked at Six, tilting my head slightly in surprise, then said what occurred to me at that moment: "A star in the library? You know, Six, I thought we were only six stars in the school."

(2)
(The page now turns to what followed the scene at the end of the second chapter.)

In the pale moonlight that reflected on the damaged floor, we all looked like trapped inanimate objects inside the remains of our wounded ship. Its rays then crept through the cracks and fractures just as fear crept into our hearts, heavy with regret and anxiety, causing us to sit in a silent circle, each star looking into the void as if searching for an answer that circumstances had not helped her find. It was clear from our tired and tense features that the discussion had not yet begun, but its exhaustion had already preceded it. In the middle of that circle, Star Three stood, her back straight despite the turmoil betrayed by her trembling fingers, and even her eyes, which glowed with a feigned resolve that did not hide her confusion. Behind her sat Star One, silent, contemplative, as if trying to remain neutral. But her mere presence behind Three without objection raised my suspicion: Did this mean leadership had transferred to her? Or had Star One, the leader who had always been our support, decided to voluntarily hand over the helm? No, it couldn't be that simple. One look at Star One confirmed to me she was not as we knew her; she was different, exhausted, as if completely drained. On the opposite side was Five, standing like a mountain of anger, her fists clenched and her face almost burning with resentment. And if everyone was drowned in fear and tension, she was the only one who decided to confront the matter with resistance. When Star Three began to speak, her voice was stern and decisive, as if she wanted to end the discussion before it even started: "We have made the decision. Exile was necessary. They pose a danger to the group, and we cannot tolerate more recklessness. We need order if we want to stay alive."

The impact of her words was harsh, like a sentence declared by a court that accepts no appeal. But Five did not back down. Instead, she took a step forward, anger flaring in her voice:

"You call this order?! You just got rid of them because you couldn't deal with the consequences of that disaster! To push the guilt off yourself, you sacrificed them by placing the responsibility on them!"

Before Three could reply, One intervened in a quiet voice, though it sounded weary as if it had exited her chest with great effort: "Five, please, let's not make things worse than they are. This decision wasn't easy for anyone. We are all trying to do what is best..."

But Five was not ready to hear any justification. Her gaze shifted towards One, a deep look, burning more with disappointment than with anger: "And you, how could you agree?! You were always the leader we trusted. How did you allow this? Have you now become just a shadow of Star Three?"

Three lifted her chin stubbornly and replied with a cruelty that seemed to be trying to bury her hesitation in a sharp tone: "Yes! I am the one in charge now. Leadership requires making difficult decisions, and I will not allow the group to be turned upside down because of your excessive emotion. So, stop this, Five."

Five laughed a short laugh, without mirth, without life, before retorting sharply: "Difficult decisions?! Are you that blind?! With that ridiculous decision of yours, you pushed three of our elite to their doom! Three whom we desperately need if we want to survive. We need each other. What you are doing now is not called leadership at all, it's madness!"

Anxiety and tension grew more visible on everyone's faces. Wary glances were exchanged among the Stars in silence, until murmurs began to slowly creep in, as if everyone was searching for an explanation for what was happening, while eyes darted between Star Three and Five amidst a charged atmosphere that didn't suggest a good end to this argument. At that moment, Star One rose, trying to calm the situation, but her tone was faint and hesitant, so much so that I wasn't sure if her words would reach them or be lost amidst this harsh tension.

"Stop now, both of you! We are going through a difficult time, and we cannot tolerate division. Three is trying to maintain the group's cohesion as best she can, that's all there is to it."

But her voice wasn't decisive enough to stop the storm that was escalating. Five was still blazing with anger, and her cutting voice carried no intention of backing down: "She's destroying it! Those you exiled were a part of us. How will we bear their loss? Who among us will be the replacement? And what will happen when Three decides to get rid of us too?"

Three stepped back slightly, staring at Five as if she couldn't believe what she had heard. But she quickly composed herself and went back on the attack: "I am only doing what is in the group's best interest. If you can't see that, then that's your problem, Five."

I felt the air in the room become heavier. That was a catastrophic declaration from Three, as if she didn't realize that with these words, she had confirmed Five's worst fears and given her the proof she was looking for. Five took a single step forward, confronting Three face-to-face, as if challenging her decision. Her tone was calmer, but every word was filled with deadly certainty: "No, it's your problem. I bet this leadership of yours will lead us all to ruin today before tomorrow."

Three couldn't respond directly, but instead of escalating, she retreated with calculated steps, as if refusing to be dragged into a bigger battle. A tense moment of silence passed between them, in which no one moved, before Five suddenly turned and walked out of the circle with angry steps. She didn't need to say anything else; her stance was enough to make things clear to everyone. Star Six didn't hesitate and joined her immediately, as if she had been waiting for this moment. With their departure, I felt as if something in this place had broken, as if the rift that began to widen would not be easy to repair.

I knew this was a pivotal moment, and that we now faced two paths, each carrying consequences that could not be predicted. Five might have been the only one who dared to speak the truth, but she was now in the position of the dissenter, a position that would be considered a threat to survival, not a warning for it. Before Star Five left the room, Three cast a decisive look at the rest of the Stars, then said in a cold and firm voice: "If Five cannot work with us, then let her do what she wants. As for us, we must focus on survival. I will not allow this rebellion to destroy us."

Then she returned to her place and sat, as if she had finished the final chapter of this confrontation. But I wasn't confident that this was the real end; rather, it seemed to me this was just the beginning of what was worse. The other Stars began to slowly move towards the exit, and the atmosphere in the room became gloomier than it was when the meeting began. One remained standing, her eyes fixed on the door through which Five and Six had left, her face filled with worry and regret, as if she realized that this decision might be the beginning of the end.

(3)

When I went out, the morning had already arrived, and the sky was cloaked in dark orange hues, heralding a turbulent day. The wind was cold, toying with the dry grasses and hastening the scattering of the heavy clouds, as if the weather itself reflected the chaos we were living in. I stood for a moment at the ship's entrance, hesitant to take any step, my eyes searching for a shelter amidst these conflicting emotions. There, on a large rock in the middle of the grassy plain, Star Five was sitting, staring at the horizon with strained eyes, as if searching for an answer within the folds of the volatile sky. As for Star Six, she was sitting below her, preoccupied, her hands fiddling with some fabrics and tools she had brought. But I felt that she, like all of us, wasn't sure what would happen next.

I looked at them from afar and felt a conflict pulling me in two opposing directions. A part of me wanted to stay, not to object to Star Three's leadership, to be part of what remained of the system. But the other part, the part that could no longer bear the silence, wanted to hear Five's opinion, to understand where we would go if we chose to leave. I moved without realizing it, as if my feet led themselves to them, until I was standing before them, listening to Five's voice which carried an unshakable certainty.

"I can't stay there. I won't allow myself to be part of her failure. Three will lead everyone who stays to their death with her stubbornness and her ignorance, no doubt about it."

Six raised her head, looked at her while turning the words over in her mind, then said with hesitation: "But are you sure? Leaving now means we lose all our rights in the group. We'll become rebels, and we'll be out there alone, wrestling with death."

"Dying in our solitude is better than staying under the leadership of someone who only cares about imposing her control. We can live on our own; we have the skills and the intelligence. We don't need Star Three to decide our fate."

Her words carried a clarity that was hard to argue with, but she had forgotten one thing: the matter wasn't just about her or me or Six. We were part of a group, and our responsibility extended to those who remained there. I stepped forward cautiously, my voice coming out hesitant, but it carried with it everything that was going on inside me: "What you said was great, but what about the rest? What about the Stars we left behind there? If we leave, if we separate, who will protect them if you're not there? We are here to be together, isn't this what the Sun used to say? Each one of us possesses something unique that makes her an indispensable part of the whole. The leader needs an explorer, the captain needs an engineer, and the protector needs a doctor. All of us exist to light the way for each other, not to say that death here is inevitable and then leave them to their death."

Five didn't say anything immediately. Instead, she left her rock and approached me. Her eyes were steady, but behind that steadfastness, there was a conflict. She looked at me for moments, then said in a calmer tone than I expected: "Even if we stay, we won't be able to help them when the time of need comes. Were we, for example, able to oppose the decision to exile our sisters? And we will remain stuck in the same vortex that Star Three has created. If you want to do the right thing, come with me, and I won't let you face their fate alone."

I hesitated. Her words carried a clear logic, but they weren't enough to extinguish the doubts within me: "I don't want to separate, I don't want to leave them, but... I don't want to die here either."

Star Six raised her head, looked at me with a faint smile before saying: "Then, come with us. We're not abandoning them; we're just making a place for ourselves where we can do something when things go wrong here. Isn't that better than standing and waiting for the end?"

I looked at her, then turned to Star Five and asked her again, as if I needed one final confirmation before I decided: "And will you return if they need us?"

"If we can do something, yes."

Then she added in a softer voice, but still filled with distrust: "But not under the leadership of Star Three. I don't trust her."

A long silence passed. I looked at the wrecked ship we had left behind, at that entity that seemed to be dying, telling us the story of its final days. Then I looked at Five and Six, at this new path opening before me. In the end, I stepped forward and joined them. But I couldn't resist one last question, as if I needed a final confirmation before I moved on: "We will return if they need us?"

"We will return if we can do something."

Star Five said it firmly and nodded her head, as if she saw in my decision a sign that something had begun to change. Finally, I turned and began to walk towards them, step by step, until I was beside them. We were three shadows stretching long on the cracked green earth, proceeding on an unknown path, while the wind intensified around us, whispering to us the stories of those who left before us.

(4)

We were walking south without a specific destination, like homeless wanderers lost in a world full of things that could take our lives in an instant. But the problem wasn't the possibility of our death, but our ignorance of the things that could cause it in the first place. For this reason, I established my first rule in this unknown: Don't touch anything, no matter how shiny it looks. As we advanced, I remembered that Star Five had mentioned finding caves in the south last evening. Did this mean we were heading towards them? The idea crept into my mind before I voiced it aloud. Star Five then answered in a quiet but decisive voice: "Staying in the caves would be dangerous with the wolves present. We will bypass this option for now and return to it only out of extreme necessity. You feel the wind picking up, don't you?"

I looked at the sky, at the black clouds coming from the east, then nodded: "Yes, it seems a storm is looming on the horizon."

"And that means the wolves will resort to hiding in the caves, especially since this area doesn't have dense forests that could provide them with better shelter."

I hadn't thought of that at all. I looked at her with fascination before saying with admiration: "You're truly a genius when it comes to survival."

From behind, I heard Star Six's voice as she slowed her steps and looked at us with curiosity: "Don't forget that you're a genius too when it comes to illnesses, Thirteen."

Then she directed her words to Five: "But, I thought you wanted to hide in a cave. Why are we heading south then?"

"The matter is clear, because I have scouted these areas previously. I will not risk your lives in places I haven't explored yet, especially in our current state."

I felt a sudden reassurance upon hearing that, as if I had been over-analyzing the situation then. We were with the leader of the Safety Squad, the person whose abilities I could trust most, a star trained to endure situations far more dangerous than a mere wolf attack. Yet, my mind was still buzzing with questions: Where should we go? How will we avoid the storm? Are these the right decisions? It was as if I were the main character in this story, even though I knew for certain that I was not.

But that momentary feeling of security quickly dissipated when I remembered the truth I had ignored until now: in our absence, no one was left with the group—and I mean that literally. The leader of the Exploration Squad and her deputy, Star Two and Six; the leader of the Engineering Squad and her deputy, Star Four and Seven; the leader of the Safety and Health squads and her deputy, Star Five and me—all of us were outside. The only older Stars left there were One and Three, and I don't need to think much to realize that this alone is enough to cause chaos.

At this moment, I saw all thoughts related to returning completely vanish before me. Every star is now trying to impose her point of view on everyone, each one refusing to cooperate. Clinging to her opinion has become more important than survival itself, and this is what makes staying together difficult, and returning impossible—unless we reunite. And yet, something tells me that Two and Four are not like us. They wouldn't think selfishly; they wouldn't seek only to survive as we are doing now. They must be observing things in a different way. They must be making a plan that includes not only themselves, but all of us. Why didn't they object to the exile decision at all? It's as if they saw in it a golden opportunity to explore this world that surprised us with its danger, as if they didn't see in it an end, but the beginning of something else.

(5)

Throughout the minutes of our walk, I was trying to formulate the ideal way to explain the problem of our departure to Five. I know she has to think about it again, and perhaps if she refused to go back with me and Six, that decision might push her to reconsider and return. But what could I do besides think while we crossed these empty plains? Sing? That's ridiculous. Only now did I realize the reason Five approached the mountains and explored the caves: she was looking for a shelter, a place for us to hide from the coming storm. But with the dark clouds looming on the horizon, it seemed to me that trying to enter the caves now would be nothing but a stroke of foolishness. Six cuts through my reverie when she noticed my expression change: "Is something bothering you?"

I'm not ready to talk right now. We don't need additional problems before we find a place to settle.

"No. I just like the view of the plains, nothing more."

"The plains? That's strange. You know? You looked cu— very beautiful during that."

She then raised her eyebrows slyly, as if testing me. So, I said: "Is that right?"

She narrowed her eyes, looking at me with suspicion, before exclaiming: "Something is really bothering you!"

Before I could reply, Five interrupted us in a calm tone: "I'm sure there's a narrow mountain crevice near here. It will be a good and safe place to stay until the storm is over. We can discuss your problems in it."

She paused for a moment, then added in a softer tone: "Is that alright? I hope I haven't burdened you two by walking this long distance."

Despite her usual confidence, her voice at the end sounded as if she feared she might have pushed us beyond what we could bear, as if, despite her firmness, she was watching our steps with a hidden concern, wondering deep down whether we were able to continue, or if her decisions had placed a greater burden than necessary on our shoulders.

(6)

The wind was raging, carrying everything in its path, and the rain began to fall heavily, cleansing the earth and devouring every trace that had been drawn upon it in the old days. I truly hope our ship isn't one of those traces. We stopped walking then and started running. Although the body becomes slow under the weight of the cold, I didn't dare to stop; none of us did. Five was in the lead, her heart pounding with a force that gave her an unusual flame of activity due to anxiety and stress. Perhaps that's because she knows very well that fear doesn't exempt her from her responsibility, nor had any of us overlooked it. With every step, her eyes would glance back towards us to check on us, then return to scanning the sky, not the ground. With her sharp movements, it was clear she knew exactly how to handle the storm and where we were headed.

Then suddenly, out of nowhere, a narrow opening appeared before us in the mountain. It must be the crevice she spoke of, but it was extremely narrow, more so than I imagined. It barely allows you to pass through by crawling. That's why I didn't understand how this place could be our shelter from the storm from Five's perspective. I looked at her with surprise as I gestured with my hand towards the narrow crevice. She replied, trying to make her voice as calm as possible: "We'll shelter here until the storm ends. It's not a luxurious place, but at least it's safe."

I gestured again towards the crevice with clear objection: "But it's just a small crevice."

"Yes. That will make it warm inside."

She said it as she was lowering herself to the ground to crawl through the narrow opening, and she really did it. I then turned to Six. I'm sure she would have refused to crawl on the ground if given the choice, even if it were for a necessary matter, but now she was forced to do it, and this gives me an irreplaceable opportunity to be sarcastic with her. The time has come to repay the debt for the silliness she said to me while we were walking earlier. I smiled with obvious sarcasm as I pointed to her rain-soaked clothes: "At least the beauty won't worry like the cute one about her clothes made of celestial silk."

Her eyes flashed sharply, and she replied without hesitation and in a clear tone: "Of course she won't worry when the beauty's tailor is with her, but the tailor herself has no replacement."

I raised my eyebrows with clear defiance: "So what's your plan, cute one?"

"I'll take off my clothes and then go inside."

I thought she was joking as usual, so I smiled with disbelief: "Is this another joke?"

"No. I'm serious about what I'm saying now."

I felt genuinely worried by her seriousness, so I took a step towards her: "You'll get hurt, and you might catch a cold."

"It's alright, the wounds will be under the clothes."

I wanted to provoke her stubbornness to test her seriousness, so I said with an explicit challenge: "Then, I dare you to do it."

She replied immediately with a stubborn tone: "But I really will do it."

"I'm sure you won't. Sacrificing your body for clothes! What a ridiculous decision."

She began to touch her elegant, wet shirt gently, her slow finger movements revealing how hesitant she was, carefully pulling the fabric from her body to take it off delicately. Even while doing so, she was trying to preserve the shirt's details as if it were something truly precious. Her gaze didn't stopdarting between the mountain opening and my eyes, as if waiting for me or Five to stop her, but that didn't happen. When she was about to take off the first parts of her shirt, despite the grandeur of the sight of her gleaming eyes doing it defiantly, and that internal resistance visible on her face, I stepped towards her and gently but firmly grabbed her arm, preventing her from completing what she had started. I let out a long sigh as I shook my head: "Are you serious? Sometimes I feel you're a child because of these actions."

She stopped moving and looked at me, feigning displeasure, before a faint smile formed on her lips, hiding behind it a clear feeling of relief. The whole scene was ridiculous, funny, and warm at the same time. It reminded me that we are not just survivors in a harsh world, but sisters who bear responsibility for each other. With that long sigh, I lowered my head to the side and closed my eyes, but I was now certain: if she was truly ready to take off her clothes to avoid staining them with mud, this only indicated their precious status to her. I might be an opportunistic friend for sarcastic scenes, a lover of revenge, and a refuser of submission when it comes to Star Six specifically, but I also extend a helping hand when my sisters are in need and distress. This was one of the first things I learned from the Sun, and from Star Five as well, the leader of our squad.

I finally spoke in a quiet voice, trying to reassure her as much as I could: "The place must be warm inside, so I'll pass my coat back to you after I go through. It's a bit long on me, so I'm sure it will cover your uniform completely. Is that alright?"

She looked at me intently, her eyes filled with confusion and gratitude. She was fidgeting with her fingertips between shyness and doubt, but when she saw my confident, calm eyes, she felt a sense of appreciation and whispered: "Thanks. I didn't expect that from you."

I smiled lightly as I replied with a gentle joke: "My pleasure, cute one."

With that, my work outside was done, and it was time for me to enter the mountain. I threw my body to the ground, put my head inside, and began to crawl. It was difficult with this large body—oh, how it becomes a burden in situations like this despite its advantages—but with this, I was now sure that Six would be able to pass through easily with her slender body. From the inside, the tunnel was like deaf, cold walls, and step by step it grew narrower to the point I imagined my chest would be the only thing preventing me from entering in the end. I even imagined the mountain slowly swallowing me as I passed. Then suddenly, a faint light appeared from the other side, which was only one last step away from me. And there was the end.

The inside of the place was no different from the tunnel. It was more like a rectangular, box-like room with solid, engraved walls, and not large in size—just enough for the three of us to sit and light a fire in the middle without its flame posing a danger to us. I sat on the floor as soon as I passed through, leaning against one of the walls. I couldn't stand up due to the low height of the ceiling. I then took off my coat and passed it to Six, who was waiting outside. I settled down to catch my breath for a few moments, but I couldn't stop for long; the need to warm the place was more urgent than our fatigue. After Six crawled inside, I sat firmly in the middle, as if I had become the temporary leader of this small group while Five sat quietly in a solid corner. I gathered my breath and gave instructions in a steady voice: "Star Five and Six, first take off your wet uniforms; we'll leave them aside to dry. I'm going to light a fire, so put the sleeping covers around you and sit beside it so you don't catch a cold. I will check on you after that. If the storm lasts longer than lunchtime, we'll sleep to save time."

Five looked at me with calm eyes, then nodded in agreement. As for Six, she raised her hand hesitantly, handing me my coat whose color had turned from white to brown because of the mud that stuck to it during her passage. When I took it from her, she whispered shyly, trying to avoid my gaze: "I don't wear anything under my uniform, so it would be a bit embarrassing to take it all off, and it's not that wet so..."

My eyebrows rose in surprise, then I answered her seriously: "Your clothes are the wettest among us, what are you talking about?! The dampness will quickly absorb your body's warmth, which will increase the likelihood of you getting Star hypothermia. Even I don't wear anything under my shirt, so we are in the same predicament."

She looked at me with disapproval, then grumbled in a low voice: "Why do you think telling me that would reassure me?! This only makes it more embarrassing."

I sighed in despair, trying to suppress a sarcastic smile: "Oh, my luck with you! I think I have a padded vest; you can borrow it until your uniform dries."

Her eyes began to sparkle a little as she said in a half-surprised tone: "How generous of you today. You would have refused to give it to me if we were at the school."

"Of course I would refuse! Our room's wardrobe was so full of your worthless experimental clothes that you forced Seven to put her clothes under her bed. So why would I give you my vest then?!"

She smiled a small smile, her eyes twinkling with that old competitive streak that hadn't disappeared even in circumstances like these: "Have you forgotten that your vest, this coat, and even the shirt you're wearing now are all from my sewing, because of those experimental outfits?"

This conversation would never have ended no matter how much we talked, so I had no choice but to cut off her argument with silence. I lowered my head to the side, closed my eyes, and let out a long sigh that was like an attempt to get rid of all the chaos that had begun to accumulate inside me. Before I could complete my surrender, I felt a warm hand touch my shoulder. It was Five; she had approached without me noticing, passing me her heavy leather coat and her skirt while whispering in her familiar, quiet voice: "I didn't know your relationship had reached this level. How impressive and cute."

Hearing those words from her was surprising, embarrassing, and validating all at once. A quiet, unexaggerated smile formed on my lips as I tried to hide the embarrassment I felt, but my eyes couldn't ignore the expression of delight that filled her face, while her eyes burned it with a look that held a deep, hidden sadness beneath the surface. It was easy to know the reason for that. My relationship with Star Five was one of the most affectionate for her, even though we only met in regular school classes or at meetings of the Safety and Health club. She always showed her concern for taking care of each one of us. She wasn't reclusive like Two; she didn't avoid making friends or connecting with others. She even played with us sometimes, even if the play was always interspersed with a kind of chaos. No one liked playing with her at first, then they started to constantly make fun of her when she tried to join them. Yet, she never stopped herself from continuing.

She always displayed the personality of an older sister to everyone, giving advice nonstop, as if she considered herself responsible for everyone. The sight of her sitting in the garden sipping tea while giving advice to the little Stars was a common scene; she was their first choice when the Sun was absent, the safe haven they turned to for her counsel. But, even at those times, no one really tried to spend time with her. Even I, her deputy, would only watch her from afar, perhaps because I considered her strong enough to bear all that without needing anyone.

No. That's not entirely true. Recently, she had been spending most of her time with Four, likely due to both of them being busy with the same tasks in preparation for the journey. It must have been Four's exile, far away with the others, at a time when we specifically needed them, that plunged her into this tragedy. And seeing us outside as well only increased her sadness until she was unable to hide it despite her toughness, while having no solutions except escape, knowing it's futile, and thinking about helplessness.

(8)

How I hate these hours. My last word left me confused even after I had dozed off. I tried to grasp something different, but all thoughts led me to this point: Everyone is actually incapable of finding a way out of what we're facing. It's the second day! Everything that has happened, and we are still on the second day. And what did we have other than arguing and casting blame? Nothing. What have we done to survive and try to leave this nightmare? Nothing either. This is the bitter reality we are living in amidst all these disagreements, without realizing it.

When I woke up, Five was already sitting up, but her mind was wandering in a distant world, thinking, so she never noticed my waking. And Six was still sleeping peacefully despite what was befalling us. Oh, how relaxing ignorance is. I put on my shirt and sat beside her. I saw that this was the right time to talk about our problem in more detail: The older sisters remaining in a state of constant argument and separation will leave the younger Stars no choice but to fall into an abyss, one most of them have already fallen into. I thought about opening the conversation, but I was searching for the right words. Suddenly, I spoke at the same time she did. It seemed we both wanted to talk about the same thing: "I want to talk to you for a bit about returning."

"Do you want to talk about leaving?"

And it became funny when we both fell silent out of respect for the other to complete their sentence, which left an opportunity for a long quiet to spread without anyone speaking. One of us had to bravely break it to talk, and neither of us possessed that kind of courage. In the end, as usual, Five broke the silence and continued: "After thinking about it, I realized it too. Leaving the ship at this specific time was a bad choice given the approaching storm. I didn't expect it to hit with such force. Was this what was bothering you while we were walking?"

I shook my head in denial and answered: "No. I still think leaving was necessary to teach Three a lesson about cohesion, and that a quick wave of rain would make her understand the difficulty of surviving away from her illusions. But I never imagined it would turn into a strong storm lasting for hours. The endurance of the damaged ship's hull in this weather is a miracle. Without the ship, it would be impossible to find another shelter quickly, and they would be forced to take cover in the dense forest, which is more dangerous than the cold."

Five was looking at me with concentration, as if rearranging her words in her mind, then she said cautiously: "So we should return as soon as the storm stops to help them survive. Is that good?"

But I felt some hesitation, and I knew another idea was forming in my mind. So, I told her in a quiet but firm voice: "Our going would be pointless. We aren't capable of changing anything in that scenario; we would only perish along with them. We will go find the exiled ones. Star Four and Seven are the only ones capable of knowing the ship's condition and what it needs to endure the storm. We must agree that there is no shelter like it, aside from its importance for returning later."

This wasn't entirely true. There was a much better idea than this, an idea that gave me a sense of peace.

"No. The Stars are now without a guardian. You must return to them with Star Six and help Star One manage this crisis. I will go search for them alone."

I wasn't sure of her response and was prepared to hear her refusal, but her silence was surprising, before she said slowly: "I trust your decisions, but are you sure that's the best option for us right now?"

I looked away, feeling the weight of the words on my chest before I answered: "Not really, but as long as you are there, I will rest assured about the Stars until my return, no matter what happens. It's just a selfish wish of mine, isn't it?"

How did I become so blunt as to say such a thing?! It seems my heart had weakened to the point that I wanted to escape from everyone, weakened to the point I was no longer able to hold back such ridiculous desires. I could have changed the phrasing of the matter to turn it into an indisputable fact, but I preferred to say it in its explicit form, even if it was embarrassing. Five would surely reject it now because of that. I looked away, on high alert to hear her refusal after the current silence.

"But are you sure about going alone when you could leave accompanied by Six?"

I hesitated for a little, then spoke with a false confidence I was trying to affirm more to myself than to Five: "Searching alone will be lighter and faster than going with her, and you will definitely need her amidst the crowds of Stars if you want positivity and calm amidst the frightening, decisive moments."

Five raised her head, and the same expression I saw at the beginning of the journey appeared on her face, a mixture of confusion and confidence. Then she said quietly: "We'll do what we can there. Find them quickly and return to the ship before it's too late."

I was surprised by her accepting tone, so I asked with hesitation: "Wait... does that mean you agree to it?!"

Then she smiled lightly and replied: "To survive, we need everyone, isn't that what you said earlier? That's why we will all gather again at the ship, and we will force that upon Three. Since this is your decision, I will respect it. We're counting on you, Thirteen."

Her smile, despite its paleness, carried within its folds the warmth of the Sun that had recently been absent from our sky. I felt a different feeling, a mixture of confidence and fear, but I knew there was no longer any room for turning back.

(9)

I immediately prepared my luggage, keeping only my essential belongings and emptying my bag of anything related to provisions. It would be more important for them than for me, and I had to be as light as possible. I don't know how long the search for them will take, when the storm might stop or strike, or where I will have to spend the night during that. Amidst all this, I remembered that my absence would also be a problem, but I can be replaced by notes. If I'm not here, my written words might be their only support, like a shadow of me that stays with them if my absence is prolonged.

I took my journal out of the bag and wrote in it the most important illnesses and problems that can affect the Stars and their methods of treatment in detail, adding guidance notes for facing any emergency situation. When I finished, I put the final touches on my preparations, then approached Five with hesitant steps, holding the book whose weight I felt more than usual, and the bag hanging on my back. Five raised her eyes towards me, the signs of worry clear on her face: "You're leaving now? The storm is still strong outside."

"They will probably be hiding now like us; that will reduce the distance gap between us quickly. I will manage somehow, don't worry."

"And do you know anything about their location? This land is vast, and I don't want you to get lost."

"Two talked about ruins of a city near the ship's location when she was interrogated about the matter of her going out with Seven at night. And if I know Two and Four well, they will definitely be there looking for a place and equipment to repair the ship."

Five hesitated for a moment, then said in a worried voice: "Don't you at least want to inform Six before you leave? She will worry about you as soon as she wakes up and doesn't find you here."

"Just give her my coat then. That will be what she needs from me when she wakes up."

"I don't understand, but I will do it. And what else... yes. Take good care of yourself, Thirteen."

Her final words weighed my heart down with longing, as if she were asking me to stay. For a moment, I almost gave in, but duty was calling me more strongly. She made me imagine that she, for some reason, was the Sun standing before me, with those kind features and her eyes full of both confidence and sadness. I wanted to stay with her a little longer, perhaps just to reassure her, but I had to hurry and leave now, and that's what I did.

(10)

I stepped out of the crevice with heavy steps, the wind lashing my face from the first moments of my exit as if testing my resolve. The storm had not subsided; rather, it seemed to be growing fiercer, its shriek like the creaking of doors slamming shut nonstop, masking the sound of my footsteps on the damp ground. For this reason, I had to concentrate on every step. The path was rugged, and the scattered rocks, like thorns, were waiting for a small slip from me to devour me. I tightened the strap of the bag on my back and advanced with difficulty.

Despite the breaths of the storm, I felt an inner warmth as I thought of them, my sisters. In this endless expanse of loneliness and loss, I remembered Five's words and her final look. Sometimes, even the sun that rises on my heart leaves a place for shadows, but they are shadows that give me strength.

With every step, I scrutinized the land stretching before me, searching for any sign indicating the ruins Two had spoken of. This land, which looked like an endless dry sea, breathed its harshness in my face with every gust of wind that carried dust as sharp as needles. The shifting sand under my feet made faint sounds, as if conspiring to confuse me, and the barren plains extended mercilessly, covered with scattered rocks that had taken on strange shapes, like frozen ghosts watching me in silence. Some were small like scattered pebbles, and others huge like the ruins of ancient temples, bearing the traces of a time erased by oblivion. I tried to analyze every detail: the lines the wind had drawn on the sand, the tracks of animals that might have passed here days ago, the remnants of armored vehicles that had turned black despite their toughness, and the shadows of the rocks that seemed to be pointing to something distant, in an attempt to find any clue to them. With every step, I listened attentively, but silence was the master of the place, except for the sound of the wind that raged in my ears like faint whispers warning me.

Sometimes, my vision deceived me. I would see something moving in the distant horizon, like a person or a living body, but when I got closer, I would find it was merely a mirage or shadows played by the sun on the sand. Despite the harshness of the scene, I couldn't ignore its strange beauty. The gray sky, pierced by lines of faint light, left a glimmer of hope on this expanse. And between the rocks, there were rare plants barely clinging to life, their pale leaves wrapped in winding brown lines like dying veins, but still resisting, as if challenging the wind itself, as if fighting to survive in a merciless world—one that fate, unfortunately, chose for us to be stuck in. And the deeper I ventured, the more I felt as if the earth itself was hiding secrets, perhaps the footprints of those who passed here before me, or signs indicating the ruins I was seeking. Everything in this labyrinth of rocks, sand, and metal seemed like a puzzle I had to solve, and I was searching for the first thread that would lead me to the truth.

After hours of walking, the storm began to subside, as if nature had decided to grant me a short respite. The sky, which had been obscured by thick clouds the whole time, finally revealed its majestic, blackish-blue color, illuminated by the paleness of the sun, which seemed to be gazing at me with worry. As for the wind, which had defied me with every step, it had now retreated to faint whispers as if watching my silence. I used this calm to take a moment's rest beside a large rock, with rough edges, that looked as old as the earth itself. I took the water bottle from my bag and drank a few small sips, carefully touching them to my lips, while allowing my eyes to wander across the horizon. The place was vast, a sandy expanse meeting the sky at an unclear line, but it hid within its folds something I felt belonged to me. I stood up again and began to look around, searching for any sign that might lead me to them. The scattered rocks, the dry earth bearing ancient, time-covered traces, and even the shadows of the distant mountains—everything I observed seemed meaningless. I felt as if this land were deliberately hiding its secrets from me, swallowing every clue that could lead me to those lost ones.

(11)

As time passed, and the sun slowly descended towards the horizon, it cast long shadows on the barren land. I was moving randomly, without a clear direction, my heart heavy with worry and fear that I might have lost my only chance to reach them. Every step added a new burden to my soul, and every passing minute made the probability of finding them seem impossible. Suddenly, in a moment where despair mixed with a deadly calm, the air split with the sound of a huge explosion that shook the ground from under my feet. I stopped in my tracks, and I felt my heart freeze for a moment, then it began to pound madly. The sound was close, and its power made me realize it was no ordinary explosion. I raised my head towards the horizon and saw a dense black cloud rising slowly into the sky, like a dark fist piercing the atmosphere. The scene was shocking, but it was also the answer I was searching for. There was no doubt; that explosion was the only proof of their existence. But are they okay? This explosion was nothing but a sign of imminent danger. I knew then that I must get there quickly, whatever the cost.

I started running unconsciously towards the source of the smoke, my feet sinking into the sand at times, and on the grass at others, my heart moving with greater haste than my mind's analyses. The path was filled with debris and the remains of machinery, but fear mixed with hope pushed me to continue without feeling fatigue or concern for what I saw. The closer I got, the more the features of the land were changing. The remains of destroyed buildings appeared before me, then corroded metal structures—clear signs that this area had witnessed an unforgettable war. Then from the top of a small hill, I saw before me a site resembling an old airport. The huge iron structures that survived the destruction stood like silent ghosts, while the thick smoke emanated from one of the side warehouses. I stood there for a moment to catch my breath, my eyes scanning the place nonstop. The atmosphere was enveloped in a silence charged with danger, as if the earth itself was warning me of what I might find inside. I screamed at the top of my lungs: "Two! Seven!"

I repeated it over and over, but the echo was my only reply. At that point, I had no time to hesitate. I gripped the bag tightly and rushed towards the warehouse, where the answer to all my questions seemed to be waiting for me inside.

(12)

I reached the ruins of the warehouse, thick dust filling the air. The black cloud I had seen from afar was hiding the aftermath of the explosion and the fire that followed, but its presence still permeated the place, mixed with the smell of fuel, burning metal, and a heat that crept onto my skin relentlessly. From a distance, amidst the debris and the intermittent sounds of small parts of the ceiling collapsing, I glimpsed her moving, leaning on the remains of one of the destroyed buildings. I approached her slowly, feeling my breath catch with every step. And there I found her, the dreamer, Seven. Her face was covered in soot, her clothes torn by the explosion, and burns covered her left arm and part of her face, while her right leg was twisted at an unnatural angle. I knew immediately then that her foot was broken.

I screamed her name and ran towards her. When I reached her, I knelt cautiously beside her, my fingers trembling as I tried to make sure she was still alive. Her chest was moving slowly, her breaths weak but present.

"Thirteen?"

She whispered in a barely audible voice, her eyes half-open, as if she couldn't believe I was here.

"I'm here. I'm with you now. Don't move!"

I tried to sound strong despite the anxiety tearing me apart. I quickly checked her body; the burns seemed superficial but painful, and the fracture was clear from the swelling. I had no time to hesitate; I had to act quickly and correctly. I opened my bag and started searching for anything that could help. I took out a clean cloth I kept for emergencies, then poured a little water on it to clean the burns as much as possible. Seven groaned in pain even though I tried to work as gently as I could.

"I need you to endure a little. We're getting out of here together, but I have to treat you first."

Then I moved to her broken foot. I didn't have specialized medical equipment, but I know the basics and can simulate them. I bent a piece of a small metal rod from among the debris, wrapped it in a piece of cloth so it wouldn't hurt her more, then used it as a temporary splint, and tied her leg to it using my belts.

"This will hurt a little, but we have no choice."

She screamed in pain when I started to tighten the belt to secure it, but I continued, because if I didn't, her condition could worsen. After I finished the first aid, I took a deep breath and tried to assess the situation. I was reassured that Seven was in a relatively stable condition, but the worry for Two and Four was setting my chest on fire, and I had no choice but to act quickly.

"We're getting out of here, but you have to tell me, where are the others? Are they okay?"

"The warehouse... we were there..."

She sighed with difficulty before continuing: "Two was here... she might be somewhere nearby... looking for Four."

"Seven, I'm going to leave you for a short while. I'll look for Two and Four and come back. That's a promise."

She looked at me with exhausted eyes and tried to nod in agreement, but the pain stopped her.

"But be careful... please."

"I'll be fine."

I said it, although my heart wasn't entirely confident in my words, and I started to move quickly. My eyes searched the horizon for any sign indicating the presence of Two or Four, but the rocks and smoke all looked the same. So, I tried to focus on the small details: footprints that Two might have left, or any unnatural sign that might indicate buried living remains. I passed through areas where the debris was denser, burnt metal remains and destroyed walls, but I found no trace of the Stars. Then the wind began to gradually return, carrying with it faint sounds from afar. I listened carefully, hoping to hear a voice or a call, but everything was still.

As I was moving through a small valley between the metal sheets, I noticed something strange on the ground: a small, torn piece of cloth, its color matching our uniform. I picked it up quickly, and my heart began to pound forcefully. This was a clear clue that she was nearby. I looked around cautiously and tried to estimate her direction.

I screamed at the top of my lungs: "Four!"

But the wind stole the call away. I waited a moment, hoping to hear a reply, but there was only silence. Nevertheless, I wasn't ready to stop. I continued moving, following the small tracks she had left, determined to find her and Two, no matter the risks. Deep down, I knew that time was not on my side, but hope was pushing me forward. I will not leave them behind.

Before I took the first step away, I felt something touch my back. That touch sent terror deep into my heart in an instant, and I fell with an unending scream between the black rocks and the foul-smelling sand. The smoke prevented me from seeing her at first, but after she lowered her head and extended her hand to lift me, I saw her up close, clearly. It was Star Two, her serious, steady features standing out as usual. I was catching my breath with difficulty, especially in this airless area, so I rushed to scream at her: "You should have answered me when I was calling! For your Mother's sake, why did you do that!"

"I saw no point in shouting and replying to you from a distance. I thought approaching was better."

That was her habit, and I didn't really expect an answer beyond what she said. I gripped her hand tightly and pulled myself up by it. As I was dusting myself off, she continued: "Of all people, I was hoping you specifically would be here, and here luck has brought you to us. You must have met Seven at the entrance, right? How is her condition?"

"She's stable; she'll recover with some rest, besides a broken foot. And how are you? What was the cause of that explosion?!"

"I wasn't hurt; I happened to leave minutes before it occurred. Its cause can only be disclosed to you by Four and Seven, who were inside. I can guess what happened, but the matter requires a long narrative and a lot of explanation for you to understand it. Let's find Four first."

That's right, let's find Four before anything else. I stepped forward with steady steps that quickened with my heartbeat, the dust surrounding us like a gray curtain hiding the rest of the world. Two was by my side, silent as usual, her serious eyes scanning the horizon as if searching for something only she could see. The heavy air, thick with smoke, pressed on my chest, so there was no room for words. I felt that talking now would be a waste of precious breath we might need later. With every step, the silence grew heavier, as if the world were anticipating another explosion. Suddenly, Two stopped and raised her hand as a signal for me to stop. I looked at her and found her eyes fixed on something distant amidst the ruins. I followed her gaze and saw a shadow moving lightly between the rubble. Involuntarily, I called out in a voice mixed with hope and fear: "Four?!"

But the shadow didn't reply. We approached cautiously, our steps creating a screeching sound from the charred debris under our feet. With every step, her features began to manifest. She was sitting on the ground, her back leaning against one of the collapsed pillars, her head tilted to the side, as if she had been awake and then lost consciousness.

When we approached her, I immediately knelt beside her. Her face was pale, her lips as dry as if they hadn't touched water in days. She didn't open her eyes, but her chest was moving slowly, and her slow breaths were all that confirmed she was still with us, which reassured me a little. I placed my hand gently on her shoulder and shook her slightly, but got no response to speak of. She was sunk in a deep coma, as if having escaped from this world to another place. Then I placed my hand on her forehead; it was cold despite the heat of the place at this depth. Her body was losing its strength little by little. I turned to Two, who had remained standing a short distance away, watching the scene without intervening. Her silent eyes were enough to convey the question she didn't speak: Are you going to leave her here? At that point, I could no longer bear the silence that was suffocating us, and I said in a low but firm voice, as if answering a question I didn't want to face: "There is still hope for her survival. I will not abandon her."

Two advanced with slow steps and cast a quick glance at Four. During this, she took some water from a bottle she had and wiped her face with it, then said quietly, in a dead tone, devoid of pleasantries: "If we carry her, we will be slower. Time is not on our side."

I felt the weight of her words, but she was right. Carrying Four in this difficult state might make us lose the time needed to reach the group, thus losing other stars. Yet, the idea of leaving my sister here, alone amidst this destruction, was not an option I could bear. So, I said with firmness, though my voice trembled due to my hesitation: "I will not leave her."

Two replied without changing her tone, but she bent down to help lift her: "Then you will bear responsibility for her. I will not wait for her. I will leave with Seven when she recovers."

I ended up lifting Four out with Two's help. What would fall upon me later was to take care of her alone until her condition stabilized before returning to the group. And as we moved her, I felt a weight not limited only to Four's body, but to the hope I had pinned on her. Deep down, I knew we might lose everyone because of this, but I was offering something else: Stars don't abandon each other, even if the sky grows dark.

(13)

With great difficulty, we managed to get Four out from among the debris and move her to the nearby plain. Our steps were arduous, but the weather seemed to be gradually changing. The storm that had been battering the place with all its ferocity began to melt on the horizon, and the sky that had been filled with smoke cleared to reveal a warm sun, as if merciful nature itself wanted to grant us a new chance. Under a lone tree standing in this deserted plain, we carefully laid Four down, then I followed with Seven, whose condition was more stable, but she still needed rest. I looked at them, my heart growing heavy with worry, as if the burden I had been carrying the whole way had now doubled as I saw them lying there, weak, under the shadows of the tree. I caught my breath, then took out what little equipment I had left to try and wake Four. Two was standing nearby, her arms crossed, looking at me with impassive eyes, as if observing me from a distance to evaluate my attempts. She said nothing; she didn't need to. Her previous words were still ringing in my ears. But I won't be able to live with the idea that I didn't try.

I began by cleaning the wounds. The water was barely enough to remove the clinging ash from her skin, so I focused on the deeper wounds, trying to sterilize them as much as possible. But everything I did seemed to be in vain. The bleeding didn't completely stop in some areas, and the burns were severe, to the point that the flesh was charred in many places. I placed the damp cloth on her arm, on her leg, on her cold forehead, but there was no response. In the end, I whispered in a broken voice, as if trying to awaken her spirit with words, despite my disbelief in such things: "Four, wake up. Please. Fight for us."

But she remained still. There was no movement, not even a small tremor to indicate she heard me. Her pulse was so slow that I felt it disappearing between my fingers. At that point, despair began to seep into my depths. Two approached and sat beside me. She looked at Four, then at me, and said in a sharp tone, devoid of pity: "It's useless, and you know it. Every minute we spend here means a greater risk for all of us."

I raised my head towards her and found myself screaming without realizing it: "How can you say that? She's still here! I can hear her pulse; I can feel it! How can you ask me to abandon her?"

She looked at me coldly and said in a steady voice: "You 'feel' it? That's not enough. Her pulse doesn't mean she will survive. If everything you did couldn't save her, what can words do?! We are in the heart of hell, and every minute we waste here means death is approaching all of us."

I turned my face away from her and continued my work. I took the piece of cloth and tied it around a wound on her leg, trying to stop the bleeding, but the bandage kept slipping, as if I had forgotten how to do it, as if everything was refusing to cooperate with me. I was trembling, not just from exhaustion, but from the feeling of helplessness. I found nothing left to do but call her name in a faint voice, over and over, but with no answer. After all those desperate attempts, my body grew weak. My hands fell onto her chest, then my head, and I said in a broken voice, accompanied by tears that would change nothing: "I promised her... that I wouldn't leave you. That I wouldn't let anyone suffer."

Two moved away a little but didn't go far. She was watching the horizon, waiting for me to make my final decision. I felt torn between what I know is right and what I cannot let go of. Yes, I am not ready to abandon her, even if all the evidence points to the nearness of her end. I knew deep down that I would stay with her until the end, whatever the result.

Silence began to settle over the place, as if the whole world had stopped under that lone tree. Four lay before me, her body pale, her breaths barely audible. I remained kneeling beside her, my hands limp, as if all the strength inside me had seeped out with the tears that flooded my face, until my eyeliner ran like chaotic black lines on my cheeks, reflecting the brokenness within me. I had nothing left to do but look at her impassive face, while Two stood in her place, still as a statue, her sharp eyes watching me without any sympathy, just waiting for me to give up, to accept what was inevitable.

And before the silence could stretch on any longer, a faint sound came from behind us, a groan that was almost buried under the sound of the weak wind. I slowly raised my head and saw Seven trying to stand up. Her broken leg was trembling under the weight of her body, her face distorted with severe pain, but she insisted on getting up. I screamed as I ran towards her to prevent her from moving: "Seven! Sit back down! You're not okay!"

But she pushed my hand away stubbornly, her pain-filled eyes glowing with a strange determination. She looked at me, then at Two, before saying in a trembling, firm voice a mumble that no one heard, then repeated it louder and in a more intense tone: "I said we're not leaving her!"

Her words were like stabs in the air. Even Two turned towards her, a hint of surprise on her face despite her attempt to maintain her frozen expression.

"Seven, sit back down. That's enough. We did what we could, and time is not on our side."

Seven took a step forward, accompanied by her heavy, hesitant breaths in the air. Her face was distorted with tears, but she didn't look weak. Instead, she was like someone who had decided to face the world to change Four's fate. She screamed in a voice that was trembling but filled with anger and determination: "You say time is not on our side, but what about all the time she gave us? She was always by my side, my teacher, my leader, my friend who put up with my ignorance and my neediness no matter how hard it was. She never stopped thinking about all of us and was ready to sacrifice herself to save us. Even after she was warned about the danger of tampering with the central administration computer, she went back to it again to make the warehouse a perfect haven for us. And now you're asking me to leave her here? I won't do that, no matter what happens."

Two replied, her sharp gaze indicating she wanted to end the discussion: "Seven, you can barely stand. If you think you can carry her, you are delusional. What you are asking for will kill us all."

But Seven didn't back down. She raised her head higher, as if challenging the pain that was gnawing at her body.

"If you see her as a burden, I will carry her myself. I'll put her on my back and walk, even if the road takes me years. I will not leave someone who was always here for me, and for all of us."

Her voice was trembling, but it was filled with a determination that made me feel ashamed of my weakness. I stood up and took a step towards her to support her; her eyes were filled with tears she wouldn't allow to fall. I tried to speak, but my voice got stuck in my throat. Two cut me off with a sharp voice: "You don't understand! If we lose time here, you are the one who will pay the price."

"And I don't care! If you want to leave, then go, but I'm not moving from here without her. I couldn't live with myself if I did."

Two froze in her place, as if those words were an unexpected slap that robbed her of all the options upon which she was building her next decisions, leaving her no choice but to build a new plan that included Four, who looked like an unconscious corpse. Although I know that the chance of her survival and waking up is closer to impossible than possible, I couldn't bear to leave her or accept the truth, and Seven was stubbornly pushing me to escape from that reality. How emotional and foolish I am. What we're doing now is nothing but stubbornness that will cost us a lot later, and I will remind myself of these words when we get there—if we get there at all.

Chapter Six:
The Funeral of the Stars, Its Time Has Come

This time, Star One writes the story for you — we take you back a little to the distant past, the early school days.

(1)

When I opened my eyes for the first time, I found myself in the middle of a deserted garden, its silence as absolute as the echo of an ancient explosion never heard. Everything was still, as if time had stopped in an absurd moment, and all forms of life had vanished except for a single trace on the horizon. The garden, if it could be called a garden, seemed more like a void reflecting only my loneliness, a vast space devoid of meaning, as if the entire world was created just to be a witness to my singular existence—alone, without a companion or even a sound. But in the heart of this silence, amidst the ruin, I noticed that one lone flower. A flower with wilting leaves, touching its end quietly in deference to the garden. Its thin stem was half-sunk in the dirt, the other half suspended between life and death, struggling to remain standing despite its fragility. I stood contemplating it for a long time, my eyes fixed on this small being that seemed like a silent challenge to the void. For a moment, I felt that the entire universe had condensed its existence into this flower, as if it were a mirror reflecting the deepest corners of its soul.

So. I am the first...

I knew it instantly, as if the idea occurred to me the moment I thought of it.

Like this flower, I stand alone in this void. The first is always alone. The summit that everyone thinks is a privilege is nothing but a naked point, exposed to every wind and eye, a point without protection. Everything around me will expect me to carry it myself.

I began to approach it slowly, with cautious steps as if I feared disturbing the flower or losing this strange feeling of connection. With every step, I felt something inside me changing. The weight of loneliness grew clearer, but at the same time, it was revealing new meanings. I finally sat on the ground before it, my eyes staring at it as if interrogating it with silence.

Being the first is not a privilege as everyone thinks, but a burden. Like the burden of always being alone at the forefront, of facing the winds by yourself, and of being their role model and their safety, while inside, you are as fragile as this flower. Will they see my fragility? Will they realize how the wind breaks me, even as I appear to be standing?

But I felt something else, something deeper: that flower, despite its fragility, did not disappear, was not defeated. It remained. It was a witness to the ruin, and yet, it was still here.

Despite everything, it did not vanish. Perhaps being the first is not just a burden. Perhaps being the first means being like this flower, to stand, even when everything around me breaks, to be a witness to survival, despite all that will collapse.

I raised my hand slowly and touched the flower's stem with my fingertips. The roughness of its dryness captured my feelings as if reformulating a truth I didn't want to admit. The strength one shows to others is just a fragile mask behind which a hidden weakness hides. What will the sky and the Stars who will depend on me be like? Those who, despite their apparent strength, will draw their stability from my existence.

The strength they claim to see in me is nothing more than a reflection of them. They are my roots, and my fragility intersects with their strength. Weakness, like this flower's, is not an end; it is what makes survival possible. Perhaps I, just like it, need others to remain standing.

My thoughts began to dive into a deeper spiral, as if the flower were gripping the lapels of my soul and revealing truths of which I had only seen shadows.

Are we weak because we need others? Or are we strong because we draw our existence from that very weakness? Is strength to remain standing alone, or is it to know when to lean on those around us? Perhaps my being the first is both a curse and a blessing: a curse with absolute loneliness, and a blessing with gradually understanding others—their need for me, and my need for them.

I returned to silence, staring at the flower for a long time, before gently wiping the dirt from around it. It seemed as if I were granting it a moment of care, as if sharing a part of its weakness. Then I whispered, as if talking to the flower, or perhaps to myself:

We live as you live. We do not live alone, but in each other's shadows. We live by what we lose and what we keep. You are standing here, not because you are strong enough, but because you are weak enough to need the earth that supports you, the roots that no one sees, just as I need the Stars who will carry me while I pretend that I carry them.

When I finally stood up, I felt the garden was no longer empty. This lone flower, despite its fallen leaves, was not just an ancient trace, but a testament to what it means to be alive: loneliness that creates strength, and weakness that makes survival possible. I raised my head towards the sky, took a deep breath, and finally said to myself:

To be the first means to start the path, but the path is only completed by the shadow of others. We are like this flower; we remain not because we are perfect, but because we carry in us what others have left, and what we have left for them.

I left the flower behind me, but I realized that I would not be leaving it, because this flower will be a witness to my loneliness, a witness to my endurance, and a witness to the truth that I, like it, draw life from everything I thought I could live without.

But something in the stillness suddenly changed. The sound of light footsteps broke the silence, and I felt another presence. I raised my head and looked towards the neglected glass gate that stood at the edge of the garden. There, amidst its distorted reflections, stood a star. She wasn't just a stranger; she was something closer to a familiar image I had never seen before. Her calmness was absolute, her facial expressions as impassive as a rock that does not tremble. That steady gaze she held concealed something deeper than mere appearance, something akin to a mirror reflecting what I was trying to escape from: the truth.

I advanced towards her slowly, as if an invisible thread between us was drawing me to her against my will. With every step, I felt an internal tremor intensifying. When I stood before her, I looked at the number engraved on her chest. It was two, the number I thought didn't exist, a number that contradicted everything I had felt the moment I believed I was the first, that I was alone. Who is this? And why? It was a shock that began to tear me apart inside. She finally raised her voice, a quiet voice that held a depth akin to the mystery of the night: "You think strength and weakness have meaning. You think that being the first gives you an advantage, or places a burden on you. But strength and weakness are both a lie. They mean nothing, because the Stars, no matter how bright their light shines, will end. They will disappear as all things disappear, and will be forgotten just as this flower will be forgotten. Even the Great Sun, whom we consider a perfect, ideal mother, is nothing but another flower on the verge of wilting. One day she will be buried, and then no one will remember her."

Her words pierced me like cold arrows. I tried to reply, but my voice stumbled midway: "The Sun is not just a flower! She is the foundation of our existence! She is the one who gives us meaning and life!"

My insistence was closer to a desperate defensive cry, but I realized, despite everything I was saying, that her words had seeped into me. The truth in her voice was painful, but it was convincing me against my will.

"And what is the use of life if its end is oblivion?"

She said it as she took another step closer to me, then continued: "You speak of strength, of bearing the burden, of survival, but you don't realize that all of it is an illusion. The Stars, the Sun, the flower—everything is fated to perish. Nothing will remain."

I felt anger rising inside me, but it was a fragile anger, an anger stemming from my fear of what she was saying, not a rejection of what it meant. I advanced towards her, trying to defend my view of life, the meaning of survival despite its fragility, but her features didn't change. She was like a wall against which everything crashed without a tremor. That didn't stop me from saying my words in a voice I tried to make firm: "Even if our fate is to perish, that doesn't mean our existence has no value!

Even the flower, despite its death, is a testament to a life. The Sun, too, is not just an entity that will end; she is a source, she is a beginning, she is proof that something was here."

But she didn't argue. She merely remained silent, looking at me, as if her words had completed their mission. And despite my defense, I felt I was dropping my weapons one by one, for every word she said was as if it were carving an idea inside me, I hadn't dared to think of. Perhaps she was right. Perhaps strength and weakness, survival and demise, truly have no meaning in the end. Everything will be forgotten, everything will end. And yet, a part of me refused to surrender to her idea completely. In the end, I stood silent before her, while she turned quietly and left, leaving behind the echo of her words reverberating in the garden. I felt then that the garden had changed. The flower was no longer just a flower to me, and the void was no longer just a void. Everything around me carried a new and strange meaning, a meaning that pulsed with a weakness no one sees, but that moves everything.

I sat beside the flower again and closed my eyes. For the first time, I felt I wasn't alone. But at the same time, I wasn't sure if the loneliness had truly left me, or if I was beginning to accept it as part of my existence. I find myself saying after she had moved away from me, in a low voice so she wouldn't hear: "Perhaps you are right, but even if everything will disappear, I am here now, and you are here now, and that alone is enough."

I took a few steps back after she left, as if I had sunk into a heavy silence that swallowed any desire for confrontation. But a sudden idea flashed in my mind. I felt it course through my blood like a fleeting glimmer that illuminated the darkness of my questions: Why don't we create something that immortalizes our existence if oblivion is what strips life of all its value? I wondered with a kind of enthusiasm that awakened a new resolve within me. That idea was capable of changing the entire course of the discussion, even if it seemed feeble before Star Two's certainty in the futility of everything.

I couldn't bear to see her cold back moving away from me like that. I rushed towards her, passing the flower and the distance that separated me from the dark glass corridor leading to the school. It seemed to me the sound of my footsteps was louder than usual, as if imploring her to stop. And indeed, she stopped in the middle of the corridor, but without turning her face towards me. She still held her usual calm, standing in her place like an unmoving statue. I took a deep breath, gathered the fragments of my thoughts, then called to her: "Wait! Just hear me out before you go."

She paused for a moment, as if silence had become her preferred language for responding to any attempt at discussion. But I continued with the stumbling rush that I fuel with what little hope I have left: "If oblivion makes everything meaningless, why don't we leave behind an unforgettable trace? A story that remains a witness to who passed here, to our existence? That we tell it, or write it, or paint it, so it remains alive after us?"

I thought I had moved something in her. I felt my breaths coming in quick succession, afraid of her logical, stern response, but she remained as she was, impassive, unmoving. Finally, she turned her head slightly, one eye staring at me through the reflection of the gate's glass, as if wanting to confirm my madness or my sincerity. A cold look that held no emotion, yet it encapsulated enough questioning: "A story?"

She uttered the word quietly, tinged with doubt, then continued as she turned her gaze forward again: "And do you really think a story can save a star from its death? Or save the Sun from its inevitable demise? Even stories are forgotten with time. They are erased from the memory of those who read them, and their texts mix with hundreds of other stories until they no longer have meaning."

I hesitated for a little, but I kept my head held high, facing her: "Perhaps they are forgotten, perhaps a part of them is lost, but some stories live long enough to make us believe we did not live in vain. Even if the story is forgotten in the end, it's enough that we will be carried with it in its remaining moments."

I took a step towards her, trying to make her turn around completely. I needed to see her eyes, hoping I might glimpse a shred of belief or hope within them.

"You said everything will end, so what's the harm in trying to preserve it for a little extra time? At least let's not let oblivion consume us now while we are still alive."

For a moment, I thought I saw the corner of her mouth twitch. I didn't know if it was annoyance or a suppressed laugh or just a fleeting movement, but her answer came in her rigid body language. She resumed walking towards the end of the corridor, leaving me to watch her back again.

"If you soothe your conscience with the words of your story, that's your business. As for me, I won't cling to another illusion."

I felt a prick of pain knock at my heart, as if what she said confirmed that she still rejected the possibility of salvation in any meaning we create for ourselves. I tried to gather my voice for the last time: "I'm not saying it's an illusion, but it's hope..."

She didn't answer me. The sound of her footsteps on the hard floor was stronger than any other word trying to escape my mouth. When she passed through the glass gate, her features disappeared into the shadow, leaving the place as she had found it: silent and without explanation.

I stood in my place, having realized I hadn't convinced her, and perhaps I hadn't even convinced myself. But the idea of the story remained alive within me, igniting in my chest a small flame of rebellion against oblivion. I realized in that moment that even if I couldn't change Star Two's mentality, I might have begun to change my own view of many things: to fight transience and inevitability with my brush. It might seem like a feeble idea, but at the same time, it was enough to give me the meaning I was searching for amidst this void.

I looked at the gate that had swallowed her and remembered the lone flower on the other side. Perhaps the painting won't change the flower's fate, nor will it change the Sun's fate, but it will keep the spark of the soul alive and prevent us, if only for a little while, from falling silently into the abyss of nothingness. And as Star Two walked her path, I too was preparing to write my own story, hoping it might become a lifeline between our weakness and our strength, between our fleeting moment and a memory that might not be forgotten.

(3)

My wait at that glass gate was so long that, at one point, it seemed my life had become an extension of it. Every day I would stand nearby, staring at the reflection of my face on its glass, reliving in my silence my debate with Star Two. I still see her impassive form in my imagination, as if she were present behind it all the time and had never left. Sometimes, when I closed my eyes for moments, I would imagine the gate had actually opened, that I could hear her quiet footsteps approaching. But when I stared harder, I would discover I was still alone; only the void stood behind the glass.

The years passed like a relentless gust of wind, and with them, the silence of the garden gradually disappeared, replaced by the clamor of life. The garden filled with Stars of all numbers, becoming a large playground filled with the noise of laughter and the sounds of running and racing. These transformations were enough to instill some warmth in my soul. Seeing life glow where silence used to dwell seemed to me like a small story that had begun to fade, for a new story to be born from its womb. And yet, the glass gate remained fixed in its place. No one approached it except occasionally, as if the path leading to it were hidden, only visible to one who intentionally searches for it.

There was an urgent feeling inside me that I had to create a trace that would remind me, and others, of that moment with Star Two, the moment of the first debate that shook my convictions. Her words continued to ring in my mind for a long time. So, one day, I took my brush and began to paint the flower on a large canvas, with a size rivaling the scale of our debate back then. I added to it all the details of the silence and stillness, everything I felt of sorrow and the desire to keep the story alive. I was painting the flower at the peak of its wilting, yet still resisting, still holding within it a mirror to my old loneliness. When I finished, I kept the painting in one of the school's side corridors. I wanted to show it to Star Two when she returned, to tell her: Even if the flower died, there is one who will remember it.

But she never came, or so it seemed to me after the years passed and the faces changed. While I was absorbed in my daily routine among the Stars, a small star suddenly appeared, no taller than my shoulders. She carried the number seven, and this alone was enough to arouse my astonishment and everyone else's. We were used to numbers being granted sequentially according to appearance, with rare exceptions, but it seemed there was something different about this girl that made the Sun choose to finally grant her the lost number seven. At first, she didn't believe her number meant anything; she was skeptical, looking at the number as if it were a myth with no proof. But I saw something strange in her eyes, and I felt that she would find her way amidst the sky in a unique manner.

And as I was watching the glass gate with my wandering gaze that day, recalling at every moment the memory of the first debate between myself and Star Two, what I never expected happened. The gate finally opened, and Two emerged from it with a quietness resembling the steps of ghosts, as if something in time had finally decided to move on after a long halt. In that moment, I felt my heart flutter, as if all the accumulated thoughts inside me raced to appear. Two's return was not the only surprise; what truly awakened my astonishment was knowing that the new one, Star Seven, was the one who had convinced her to come out. My insight was proven right then: that Seven was no ordinary star, but held in her heart a glimmer capable of breaking the stillness of others. I realized as I watched Two move away from the gate that Seven, despite her young age compared to her high number, had achieved something great today. She had succeeded in bringing Two back from her isolation and proved that her distinction lay not just in her number, but in the strength of her resolve and the sincerity of her belief in what she does.

After minutes of silence that followed her sudden appearance, I felt a light movement beside me. I turned to find Star Two had quietly stood by my side, as if she had taken her time in deciding whether to share my solitude or to go on her way as I was used to her doing. It seemed to me she was hesitant to speak, but finally I heard her whisper in a tone that maintained her serious features: "The flower painting in the corridor... truly wondrous. If the flower were alive now, it would have been happy to see it. But in the end, it's just a buried object. So, what is the use of the painting as long as you and I are the only ones who understand the meaning behind it?"

I lowered my head for a moment, recalling in my mind my first steps when I painted that flower, how it was laden with all that had passed between us of debate, certainty, and loss. I saw in Two's features something of a hidden regret or perhaps a faint admission of a value she didn't previously acknowledge. A shared inner feeling connected me to her, a feeling that what we had lost still binds us, despite our differences. I looked at her with a forgiveness I had long awaited from myself before others, and said in a voice in which warmth had regained its features: "Rather, that is what makes it special. The painting might seem meaningless in the eyes of others, but it's the only link that reminds us of the fact that our paths once crossed. It is the only thing that binds us together, even though it was inspired by a flower that was buried long ago and no longer exists."

I raised my eyes towards her, watching a fleeting sparkle in them. She didn't comment much, contenting herself with fixing her steady gaze on the void. I felt the silence between us had become more honest than any other words, as if the painting I had made spared us a new argument that might take us back to the starting point. Nevertheless, I was confident that a little calm had finally settled in our hearts, and that something of that flower was still alive, even if it was only reflected in our eyes.

(4)

This particular story, I don't know where it began or when it ended. That's not due to my ignorance, but to my earnest desire then and my insistence on forgetting it. Yet, it has returned to show its old face from time to time, like shadows looming behind the dim glass of memory. No matter how I tried to erase its details, it grew more stubborn. And here I am, despite all my attempts, I find myself uttering it in a low voice, as if it were a tale of another person who didn't resemble me at all, or perhaps, resembles me to the point of being identical.

When I say I don't know the beginning or the end, I mean that the thread that connects its events was nearly lost amidst a rubble of things I tried to ignore. But it wasn't a loud dramatic climax; rather, it was a small whisper that slowly crept into my soul until it formed a scar not visible to the naked eye. Perhaps at its beginning, I thought it was a moment from a silent scene that didn't affect me compared to an old garden and a flower that had vanished, or a conversation that became the subject of thought for a case closed without explanation.

That was until she gave me a troubled idea from her eyes and disappeared into the glass corridor, leaving an indescribable, unforgettable weight in my heart. It is just a story that began with a moment I almost never considered important, and ended with something I couldn't easily get over. It is most likely that missing link in which I transformed from Star One, the first bright Star, into who I am today: a star who sees that toughness is but an illusion we hide behind to protect ourselves from breaking.

My entire focus back then was directed towards that sad flower, whose leaves began to die little by little despite all my persistent attempts to care for it. I used to watch it every morning as if watching myself: at first, it was wilted yet bright, receiving the garden's sun with petals full of life, then with time, it transformed into a tired body that could barely lift its head towards the sky. I extended my hand to touch the tips of its withered leaves, feeling their roughness, similar to cold sand, and I wondered: *Why does nothing stay as it is? Is wilting an inevitable destiny for all that is born beautiful?*

Suddenly, a sharp scream from inside the school pierced the garden's silence. It came from the area where the back corridor meets the stairs leading to the upper floor. The sound echoed off the walls, accompanied by the hurried sound of feet as if chasing something or someone: "You're just ignoring everything as if it doesn't concern you!"

I jumped to my feet when I heard those words, conflicted as to whether I should leave the flower and go see what was happening, or convince myself that this scream concerned others with whom I had no connection, and that my intervention would be of no use. I had a desire to withdraw, to maintain my tired silence and calm, but curiosity overcame me. I felt a prick inside me, like the prick of guilt when one turns a blind eye to something happening before them. Indeed, it was as if that scream placed a confusing truth before me that pulled me in: I am not even the second Star, but the third. I took a deep breath, then left the garden with quick steps, following the call mixed with this scream.

The further I got from the flower, the more I felt as if it were bidding me farewell with a still gaze, urging me to move forward because wilting does not forgive one who is unable to understand its causes. I passed through the hazy glass gate leading to the south corridor, where the smell of old wood permeated the air, hiding beneath it layers of stories that were buried over the years. As soon as I turned the corner, I saw shadows moving near the stairs. In that moment, everything froze for a few seconds when I collided with another star who was running in the opposite direction. I tried to step back a little and lean against the wooden wall, but the force of the collision surprised me, and I found myself stumbling into a half-fall onto the floor amidst confusion as to who it was.

When I raised my head, my gaze fell on the uniform of the star I had collided with, and the number engraved on her chest seemed clear to me: it was Three. I didn't process it immediately; it took me a few heartbeats to realize she was a new star I had never seen before. Her black hair was flying in a strange disarray around her face, while her eyes blazed with a strange look combining panic and determination, as if she were chasing something or fleeing from a matter she was no match for. She stood near me, moving nervously to make sure I was okay. She wanted to speak but was stammering, as if hundreds of questions or arguments were crowded in her mind. I stayed for a moment to regain my balance and feel my shoulder and knee, before taking a deep breath, feeling the pain gradually recede.

"Sorry. I wasn't really seeing what was in front of me."

She apologized in a hoarse voice mixed with the flutter of ragged breaths. I raised my gaze to her again, possessed by a feeling that something heavy was settled in her heart. She wasn't just a lost star; the features of her face showed a mixture of haste and anxiety, tinged with an unmistakable impatience. I stood up slowly, dusted off my robe, then said in a quiet voice that might hide my confusion: "It's alright. What about you? Are you okay?"

She nodded her head quickly to confirm, though her worried features indicated she had a destination she couldn't bear to be late for. I felt that this sudden meeting of ours was no coincidence; there was a turmoil in her eyes that went beyond a mere passing stumble, and for some reason, I felt I had to go with her without discussion.

I didn't think much before I took a step forward. The issue wasn't just about a passing collision, but about the fact that I stood before a star bearing a number I never expected to exist, despite my previous meeting with Two. Three didn't move far from me, but her eyes remained directed towards the dark corridor behind me, as if she were searching for something she hadn't yet lost. It then seemed to me that her brief speech to me wasn't out of indifference, but from a burden that weighed down her shoulders, leaving her no opportunity to explain. The atmosphere around us was still, except for our rapid breaths and the sound of the wooden floor creaking under our feet. As I was about to speak, she suddenly raised her head and said in a rough tone tinged with a distress she tried to hide: "So, you are the one called Star One."

It was a sentence that wasn't an inquiry, but more like an indisputable fact. It was strange, as if she knew me beforehand or had expected to meet me right here. I didn't answer her immediately, but I involuntarily raised my hand and placed it on the number engraved on my chest, as if verifying whether I was who I had thought I was all this time.

"Yes. I am Star One. And you?"

Three lowered her head slightly, glanced at my number which appeared clearly under the faint lamplight, then smiled with a slight sarcasm I couldn't immediately understand. Another step back made her seem more at ease, but she didn't stop analyzing my gaze. The retreat wasn't a sign of fear, but more like she was waiting for a reaction from me, as if anticipating how I would act in this moment.

"The first Star, actually, but they call me Star Three."

She said it as if offering me something more than just a name, or perhaps she was waiting for me to say something specific. I continued to look at her intently, realizing that the number she carried was not just a ranking as I had thought, but meant she was a person who stands on the same line where I thought I was unique. I couldn't hold back the question that slipped to my tongue before I could think of its consequences: "And how is that?"

Her reply was simple, yet it disturbed me even more: "Because you are not the only one here, as you think."

I froze for moments as I processed the impact of her words. This wasn't just a passing encounter with another star; it reflected a reality different from what I had imagined. I had always thought I was the first, that I was the only one who carried this number and this role. But here I was now, standing before someone who shares the same space I thought was mine alone. And she didn't give me enough of a chance to absorb it. She suddenly turned and walked away with steps faster than I expected, so much so that I thought she would disappear into that corridor like the previous one while I stood here watching her. So, I felt I had to follow her, not just out of curiosity, but because a painful sensation began to creep inside me, like the loss of something precious from my hands, as if I had entered a game, I never knew I was a part of.

"Where are you going?! Wait!"

I threw the question at her before she completely disappeared. She stopped without turning to me. I could still see her shoulders moving with her heavy breaths, before she whispered without raising her voice: "If you think your number makes you the first and the highest, it's time you realized that someone has already preceded you."

I kept staring at her, while her words ran through my mind like a fleeting flash that cannot be ignored. Then she continued on her way, leaving me behind to think about the meaning of those words, trying to understand what brought her here, and what the existence of a Star Three meant in the world of First Leadership that I thought was carved for me alone. I raised my eyes towards the corridor she had walked down. I felt that her steps were drawing a path I was not ready to walk, so I stopped. But I realized that I would not find an answer to what was going on in my mind except by moving forward behind her someday.

(6)

The night was not easy. I stayed awake, staring at the narrow room's ceiling as if searching it for an answer to what Star Three had said. How could there be two stars of the same rank? This overturns everything I believed in. My thoughts were tangling endlessly, while I heard the echo of distant footsteps in the empty corridors, and the lamp's pale light cast dancing shadows on the cold walls. Sleep was not an option; I kept thinking about it until dawn broke, when the faint morning light began to seep through the window, heralding a new day I was not at all prepared for. When I got up, my body felt as if it had been through a long battle, but there was no time for rest. I put on my clothes quickly and left the room, heading to the garden where I always started my day. The atmosphere in the school was different today. I felt that there were gazes following me, eyes watching me secretly. Was I imagining it? Or was I going mad with the idea of possibly meeting Three at any moment, as if she were always watching me?

At the start of the back yard, I found her. She was sitting on the stone stairs, her back leaning against the old iron fence, her eyes fixed on the horizon. Her black hair was messy, as if she hadn't even bothered to comb it this morning, and it seemed as if she had been waiting for me there. I hesitated for a moment before stepping forward. I didn't know how to start the conversation; I knew I needed to understand what was going on. She beat me to the conversation then: "Woke up early?"

She threw the question in a low voice, but she didn't look directly at me; only the corners of her lips moved with a sarcastic smile.

"I didn't sleep at all."

"Neither did I."

She turned to me when she said it, and it seemed she was trying to weigh her words before speaking them. I took a deep breath, then said quietly: "What was on your mind?"

"I was thinking about the school, and the rules, and how things work here."

I felt there were other things she didn't say, perhaps matters related to yesterday's screaming, but I didn't want to press her. I continued to search for answers, but she was hiding them in a way I couldn't understand. I looked at her for a long time, but she didn't speak. She just let out a long sigh and turned her eyes back to the gray sky above us. I felt there that what would follow this day would not be like any other day I was used to in this school.

(7)

In the following days, the situations began to repeat themselves, and I was always trying to prove that I was more deserving of leadership. It wasn't just a personal challenge, but more like a hidden conflict between myself and Star Three. She didn't oppose me openly, but she would put me through indirect tests, as if she wanted to gauge the extent of my true ability, or perhaps she was trying to show me my limits without stating it. Then as the days passed, the atmosphere around me began to change, specifically with the gazes of the others which were not as they used to be. The reason wasn't entirely clear to me, but I felt that something was going on in secret. I would see her, Star Three, watching from a distance sometimes. And in some moments, her sharp words made me feel as if she were trying to expose a weak point in my decisions. But she never did it openly, rather in her calm, composed manner, the kind that made me feel she possessed a confidence I did not yet have. Then came the day when the first clear clash between us occurred, a moment I was not at all prepared for, but it was inevitable.

There was chaos. A group of Stars had broken the rules in an unexpected way, leaving the garden through a gap in the school fence. The situation demanded a quick decision, or so I thought. I stood in the middle of the yard, watching the scene with alert eyes, searching for a solution before things got out of control. There was no time to wait; I felt that every second equaled a lost opportunity to prove myself. I said firmly, trying to impose my decision, my tone sharp, decisive, because I didn't want to seem hesitant in front of them:

"We must move out and find them immediately. There's no time to waste!"

But Star Three didn't seem convinced. Instead, she remained in her place, her gaze steady, contemplative, as if analyzing the situation with a coldness that didn't match the tension filling the place. Finally, she turned to me and said in a quiet but strangely provocative voice: "Or maybe we should inform the Sun, before we fall into a new trap because of hasty decisions?"

I froze for a moment, looking at her with disbelief, as if I couldn't believe she was challenging my decision in front of everyone. I felt anger rising inside me, not just because I believed I was right, but because the way she said it made me feel as if I were reckless, impulsive, someone who doesn't know how to think before acting.

"I don't need your advice!"

I said it stubbornly, my hands clenching without my realizing it. My tone was louder than I wanted, but I couldn't back down now. I saw a faint smile creep into the corner of her lips, that smile that didn't hide its sarcasm, but also lacked any obvious hostility. She gave me a long look before saying slowly, as if enjoying watching my emotional reaction: "Then don't blame anyone but yourself when you need my help later."

Her words were like an unexpected blow. They weren't just a challenge; they were a hidden promise, or perhaps a warning. I felt heat rising in my face, but I didn't want to give her the satisfaction of seeing me flustered. The other Stars were watching us in silence; no one dared to intervene, as if they realized this confrontation was between her and me alone. For the first time since my arrival, I felt I was no longer completely in control of things, and that I might have fallen into a test I wasn't prepared for.

That was the first real test between us, and it wasn't the last. I began to realize that Star Three's existence wasn't just a repetition of my status, but was testing me in ways I had never been prepared for. It was like an undeclared battle, a battle with no clear loser, but it put everything under the microscope, making me wonder: Was I really ready for this role? Or was I fighting to protect something that wasn't mine from the beginning?

It was a day like any other at the school, but it was not ordinary at all. Since morning, the atmosphere had been charged. The tension between myself and Star Three hadn't subsided, but it had become a familiar kind of tension, like a shadow accompanying my every step. I was used to being the center of leadership, always in the confrontation, for everyone to feel that I was the most competent. But something in recent days was changing, and I had to admit it, even if only in silence. During the last class, I was assigned a sensitive task related to guiding a group of new, young Stars due to the Sun's being busy. It seemed easy, just a set of usual instructions, but things didn't go as expected. One of the stars was strange, not caring at all about the rules, and she had decided to challenge me publicly in front of the others.

"Again. Why should we listen to you instead of going out to play with the others?"

Her words were like a needle in my chest, and it wasn't just a question, but a challenge as she had expected. I felt then that all eyes were on me, so I had to respond in a way that didn't make me look weak.

"Because I know what I'm doing. I am here to guide you and teach you the rules of the place, not to argue with you. It will be a minute, and then we will all be dismissed."

She didn't seem convinced. Instead, her tone grew more defiant as she stepped closer, as if it were a game to see how I would act under pressure.

"Then show us how you'll do when we leave without you!"

It was fast, faster than I expected. She suddenly extended her hand to snatch the notebook from my hand, and before I could stop her, I found her pushing me back lightly—not hard enough to make me fall, but enough to show my weakness in front of everyone as she left. I felt the situation beginning to collapse from under my feet. I looked around; the eyes were watching in silence, some with astonishment, some with anticipation. I had to respond, to regain my control. But in that moment, I couldn't find the words. Before I could think of my next step, I heard a familiar voice cut through the silence: "That's enough!"

I turned to find her, Star Three, standing at the entrance, her eyes fixed on the star who had challenged me. She wasn't angry, not even displeased, but she looked as if she saw something in the scene more than I did.

"If you think proving yourself comes by insulting others, then you are not fit to even be here among us."

Her tone was steady; she didn't even raise her voice, but it pierced the atmosphere like a sword. And that one froze for a moment, then her eyes narrowed as if considering a sharp retort, but she realized at the last second that confronting Three would not be in her favor. She lightly threw the notebook to the ground, as if she hadn't been interested from the beginning, then turned and left without uttering another word.

I stopped, stared at her for a long time, and didn't know how to begin my conversation, as that was the first time she had intervened to save me. She didn't say anything immediately, just bent down to pick up the notebook, then handed it to me in silence. I took it, feeling the weight of the moment. I hesitated, then said in a low voice, not even sure if I wanted her to hear it: "I didn't expect you to help me."

She didn't seem surprised, but rather as if she had expected me to say it. She looked at me, then said quietly, as if the matter had been clear from the start: "If you were weaker than I expected, I wouldn't have bothered."

I smiled despite everything, despite the whole situation, despite my pride which was a little hurt.

"This is the closest thing to a compliment from you, isn't it?"

I saw how the corners of her lips moved slightly, but she didn't give me the answer I wanted. She just lightly averted her face and said in a low voice that was filled with a familiar tone: "Don't waste my time with your ridiculous interpretations."

I walked beside her to exit the hall, moving in silence. There was no need for many more words now. Something had changed, not much, but it was a beginning. And I didn't need to admit it out loud, but I realized I was no longer alone, and that she, somehow, was not entirely against me.

(8)

It was another day, a day when the school's atmosphere was bustling with unusual activity. Whispers echoed through the corridors, and eyes cautiously watched every detail happening in the large yard. No, today was different. The Sun had officially announced the upcoming journey, our first real test outside the school's borders, and everyone was waiting to know who would lead this adventure. The decision had been issued, but it wasn't as surprising as I expected. My name was first on the list of assignments: Star One, General Leader of the Star Squads.

There was no sound of objection, not even any tension, but it wasn't a comfortable feeling either. The title meant nothing anymore; I realized that after everything I had been through in the preceding days. Leadership is not just a position, not empty power or personal glory, but a responsibility that places the burden on your shoulders and leaves you no choice but to be the worthiest of it. As for the second name on the list, it was a name that would never be absent from any challenge concerning me: Star Three, Leader of the Command and Administration Squad.

I met her at the back of the yard, where she was sitting as usual, her legs crossed, her head raised towards the horizon, as if nothing had happened. I approached her without saying anything, and I didn't need to; she isn't one of those who like pleasantries.

"Well, Captain, it seems we'll be working together in the end."

She didn't turn to me immediately, just raised her eyebrow with light sarcasm, before saying: "If I thought otherwise, I would have withdrawn from the journey entirely."

I smiled, even though I knew her words weren't just a joke, but meant more than that. She was always the opposition, always questioning my decisions, but for the first time, this wasn't empty opposition.

"You have a chance now, then, to prove that opposition isn't your only job."

"And you have a chance to show me if you're truly a leader or just a star who holds the number one."

The next day, the training began. I was responsible for the entire squads, while Star Three was responsible for piloting the ship. And despite everything, it seemed as if we were working in harmony without even trying. She gave commands with confidence, handling complex technologies as if she had known them since eternity. As for me, I watched her in silence. I suddenly realized she hadn't been trying to surpass me before, but was just pushing me to be better. After one of the training sessions ended, we were sitting inside the ship, silence surrounding us except for the sound of the devices as they lit up and dimmed regularly. I felt something in my chest, a desire to confess, but I wasn't sure what I wanted to say.

"See? In the end, it seems the Sun chose me to be the one in charge."

Then I heard her laugh, a light but sincere laugh this time, before she replied: "And maybe she chose me as the leader of the Command team without you so I could make sure you don't mess things up completely."

That was the first time I felt we were on the same side, that we were no longer competitors, but one team. The leadership was no longer my burden alone, and for the first time, I didn't feel I was alone on this path.

This is what I thought then, and now I see only that I was a complete fool when I realized that.

And I only learned about her after the rug was pulled out from under my feet and I fell without realizing it.

(9)

*(The page now turns to what followed the scene of Star Three and Five's argument. The
moment the storm began outside.)*

The silence inside the ship wasn't just quiet; it was heavy and suffocating, seeping into the surroundings like old dust hanging in the air, filling the lungs but not leaving easily. Since Five, Six, and Thirteen left, I hadn't spoken to anyone. I didn't want to. I didn't find in myself the ability to face the eyes that were searching for an answer, nor to listen to the whispers of the remaining Stars who were looking through me for deliverance. And worse than all that, I didn't find in myself the ability to face Three.

I walked through the dim corridors, my feet stepping on the damaged wooden floor, the creaking sounds beneath them echoing in my head like a constant alarm, like a warning that I was about to enter a losing battle. I saw her before I spoke, before I even dared to think of the words I would say. She was there, standing before the cracked window, staring at the fading light outside the ship, as if she could truly see it, as if the answers she refused to give me were written on the cloud-laden horizon or in the storm that had begun to rain down on us. I hesitated for a moment, then said in a voice I tried to make steady, but it came out trembling against my will: "Three... do you have a moment?"

She didn't turn around. She remained as she was, silent, as if I weren't there. Then she finally said, in a cold voice, devoid of any trace of remorse: "If this is about them leaving, then I don't want to hear any complaints."

I could have retreated then. I could have swallowed my words, postponed this confrontation for another day, another hour, a moment when I didn't feel my heart pressing on my ribs as if it wanted to break free from my chest. But I didn't. I said, as I took another step closer to her: "They aren't complaints, but questions. Questions that deserve answers from you."

She turned slowly. Her eyes were cold, but they were not without weariness. There were small cracks in her solid facade that were not easy to notice, but they were there, waiting to widen. She said, in her steady voice that never betrays her: "Then ask."

I breathed slowly, tried to arrange my thoughts, to be clear, to be firm. Then I said: "Why didn't you try to stop them? Why did you let Five leave? You could have negotiated with her; you could have convinced her to stay. You know their departure isn't just the loss of three stars, but the loss of leaders! Do you realize how much we've left behind?"

She didn't flinch. She didn't even move. She just answered with that same provocative coldness: "Exile was necessary, One. We need order, not those who undermine it."

I felt the heat of anger rising to my face, but I didn't let it control me. I held myself back.

"Order? You call this order? Since when did banishment become the solution for everything? More importantly, what are we going to do now? We don't have enough food, and everyone is in fear and doubt about the future."

She didn't answer me then, as if she were weighing her words, or perhaps trying not to say what she might later regret.

"No one denies we are in danger, but our danger is now greater because you allowed Five to leave. Who will protect the ship now? Who will manage safety? We have lost so much because of your decisions, like Four, our best engineer; like Two, our primary explorer; and like Thirteen, our only doctor! How will we manage without them, in your opinion?!"

Her eyebrow rose slightly, but her features didn't change, didn't waver, as if my words held no meaning.

"I don't need to justify my decisions to you, One. Leadership requires making difficult decisions, not begging others to stay."

Hearing that, I laughed a short, sarcastic, and bitter laugh, for I finally understood her position.

"So that's it?! You can't even admit you were wrong?"

I took another step towards her. I felt her grow more tense, but she didn't retreat.

"I was not wrong! I was doing what was best for the group!"

"Best for the group? Look around you, Three! The ship is now half-deserted, the Stars are terrified and uncertain, and you stand here as if everything is fine. But it's not fine. We are not fine at all!"

Her chest rose and fell, as if she were about to respond emotionally, but she closed her mouth at the last moment and regained her artificial calm.

"If you don't trust me, One, that's your business. But don't think for a moment that I will back down."

That was the moment I felt the path of understanding had broken between us, and would not return. I took another step, looked her directly in the eyes, then turned, walking away. But I stopped at the door, cast one last look. She showed no remorse. So, I said in a low voice that carried a weight I never knew I possessed: "You know? I expected to hear something like this from you. But I was hoping, if only for one innocent moment, that you would be wiser than this. I hope you're confident in your decisions, Three, because I don't think you'll ever be able to bear the consequences when they start to appear."

Then I left, and didn't look back. I didn't want to see her face in that moment, but I knew, I was absolutely certain, that my words had hit their mark, that something had seeped inside her, something she would not be able to deny, no matter how she tried.

The storm continued outside, but the real storm was here, inside. The sound of the call for the meeting began to pass through the ship's cracks along with the raindrops, rising in the deserted corridors and echoing off the white walls that seemed feebler than before. Like the rest of the Stars, I left with steady steps, my hands clasped behind my back, my head filled with the echo of thoughts I couldn't quiet. The atmosphere inside the ship was saturated with tension, with tired eyes, exhausted bodies, and troubled breaths—all clear indicators that everyone knew this meeting would be different. It wouldn't be a meeting for ordinary decisions, but a meeting to try and understand the last path to survival.

Before I entered the hall, Three stopped me. She stood before me, her back straight, her eyes filled with that sternness I had come to know well. But this time, it was laden with something else, something I hadn't seen before—doubt, perhaps, or a despair concealed behind pride. I saw it through her words: "Before we go in, One, I want us to be clear about one last thing."

I didn't answer. I just looked at her with a cold silence, perhaps hoping she would back down, but she didn't.

"I have to make firm decisions now, and I cannot allow emotion to control us. The Stars need strong leadership, a system that ensures survival, even if that means sacrificing some of us to save the rest. We will divide the Stars into emergency teams: a team will go out to search for food, another team will search for a backup shelter in case the ship becomes unfit to stay in, and a final team will try to reinforce what can be salvaged from the ship. The situation is getting worse; the rains could flood the lower part of the ship within the coming hours. We need to implement a firm plan now..."

I felt my hands clench at my sides, but I said nothing.

"And so that we don't waste the meeting's time in futile arguments, you must do what you have always done. You must make everyone stand with me. This is not a moment for division, but a moment to make the right decision, and you know that very well."

I saw it in her eyes, that silent expectation that I, as usual, would be the bridge that delivers her decisions to the Stars, that I would be the one to soften the impact of her words, to justify her firmness, to make it seem like it was everyone's plan and not just her orders. But I am no longer that bridge anymore.

"No."

She raised her eyebrow, barely showing her astonishment; she couldn't hide it completely this time.

"No?"

"I will not support a plan I didn't help create. I will not make the Stars follow you just because you think this is the right decision."

Something in her face changed for a moment, something that almost made her look as if she had received an unexpected slap, but she didn't retreat, didn't budge. Instead, she took another step forward. Her tone became more insistent, sharper: "This isn't a matter of personal opinion, One! It's a matter of life and death."

I tightened my fingers, not allowing my voice to waver: "And for that reason, I will not be your subordinate anymore!"

For a second, just a second, I noticed a slight tension in her grip, as if she were about to say something that would immediately bring her down. But I didn't give her the chance, and I continued: "I will not allow you to push us all towards decisions that could mean our death. If we are to survive, we will survive together, not at the expense of one another."

She said nothing, but her eyes were burning with anger, fear, and the stubbornness I was used to always seeing in her. Then she turned and entered the hall without uttering another word.

When I entered, I felt the heaviness in the air, the mixture of tension and collapse. The Stars sat in groups, their eyes reflecting fear, hunger, and exhaustion, and the final hope that this meeting might change something. I stood in a place near the door, and there was a clear distance between myself and

Three, unlike usual—a distance that wasn't just physical, but was an embodiment of the rift that had occurred between us a short time ago, one that could no longer be repaired.

Three stood firmly, looked at everyone, and began to state her plan, her tone stern and sharp as a sword. After she finished her speech, I pushed my body off the wall, took a step forward, and said in a strong, unwavering voice: "And who among us will bear the risk? Who among us will go out in the middle of the storm? Have you thought about who might be killed during the search?"

"Everything requires sacrifice, Star One."

"Sacrifice of whom? The ones you choose, or the ones who have no chance to refuse?"

The Stars turned to us, the sounds of whispers rose, their eyes darting between us, now clearly realizing there was a blazing battle between her and me, that this wasn't just an ordinary discussion. I continued with the same sharpness: "If we are to survive, it will not be at the expense of one another."

I heard the sound of her breathing slow down; I saw that tension that began to creep into her eyes, but she didn't let it show. She didn't let it control her.

And before she could reply, the unexpected happened. I felt the floor of the hall tremble beneath our feet, accompanied by a sound like a mighty roar. The wind itself decided to pull the ship with it into the sky. In a moment, a great fissure opened in the wall. Everything turned into noise, the screams of the Stars filled the place, and some even tried to flee, but there was no room to escape. The ground began to collapse, piece by piece, in succession. They ran, but the collapse outraced them.

I tried to move, tried to scream, but everything happened with terrifying speed, as if time itself decided to rob us of the chance to understand. I turned to Three and found her looking at the chaos in silent shock, as if unable to process what was happening. Then, without thinking, I grabbed her by the arm, pulled her away from the falling rubble and out the door, just before a huge part of the ceiling collapsed where we had been standing only a moment before. I continued to cling to her tightly as we were falling, until we collided with the ground, not the walls of the corridor. My breathing was frantic, my heart pounding like the drums that announce the end. When I opened my eyes and looked around, I wished I could close them forever. I found only rubble. I found only death. The meeting hall had disappeared; indeed, the entire rear section of the ship had collapsed in an instant.

(11)

I pushed her forcefully. I was no longer able to restrain myself, no longer able to bear the silence nor the brokenness. My hands trembled, not from fear, but from the anger, from the pain that had accumulated inside me until it exploded. Indeed, my entire body, not because of the cold, for my body wasinflamed, but because of what we had lost—what we shouldn't have lost if she hadn't been so stubborn, if she hadn't clung to her opinion until the end, until the last breath.

"This is because of you! All of this is because of you and you alone!!"

The words erupted from my mouth like a scream I didn't know I possessed, as if it had been held captive in my chest all this time, waiting for this moment to be freed. Then I pointed to the rubble that moments ago was a hall pulsating with life, where we had all gathered to plan for survival, but was now nothing but a silent pit, a graveyard for a group of dreamers who remained there and would never get out.

"You could have compromised, just once! But you refused! You preferred to cling to power and drive everyone away until everything collapsed!"

I saw her eyes widen for a moment, freezing in unexpected shock. Did she expect me to be silent? Did she think I would remain that shadow who stands behind her, justifies her words, softens the impact of her decisions on everyone? No, that was over now. I am finished playing this role. I no longer follow anyone, and I no longer need anyone to decide for me or help me.

I looked at her, waited for any response from her, any word with which to defend herself, but she had nothing to say. Just silence. A heavy silence, as heavy as the terror that was clear in her eyes, as if for the first time she was realizing the evil of what she had done, for the first time seeing the destruction she had left behind her. So, I said it clearly, in a voice that no longer trembled, a voice that wasn't mine a little while ago, but became mine now: "It's over! From this moment on, I will lead alone, and I don't want you to interfere in any of my decisions anymore."

I turned, turned my back to her, and didn't look at her again. I no longer needed to see her face. I no longer needed her approval, or her confession. I no longer cared if she saw herself as guilty or not. All that worried me then was: Will I even find any stars waiting for someone to lead them away from this devastation?

I inhaled the stormy air, filled my lungs with the smell of loss and rain. Yet my hands did not stop lifting the remains of wooden planks, searching that dilapidated mountain. And behind me, Three remained in her place. I heard no sound of her breath, saw no movement from her, just stillness, as if her ghost remained stuck between the rubble and the water, between the past that had ended, and the future where she no longer had a place. She is still there, but she will no longer be a part of the story.

I continued the search as the rain still poured down on us. Our feet, and the ship behind us, sank more and more into the mud and water, as if the earth were slowly swallowing itself with us, as if it knew it could no longer bear our weight.

In the end, I saw myself alone amidst this destruction. It wasn't surprising, not as shocking as I had expected it to be. Rather, it was silent, slow, as if I were living the moment the soul leaves a dying body, a slow tide that takes everything with it and never brings anything back. I struggle with it alone, along with the ghost of Three, the wreckage of the ship, and the battle for leadership that no longer had any meaning.

Around me, everything was tilted, shattered, fragmented into pieces, like the remains of crushed seats, metal edges bent like broken ribs, and torn uniforms that were once the only thing that connected us to home. Indeed, everything around me was shattered except the void; it alone remained standing, solid, stubborn, steady amidst this crumbling world. I could hear the sound of my breathing. I could feel the mud weighing down my boots, the rain that began to gradually lose its momentum, receding drop by drop, as if it realized too late that there was nothing left to wash. Then the storm began to calm.

I froze, stopped moving. There was nothing left to be moved anymore. Even Three hadn't spoken since she fell silent. Or perhaps she was speaking, but there was nothing else I wanted to hear from her, and there was nothing else for her to say, because in her eyes, there was no one to answer her anyway. For that reason, in the end, I wanted to say something to her, anything, but I found no words that had forgiven her.

Then suddenly, the horizon split, and the light came. It wasn't bright, not glowing as in the old paintings, not a glorious birth of a new world. Rather, it was faint, shy, like the touch of a hand on an exhausted forehead, hesitant like words that do not yet know if they should be spoken. The Sun was trying to pierce this ruin to touch my faith, which had disappeared since the first day with Three's scream, to seep through the gray sky and find its way between the heavy clouds that still hung above us like an old threat that had not yet passed.

Then I saw them from the horizon, from the distant fog, from where I thought there was nothing left. I saw Star Five first. She was walking with speed and certainty, as if she knew she would reach me no matter how late she was, as if she hadn't doubted for a moment that she would find me here, standing among what remained of our dilapidated world. Then I saw Star Six. She was walking beside her, her steps heavy. But that wasn't the only thing I noticed, but also the coat—Thirteen's coat. It was draped over her shoulders, covering her body as if it still carried the weight of its owner, as if it were trying to hide her absence, as if remnants of her spirit were still clinging to it, refusing to disappear completely.

I wanted to run towards them, but I didn't move.

I wanted to shout their names, but my voice wouldn't come out.

I wanted to cry, but even the tears had dried up inside me.

Then everything collapsed when I heard a low, crumbling sound, rising as if the ship had decided to breathe its last breaths, as if what was left of it decided to fall now. Only now. Now after I had found something I could hold onto. I saw what remained of the ship collapse before me, collapsing with its full weight, with its full tragedy, breaking, tumbling, shattering as it should have shattered from the beginning.

Then came the silence, and nothing remained but it.

We were left without walls, or corridors, or halls, or places to return to. Nothing but rubble.

It was then I fell to my knees. I didn't know if I had stumbled, or if my legs had finally failed me, or if I had chosen to sit. But I found myself there, between the mud and the cold water, carrying alone what remains of this place, what remains of this journey, what remains of me.

Chapter Seven:
A Painting for the Lost Ones with a Brush of Sand

(1)

The boom of the wood as it split, the sharp shriek as it tore through the air, and the deafening impact when everything collided with everything, when there was nothing left but an eternal fall for me and for her. I was there when it happened, a witness to every part of the moment. But the sound didn't disappear; it didn't leave as everything else left. It returned, replaying in my head, stronger than it was, and my mind kept replaying it, again, and again, and again, until I could no longer distinguish between reality and memory. I no longer knew if I was still there amidst the collapse, amidst the fall, amidst the end, or if I had actually moved away from it. I closed my eyes, but the sound didn't disappear. I covered my ears, but I still felt its collapse continuing behind me. In the end, I was a coward. I couldn't restrain my fear and stop the scene, for that meant replacing it with the reality that it was over forever.

And was everything over? I didn't know. I felt nothing but the trembling inside me, as if my ribs were vibrating under my skin, as if my soul itself was cracking. Then came absolute silence. No sound, no movement, nothing, as if the world had suddenly vanished. I opened my eyes and saw only blackness. I closed them again, but the blackness didn't change. Was everything truly over? Or was I mistaken when I thought I was still here? For there was no longer any wind or water or life, not even the echo of the wreckage I had heard a little while ago. I wonder, had the earth finally swallowed me? For although I was standing, I couldn't feel my feet; I felt nothing but the void that stretched within me, in my chest, and in my head.

Then suddenly, the sound struck me—with the sound of rain. It almost tore me in two. It was sharp as if striking directly upon my head, as if the sky had fallen on me with all its wrath. It wasn't just rain falling; it was lashing down like whips, wanting to drown me in the place where I stood. I felt the water swallowing me, saw the ground flooding, overflowing, turning into an endless black pool, until I could no longer breathe. I gasped forcefully, moved backward, and then, somehow, there was no more water. There wasn't even rain. The ground was dry under my feet. Only the shock was toying with me, tearing me between what I saw and what I thought I was seeing. And I was about to surrender to it, about to believe I had truly drowned in this illusion, until I saw her. Star Five. Standing there. She wasn't far, but her presence was strong enough to demolish everything I had believed for a moment.

In her presence, there was no rain, no flood, no swallowing of the earth, no absolute end. She was just there, standing amidst the ruins, observing what was left of our world with her sharp eyes. She was real, and because she was, I had to face the truth this time. I wanted to move, to call her, to say something, anything, but I couldn't. I thought she would look at me and start screaming. I thought she would say it out loud: This is all your fault, One! while placing the entire blame on my shoulder, because I was the one who let everything happen. But she didn't say that; she didn't say any of the things I expected. She just responded to all my thoughts with a quiet voice that revealed my blindness: "So, we can't stay here anymore..."

Her words came to me like a message of realization, without being a scream or a reprimand. I understood then that the matter was no longer about blame, but about what comes next. I screamed unconsciously, without thinking, without hesitation, as if trying to scream on behalf of all the Stars who were no longer here, with what they would have said to me then: "And where will we go?!"

I heard my own voice then for the first time since the collapse. It was terrifying, laden with anger, with grief, with the futility of what we had done up to this point—the voice of a star who doesn't know where to go after losing everything.

"There's no place for us to go anymore!"

And this was the reality I saw before me, wasn't it? Weren't we now without shelter, without a plan, without a ship, and worst of all, without hope. But Five didn't look at me, didn't turn fully towards me. She just glanced at me from the corner of her eye as she stepped forward, as if she hadn't lost her confidence in anything. Then she said clearly, in a voice that left no room for doubt or debate: "To find the place where the remaining Stars are."

The remaining Stars? You mean the ones we left and then lost in our most difficult times? The ones we didn't search for when we could have? Then all I thought of after that was: How will I face them with the news of the ship's fall and the death of all the Stars because of my weakness? I realized then that I hadn't just lost this ship; I had also lost what was left of me. And for the first time since all this, I felt my feet were not on the ground. I felt that I too, Star One, was lost amidst all this ruin. For a moment, the title of this chapter became what I said to myself, and to her by mistake: "Is everything over, or is everything just beginning now?"

(2)

I couldn't distinguish between them. Between one moment and the next, I found myself like a newborn opening its eyes to a world it does not know, in which it knows no familiar face nor a safe home. The earth beneath my body was cold, resembling a charred expanse left by the previous storm in its path, but I felt a strange inner warmth, as if something deep inside me was lighting up for the first time. As we stood, I was stripped of everything—my emotions and my thoughts—as if they had fallen with me when the ship collapsed, and fate had left me with nothing but my trembling body and two empty eyes looking at a sky I had never heard of except that it was blue. But above me, it wasn't a pure blue, but a color tinged with dark gray, as if heavy cloud masses had gathered to announce a new catastrophe. And yet, the color wasn't a reason to increase my fear. Instead, I calmed when I saw a sliver of blue horizon trying to seep through from behind the fog, a ribbon looming in the distance like a hope I had previously denied. The scene looked like one was looking at an upside-down sea; instead of the blue extending beneath me, it was suspended above me in the sky, wandering in its height, promising me something I do not yet understand. I imagined that if I raised my hands towards that blue ribbon, I would touch its edges, feel a lingering dampness from the last storm, and complete this strange birth with a scream that did not come from me: And do I have the right to cry?

Then I didn't cry, nor did I make a single sound. Perhaps because the tears had dried up with the rain that had run out since the last storm, or because fear was the only thing remaining, crouching inside me like fog over a stricken city. From that scenery, the world seemed vast to me before I even took the first step, more so than I had ever thought. And despite all this expanse, I felt I had no place in it, which led my soul to tell me: Perhaps the only place you ever lived in has vanished. So, will you cling to this rubble with a past that will not return, or will you leave it to chase that blue line in the sky?

I had lost my ship, my family, and my old face. There was no one left who knew me except the me that fell, and this terrified me more than anything else: that I had become a zero, without an identity, without memories I could rely on, and without a clear future except before another storm looming on the horizon.

From my angle, I glimpsed the reflection of the collapsed ship's wreckage against the sky, the remains of wood and cracked glass. I saw it sprouting from the earth like the roots of an inverted tree, showing our weakness before nature and the merciless storms. There was nothing left behind us to leave but some bodies that would later turn into skeletons, and then they would disappear. I forgot why we had lifted them before and buried them as if that had any meaning. It only told me, whenever I raised my gaze towards it, that the past was over, and that the world was now watching me as I struggled with my illusions. I tried to rise, tightened my grip on some worn-out debris, but I lost my balance and fell to my knees. I felt the pain of pebbles that dug into my skin and some shards of glass, making me feel as if I were learning to walk again.

Here I am today. I saw myself in the open air, with no roof to cover my head but those heavy clouds, and with no being to keep my loneliness company except the echo of my thoughts. Everything seemed desolate, but it was flowering, holding a promise of a color that might resemble life. I then repeated to myself as I stared at the horizon: Perhaps I was born again in the open, with my fears, and with my desire to grasp that blue strip defiant of the clouds. But this is only my first step, not my last.

And in that moment, a cold gust of wind came from the east, as if warning me: Get ready, a harsher storm is on the way. But despite that, I rose with a kind of feeble resolve, as if bidding farewell to my old shadow, and opening a new page of my being. I advanced without looking back, for what is the use of memories when one knows that what is coming may be more savage than what has passed? For all along, that small blue patch was still there, clinging to its place among the clouds, waiting for me to raise my gaze towards it whenever despair possessed me, so I would realize that despite everything that had happened, I was still alive.

I saw her, Star Six, extending her hand towards me. I clung to it as a drowning person cling to a torn plank in the middle of a raging sea. I didn't think I could move after weakness had gripped my limbs and weighed down my soul, but the warmth of her fingers brought me back to life. I again felt a tremor in my fingers, and a vibration in my heart as before, but this time I stood and did not fall, as if her hand had whispered to me that I still possessed a strength within me sufficient to stand. When I stood up, I immediately felt the coldness of the air strike my face, then I heard the sound of metal chains dangling from one of the ship's mast crossbars, striking one another, as if they were mourning those we left behind and those who had departed forever. I took a hesitant step, my hands still trembling, but I forgave that tremor. In the end, it is not easy to leave the place you used to call home, even if it has turned into rubble and splinters in a matter of seconds.

(3)

Star Five stood a short distance in front of me, her head raised towards the sky that had never changed for her—she always saw it as a field for the next mission or the coming battle. She didn't turn to me, nor did she check if I was ready to keep up with her. Instead, she was looking at the horizon with harsh eyes, as if nothing mattered but what the world intended to throw in her path. I glanced back at her as she began to walk, and Six and I delved in behind her in a heavy silence. The walk felt like trying to sever a thick rope of memories pulling me back, mixed with a flavor of the future's mystery. But I gathered every last breath in my lungs, and every terrified beat of my heart, to continue moving forward.

And at the farthest edge of the wreckage, where the last pieces of the ship stood like gaunt bones erect on the ground, Five suddenly stopped. It's not usual for her to stop in the middle of her path like this without reason. Did she remember something important? I imagined then that she would turn to look at the ship one last time before leaving. But instead, I saw her staring into the void with a coldness, as if seeing a ghost that no one else saw. Then I heard her say with harsh clarity: "If you're going to stay here, then that's your problem."

289

I immediately noticed she wasn't directing her words to me or to Six; she was uttering them to a silent ghost squatting there. In that moment, a shiver ran down my back when I noticed the presence of a star there named Three, almost hidden in the gloomy shadows, hunched near the wreckage that had collapsed the moment I had pulled her from my arms. I thought she might raise her head and reply, or beg Five to pull her out of the abyss of silence, but she did not. She remained resigned, as if Five's voice passed beyond her senses like air through a dark tunnel. So, she moved again, with Star Six beside her, without looking back again.

I stood there, motionless, my eyes darting between Five and Three. I hoped deep down that the latter would show any sign of rising or a faint cry for help so I would stop them. I was even about to take a step back towards her, but my feet were stuck to the ground, lost as to how I could possibly wake her, while I, deep down, am fallen.

I waited there for a few moments that stretched on as if for a whole eon, hoping she might move a muscle, but Three was like a statue that had lost its sense of life. She was no longer that domineering leader nor the stern voice I once knew; she was just a faint shadow of a picture that was hanging up high, fell in the blink of an eye, and broke, with no way to make it whole again. I froze for a minute, then filled my eyes with a silent farewell look, and drew on my face an expression devoid of all emotion, except for one prominent feeling: helplessness. I realized I was incapable of changing her reality. Just as Five said, if Star Three chose to stay, that was her own problem, and no one could convince her otherwise. Then I turned to follow the steps of Star Five and Six before the urge to cry, or to try and save one who does not want saving, could overwhelm me. We both had a choice, when we saw the wreckage, between perishing there or surviving with one hand. And I chose the latter.

My steps followed theirs, while I heard the sound of the wreckage behind my back trembling under a new wind blowing from an unknown direction. Would another storm come now to uproot what was left behind, or perhaps guide us to the distant light? I didn't turn to find out. All I had in those moments was a single certainty: that if I turned back again, I might never be able to move forward.

(4)

When we emerged from that forest, I needed some time to process what I was seeing. From a distance, I saw mountains of twisted metal and huge pieces of unnaturally flat grey stone, their regular appearance suggesting they were made with a repeating pattern or complex geometric plans. As I approached those enormous hills of remains, they seemed to me like the fossils of giant creatures whose skeletons had turned to rubble over time. I realized after a while that these hills were originally towering buildings that once rose to the heavens, but now they were piled up like our ship, one on top of the other, like ancient ruins, despite how high they once stood. I was astonished by the size of these structures. I felt that the inhabitants of this planet had reached an advanced level of science and technology to have erected such edifices. But the sight also makes you wonder: how did beings like these falls? And why did their entire legacy become rubble? Many other questions circled in my mind, even though I knew from my study of the few available data from our celestial archives that many comprehensive wars had occurred in the galaxy. But I had never imagined the scale of the destruction that such a war could leave behind.

We stepped cautiously on a broken surface that looked as if it had originally been a paved road, and I was amazed by its details. There were traces of old drawing or paint indicating lanes for vehicles, which in turn I saw fallen on the sides of the road like dead, brown creatures. Their iron frames bore exquisite, different designs, and complex operating systems of wires, electronic parts, and gears. I stopped at one of them to contemplate its broken lights and its front panel with strange symbols. Curiosity arose in me: how was it operated? Did it rely on an internal power source or a comprehensive city-wide power grid? Four would have surely figured that out upon seeing them; she loved to tinker with these things.

As we continued to advance, I glimpsed on the horizon a huge screen mounted on a half-collapsed building. It seemed to me that a part of its surface still reflected a faint glimmer, barely visible in the daylight, but it clearly indicated the presence of a residual power source that had not completely gone out. What technology was it that allowed this screen to endure through all these centuries of isolation and destruction? Does it perhaps run on solar power? Or a subterranean battery that is still performing its function despite the passage of time?

After hours of observation during our passage, a strange feeling came over me as I watched those great ruins: that this destruction didn't happen overnight. Rather, it seemed the catastrophe came as a destructive storm that left everything in a state of rapid shattering, followed by a slow erosion that continued for many long years, until the air in this place now carried a heavy chemical smell, indicating it was still saturated with the remnants of lethal weapons. But amidst all this dark scene, life was seeping in like a faint light through the folds of darkness. I saw green climbing plants, lush despite the ruin, their stems and branches extending through cracks in the ceilings and walls, wrapping around the edges of the dilapidated doors and windows as if reclaiming the place for their own benefit. Even in some corners of the roads, small shrubs appeared, having broken through the concrete surface to find light and space to grow. I couldn't have imagined that nature overcomes all constraints in this way. It exploits every opportunity to ignite a new spark of life. The few remaining trees in the middle of the city seemed to me like steadfast guards, with charred trunks on one side and green branches on the other, as if the plant world insists on flourishing despite all it has been through.

I continued my exploration until I stopped before the remains of a building more colossal than the others. Its facade looked like a cracked painting. At the collapsed entrance, I touched with my fingertips a hard, smooth material resembling gemstones. It occurred to me that it might have been the administrative or governmental center of this city; these stones and metal plates indicate something of importance, but who knows? And I began to wonder: What used to happen in this large building? Were meetings held here for intelligent beings who made crucial decisions that ultimately led them to this ruin? And how were these beings able to build this city with such advanced technology, then destroy it in such a painful way? They must have, at some time, reached the pinnacle of science, invented machines and devices beyond imagination, which led them to conflicts or a struggle over resources or a flawed concept of power, pushing them to unleash the forces of destruction. My mind couldn't comprehend how a being could reach this level of progress, then head towards self-annihilation.

Then I began to collect samples of what remained around me as proof to present to myself: burnt electronic parts, and complex metal tools that stared back at me with the remains of holes and corrosion from immense heat. All this evidence was screaming a tragic story: These people possessed a weapon that knows no mercy, and when they used it, the scales of civilization were turned upside down.

I continued walking along what I thought was the city's main path, and at some point, I found fragments of a massive statue that probably once occupied the center of a plaza. Nothing remained of it but a stone foot and some of its shattered toes, and it appeared to have engravings and drawings on it that might have been a language or cultural symbols for them. When I remember the millions of miles we traveled in space searching for other civilizations from whose lives we could extract stories, I feel sorrow that I found only silent ruins—cities that once lit up this planet's nights, connecting to each other with hidden wires and waves. And now, you see nothing of them but the remains of those connections dangling like severed limbs from collapsed ceilings and leaning walls.

(5)

I couldn't get past that mysterious glimmer that had once again pierced my eyes. I stopped my steps amidst the rubble and listened again to the echo of the dilapidated doors and windows as they resisted the wind in vain. At first glance, I guessed this glimmer was a reflection of the sun on a rust-covered metal surface, but my curiosity pushed me to get closer. Here, it became clear that it was the light of the huge screen, which was still working despite all this ruin. A weary human man appeared on it, his features clinging to the strength he claimed to possess. His military uniform was decorated with metallic colors and medals overflowing with boastfulness, as if he were still in a celebration of an old victory. And although it emitted no sound, the man's firm expressions and heavy breaths gave me the impression that he held an indisputable authority, and was on the verge of giving an extremely difficult speech.

I saw flashing words beside him on the screen, separated by fleeting pauses. It seemed this was the message this leader was delivering. And although I didn't catch a whisper, I felt he was addressing everyone with severity, as if he were speaking to his people at a time that brooked no delay. I let my eyes follow the words in succession, and its content became clear to me as if I were hearing it myself: Citizens, I first assure you that our forces are, at this very moment, writing the greatest achievements on the battlefield. We are making great progress, and with your cooperation, we will achieve the victory we all await. Do not believe the malicious rumors spread by the enemy as part of their psychological warfare; we are now on the cusp of absolute victory. In these critical times, we ask for your adherence to the following instructions to preserve your security, your safety, and the safety of the homeland: do not assist the enemy in spreading their narrative or deal with any suspicious data that misleads the facts. Do not leave your homes except in cases of extreme emergency; any unnecessary movement could endanger your lives as a result of the intense military operations and the volatile security situation. When you need food, medicine, or any necessary assistance, you can contact the Office of Social Contribution for your area via the fixed numbers, and you will be provided with the necessary supplies as soon as possible. In conclusion, I stress again the importance of staying away from any military or strategic facilities belonging to our forces or our government institutions. Your unauthorized approach or presence in the vicinity of those facilities will be considered cooperation with the enemy. I assure you that our defense forces will not be lenient at all with any attempt to approach their restricted areas, in the interest of protecting us all. Every necessary measure will be taken to protect these facilities from any potential threat. This is for your safety, and for the safety of our great nation. We are strong, and we will remain strong thanks to your cooperation and your standing behind us. We fight in defense of our future and the future of our generations. Stay in your homes, stay cautious, and trust that we are inevitably marching towards victory.

Then the warning repeated. It wasn't the first time I had seen a speech that mixes optimism with the stick, but here I stood, listening to it amidst the ruins of a dying city, wondering: What is the use of these words after the land around me has become a ghost of an existence from which nothing remained but remnants? What meaning does victory have when they have left ruin as a testament to a failure they never admitted? Then I said to myself: Here is a lesson in leadership that cannot be ignored. I saw how the leader stood on the screen with his chin held high, pulsating with confidence, even to absent eyes. He speaks with the tone of a victor searching for new victims for his promises, while reality mocks him in the background of the image: an empty city, ruins testifying to a resounding fall, no trace of his army nor his citizens.

And despite all that belief, I saw myself confronting another reality: I was never in a position of power like that human leader. Rather, I was a mere shadow following a decision bigger than me, not daring to oppose it, just like a soldier when the commander waves orders at him. And yet, I found myself before the rubble once again, wondering how we can give others promises of victory when we don't have the luxury of choosing between escape or confrontation. I had no authority signified by medals, nor did I ever give speeches where the throats of supporters delighted me. Instead, I lived on the margins of leadership and learned a more precious lesson there: that responsibility is not in the number of stars on your shoulders nor the medals on your chest, but in what you can save when ruin comes. We both fell then with a resounding fall, and this is the only thing the world will witness and immortalize of our actions.

And to be honest, I was drawn to his style of instruction—this sternness, this dual use of reassurance and threat together. Like warning citizens away from military facilities while offering assistance via phones that no one answers, and the absolute prohibition of any movement outside homes except for emergencies. He speaks what is supposed to be the grand plan to save everyone, but I saw no one here to believe it or even discuss it. I saw only an emptiness without a recipient. Moments passed fleetingly, and the official emblem appeared on the screen amidst a silent anthem, as if the voices of soldiers were playing only in memory. Military grandeur turned into painful sarcasm: a demolished city wrapped around the screen, with no soul and no life in it. So, who is this man addressing? Who is listening to him?!

When the lights faded for moments, only to return and repeat the message, I could no longer watch. I was thinking about the meaning of a leadership that besieges its own people with such orders and ignites endless wars. Is it conceivable that this form of patriotic vanity is what drove them to destroy everything? If the leader was truly doing what he saw as right, then where are his people now? Where are their fields, their schools, their buildings? Where are their joys and their holidays? I murmured in a voice I barely heard myself: this is it. This is what it looks like when leadership turns into a tragic illusion, like a leader wearing medals as a symbol of pride in a moment when he has lost everything of value and worth respecting. Perhaps he wanted to defeat an enemy, so he defeated his own city first.

I looked at that harsh military face, and I felt as if it were staring directly into my eyes through the screen, demanding my compliance and threatening me for inaction. But I am Star One. I have experienced before the meaning of collapse and loss, and I have understood how true leadership is tied to real sacrifice, not slogans. I am no longer a captive to orders not supported by actions that prove their truthfulness. Instead, I have learned that a leader who does not build the trust of those they lead means their words, no matter how much they claim the truth, will turn into a tool for their oppression, threatening them with it one moment and reassuring them with it another, until everyone collapses, as happened with Three and with humans in the past.

When the screen's glow dimmed again, I understood that the message would continue to loop in a vicious circle, with no one listening. I left it there, to struggle against the darkness by itself, it and the words burning themselves out repeatedly, while the city was sealed with fragments. Its fate, like the fate of its people, was apparently written in rubble. It didn't seem that anyone would come to answer this leader's call, just as I hadn't come to obey it, but to see the lesson with my own eyes: Leadership is not about delivering victory speeches, but about giving those around you a real chance to survive. So, I muttered quietly as I moved away from the screen, leaving its image to flicker uselessly in the afternoon of the empty city. I wished I could remove the medals from his chest and tell him: Strength is not a metal facade, but a responsibility. And if you have failed to appreciate it, do not lie to those for whom promises await. In the end, I left the place, my heart heavy with a clearer vision of what it means to be a leader, of what it means to bear the consequences of your decisions before your homelands fall victim to your mistakes.

(6)

I didn't expect the sun to leave us so quickly. I felt as if the day had suddenly leaped over our heads. I didn't even notice we had lost the warmth of the light until I found my fingers unable to distinguish what they were reaching for on the ground. We didn't have much time left for this day. If we continued walking like this without shelter, we would be an easy meal for any danger lurking for us. When I turned to Five to tell her, I saw her observing the edge of the dark sky with great concentration, as if studying the extent of the darkness. She isn't the type to easily admit fatigue or fear, but the slight slump in her shoulders betrayed some of her truth. I said to her in quick phrases that groaned with hesitation: "We have to stop. There's no use in confronting the deep night when we are exhausted."

She moved her eyes towards me without a word, then nodded her head in silent agreement—a nod driven more by desire than by conviction, as our current situation didn't allow her to show her usual toughness. Then the first thing my eyes fell upon was a cracked concrete building, the edges of its upper floors collapsed at an angle, intertwined with each other. It didn't look like a hospitable place, but at least it was still standing. I said to her, gesturing with my hand towards it: "Maybe we can spend the night there."

She didn't argue with me. We just started approaching the only entrance that seemed clear amidst the scattered rubble. We then discovered that its wooden door was still firmly shut, despite all the surrounding chaos. But I didn't even need to speak, for Five initiated a usual move of hers: she lifted her foot with a bit of momentum and struck the door with exceptional resolve. I heard the sound of a violent impact followed by a sharp crack, an indication that what little strength was left in this door was not going to deter her. She kept at it until an opening was forced, allowing us to pass through. Five had always known nothing of quiet ways, but in this moment her action seemed logical; she wouldn't risk a maneuver that might prolong our standing in this darkness.

I entered behind her and found myself before a narrow hallway almost suffocating from its gloom. The darkness resembled the depth of a dark well, where our only guide was a glimmer of moonlight seeping in through cracks in the opposite wall and from the door's opening. And who said walls don't talk? For in their silence, everything was shattered, as if I were listening to incomplete tales by way of symbols and paintings on the stained walls. The smell of thick dust was the first thing that hit my nose, forcing me to stifle a sudden cough. I raised my hand to cover my mouth, and then I heard from behind me a short murmur from Five, as if she too were struggling to catch her breath. I was about to apologize for the place, as it seemed to be our only choice. And right at that moment, the sound of simple music startled me, like a distorted but soft melody, emanating from a corner whose details I couldn't see. I shook my head in astonishment and wondered: Where is this sound coming from? I didn't expect to hear any kind of sound amidst what I thought was a dead structure. Perhaps there was still an electrical device working, through which the wind had carved a path to an old tune that had lost its way among the rubble. And who knows? I didn't dwell on the question for long, because the quiet melody gave us a sudden feeling of tranquility, as if it had thrown itself into our ailing embrace to ease our fatigue, if only for a moment.

I looked at Five and saw her eyes relax, so I left her there and took a step inside the hallway to search for the source of the sound, feeling small pieces of debris crumbling under my feet. The darkness spread behind me, and my awareness grew that we wouldn't be able to leave safely for another place at this hour. So, as the echoes of the tune danced around us, I leaned myself against a half-collapsed wall a little away from the entrance and began to think deeply: How many scattered treasures might we find among the rubble of this city without realizing their value? As the music intensified slightly, I moved to take off a load that was on my back—remains of our things from the journey, and items that might still be usable which I had collected from the ship's wreckage. I left it gently on the cracked floor tiles. I couldn't believe I was finally relieved of its weight. Then I heard Five say in a low voice as she approached another inner door: "I'm going to scout the place."

"Alright, I'll wait for you here for a moment."

I didn't object. Fatigue had settled over me, and an overwhelming desire not to stand, to remain seated without moving, overcame me. I contemplated the emptiness of the hallway and that strange melody emanating like a faint call resisting the void. Between every gasp and cry of my breath, I glimpsed a short flash of lightning that I hadn't expected, startling me from behind a window that was covered by a worn-out wooden plank. I understood the situation then. There was still a lot of the harsh night that would besiege us until dawn. But perhaps, in this place, we would find moments of peace, even if temporary, before we faced the morning sun again and drowned in the journey towards being lost amidst the unknown.

It wouldn't be so bad if we calmed down a little.

I said it, then breathed deeply, drawing some resolve from the music that was still struggling against the ruin and drifting in the dust-saturated air. Perhaps this will be our first gathering in places torn by stories, but it certainly won't be the last.

(7)

The darkness, like the stillness, had settled in the corners of the place. Five's footsteps quieted at the entrance, where she sat on a worn-out table under the pretext of keeping guard, but I saw her wrestling with drowsiness until it overcame her. I didn't want to wake her; I don't know how much she has suffered recently because of me, and these few moments of slumber might be all she needs to recharge her energy. Later, I found myself trying to sit as comfortably as possible. I was unbelievably tired, and my eyes were trying to close of their own accord, so much so that my head almost fell on the edge of a set of drawers stacked beside me.

Behind me, the distorted music emanating from a lost device was broadcasting sweet hums that gave me a fleeting tranquility. But what truly occupied me was the sound of fiddling with the drawers that suddenly started near me. I slowly raised my head and saw Star Six standing there, her fingers lightly diving into the cabinet's drawers, pulling out shiny objects. I didn't want to talk; I was tired and annoyed, but I didn't have the energy then to object, to stop her noise. I looked at her face as she chose necklaces and bracelets that looked as if they were from another era, trying one on her hand and on her neck with a small mirror she held in her other hand. When she felt my gaze, she turned to me with eyes that suggested some enthusiasm, or perhaps curiosity. I asked her in a faint voice, from the effect of exhaustion: "What happened with you all when you left the ship? And how exactly did you lose Thirteen?"

She laughed a light laugh, a bit silly, as she tried to fasten a short necklace around her neck: "She didn't die; rather, she left before us to search for the other Stars, with the plan that we would return and help you all. That's what Five told me, that this was the best solution to make use of the time. But we didn't know the ship was this fragile and would collapse with the first storm that hit it."

Her face suddenly changed, as if something had pricked her after this admission, and I found my own features twisting as well. I said to myself: The collapse. The memory of the ship's collapse returned to occupy my chest with a greater weight, and I felt nothing but words seeping from my mouth, with the rhythm of the faint melody in the background: "None of this would have happened if I had stopped Three from carrying out the exile decision from the beginning. We Stars are weak, and without being together, there will be no chance for anyone to survive."

Although I whispered it, Six caught it immediately. She shrugged her shoulders with ease, as if telling me not to worry, then tried to respond with her light joke: "Rather, if we were all together then, we would have all died except you! It's fate,my older sister, just fate that led us here to go through these events."

I was badly annoyed by her lightness in accepting the incident, as if it meant nothing, so I shot back at her with a sharp blame: "But I was a failed leader! I let her influence me despite my certainty she was wrong, and I..."

But Six didn't leave me room to lament further, cutting me off at once with her words: "Pfft! None of us saw you as a leader in every sense of the word. We just saw you as our big sister we could temporarily rely on to manage the affairs of our lives."

Then she continued, tucking the small mirror into her pocket: "And you had no hand in what happened, nor could you have changed it no matter how you tried. Perhaps that was the end of one story and the beginning of another, and you will still play the role of the older sister in it, not the leader."

I felt an uncomfortable tone in Six's sarcasm, which agitated my nerves. I straightened my posture slightly and was about to reply seriously, but the music at that moment startled us with silence. The disc suddenly stopped. I froze in my place, terrified of the sudden quiet, tense like someone waiting for something unexpected. After a few seconds, a simple scratching sound was heard. The disc started to play again, with a faint melody that repeated itself, like an anthem that stubbornly resumed calming us despite everything we said and did.

Six returned to smiling at me, and although I was half-angry, I found myself breathing a sigh of relief with the roar of the melody. She approached me with quiet steps, holding in her hand one of those golden necklaces she had taken from the drawer, as if she had decided to adopt a cheerful role amidst this tense atmosphere between us. She knelt carefully before me and tied the necklace around my neck, whispering in my ear as she did: "How would you paint the final scene if you held the brush? A scribble with black and red lines, a painting everyone would want to tear up? Or would fate accompany us slowly until we reach the seashore at sunset, and there we slowly sink into it?"

She stepped back a little to evaluate the scene from her angle. She glanced at me, moving her head with clear admiration: "The necklace looks beautiful on you. Don't forget to show it to Four as soon as we reach them; she will definitely like it. Maybe I should also keep an extra one for Thirteen."

I felt the cold gold on my neck, which seemed to carry the weight of ages, and I glimpsed an absent-mindedness in Six's eyes that suggested she too didn't know what the next step was. In the end, I returned to sit where I was, on the same hard floor, a worn-out wall supporting my back, and I closed my eyes in extreme exhaustion. Then after moments, I murmured with bitterness: "That's if we find them. Perhaps we are all on a journey to be lost in a vast world whose end will be the seashore as you said, because this fate... has been mocking us since the beginning of the journey."

I felt then that the distance between me and sleep was shorter than ever before, and that a distance of questions still stretched on the dark horizons around us. The melodies of the music seemed sadder this time, but they remained a friend to us in a fleeting moment of rest, before we continue tomorrow walking towards... I don't know, perhaps towards a deeper loss.

(8)

Everything began faint and blurred, as if I were falling from a high place towards a land with no shape or features. I felt my slow blood flowing in my veins, overcome by the gloom of the surrounding darkness, until my eyes began to droop against my will, like a curtain being drawn on a stage that has finished its show. I didn't try to resist the drowsiness or cling to reality; I let myself dissolve quietly into some point of the unconscious.

I found myself standing amidst a gray fog that stretched to the horizon. I saw it swallowing its surroundings with a coldness, so I couldn't discern if I was standing on real ground or if the earth had disappeared from beneath me. Then it seemed to me that the echo of distant voices tore through this fog from time to time, voices that reflected a faint repetition of words about a devastating war, and about a leader drawing promises of victory over vast ruins. I thought I was still suffering from the memories of our ship's first fall, but it soon became clear to me that I was seeing something else entirely. I saw the remains of a world that had collapsed under the blows of fire, faceless soldiers roaming among the wreckage of cities, and the vague imprints of armed factions threatening a nameless government. I didn't understand the meaning at first, but my heart clenched as I strangely realized I was witnessing a past I hadn't lived directly. I wanted to turn and flee from this grim scene, but a paralysis struck my legs and glued me to the spot. The sky then appeared to me like a painting hung across the torn clouds, half of it immersed in blackness and a blood-red that oozed violence and destruction, the other half trying to merge with a quiet sunset, touched by threads of orange light. All of a sudden, I found in my hand a brush with bristles of contradictory colors, some dripping with blackness and others coated in that mysterious moonlight color, as if I had to either paint something on this sky or leave it fractured as it was. Then someone whispered to me: "How would you paint the final scene if you held the brush?"

In that moment, words sprang to my mind, reminding me of what Six had said about the leader and the older sister, about the painting we choose to create ourselves: "Either a scribble with black and red lines, so you etch a painting everyone would want to tear up? Or would fate accompany us slowly until we reach the seashore at sunset, and there we slowly sink into it?"

Then I saw, from between the foggy fragments, lines that flashed and warned of a suffocating danger, a danger that had turned cities into rubble and made smoke the master of the horizon. It seemed like a documentation of a war I had never officially heard of before. This made me raise the brush towards the terrible blackness first, as if responding to a dark call inviting me to surrender to everything that had happened to us since we fell on this dead planet. I then saw two reflections of myself in this color. The first one screamed at me: "I was a failed leader! I let her influence me despite my certainty she was wrong."

The words came out in the dream without an echo, and I drowned in the bitterness of self-accusation. Then I felt the brush slip from my will, heading towards the quiet orange shore where the sunset was calling me: "Our end will be the seashore as you said, so there is no place for the past or for these worries."

The colors clashed in my hands until some black drops mixed with the golden color, creating a distorted painting, half scream and half tranquility. Amidst my confusion, the paper dissolved, and a faint light emanated like the dust of a sunset mixing with the clouds of war. Then suddenly, I saw the shadows of stars advancing towards me from behind the destruction, their blaming voices calling to me: "Our older sister, where are you?"

"I am not an older sister or a leader, but just a cowardly shadow who doesn't know how to face her mistakes."

I wished to cry but I couldn't; my eyes were as if they had turned to stone then. When I raised the brush again, my arm petrified too. Indeed, everything in my body was trapped in this choice between surrendering to the pains of the present or fleeing towards a deceptive sunset. As soon as I tried to move, a sudden hurricane blast struck, blowing away all the images and colors. I lost my balance and dropped the brush from my hand. I began to flounder between dark clouds that resembled scenes from past days, while the dream ground cracked beneath me. I was just sinking into a void that was pulling me towards a colorless gloom. I tried to grab onto something to save me from falling, but I found only threads of frozen air. And in the decisive moment before colliding with a bottom I could not see, the entire world shattered around me like a painting that had exploded, and distant voices kept demanding I make a decision: "Leader or older sister? A black painting or a sunset in an endless sea? You are the one who decides."

At that, I opened my eyes sharply, and in an extremely strange moment, I heard some phrases that had just echoed a little while ago in my dream. Reality was then oozing with a hoarse speech emanating from a worn-out device; I don't know where exactly it was located in the apartment, but I think it was the one that was playing music earlier. I was still half-lying near the set of drawers, Six's head resting on my shoulder in a way I had never known from her before. I sighed as I recalled the brush slipping from my hand in the dream, then looked around to make sure I had truly returned to another world, a world not without destruction but at least less painful than that nightmare. The radio's voice, however, continued monotonously: "...we fight in the name of justice and freedom. We will bring down the war government that violated our rights, and we will save humanity from its anticipated demise whatever the cost, for nothing is more important than the human being."

From that, I realized that the war I saw in my dream was part of what my mind was hearing while I was deep in sleep, and that I was just like the painting, confused between two choices: unable to determine our fate, and not yet having attained salvation. The background screaming went silent for a moment, and I thought it was time for the previous quiet music to return, but the newscast continued with a clearer voice, with more coordinated words: "...Ladies and gentlemen. We are facing today a war the likes of which we have never witnessed in our history. In the state of New York, armed factions have appeared belonging to what is called the Free and Just Humanity Squad, where they have declared a military movement seeking to overthrow what they have termed the war government. The squad's leadership claims to possess a solution to save humanity from its current crisis and raises bright slogans about freedom and justice, while asserting at the same time that it is independent, not falling under the banner of any of the major international parties or hostile military alliances. For its part, official authorities state that this movement only exposes the country's already fractured stability to more chaos, and confirm that fighting with these militants has indeed broken out in some districts of the state, causing severe damage and allowing foreign forces lurking for our country to advance without hindrance. In light of this turbulent situation, quiet voices continue to call for a diplomatic solution, but does diplomacy still have a place when the tongues of flames blind the hearts and the voice of humanity is lost among the rubble of buildings? Will the promises of those outsiders lead us to a solution that actually results in saving the people, or to more severe chaos and a new fall in the record of disasters that have fractured our country? In any case, it seems the future grows darker with every passing hour without an agreement. And here we remind everyone that the security situation is worsening, and that emergency aid may be delayed in some areas due to the blockade of a number of main roads and several sectors falling out of control. Here ends our report for today. Stay safe wherever you are. Do not leave your homes."

And the words in the background continued to echo in my ears without stopping, one bulletin followed by another of similar meaning, until I ignored everything mentioned. Indeed, I summarized it in my mind with two words: Wrong result. My awakening at that time was featureless, unclear in its direction or reason. It didn't even compel me to go back to sleep after all I had heard or seen around me. Everyone was as still as the moonlight, and no sounds needed my attention except for the newscast which later became easy to ignore. There was no particular place to go or hunger to satisfy, as if it were a moment that existed only for me to see my own reflection in it and think about my days that had passed, my days that were quickly snatched from me, from which I reaped nothing but a guilty conscience.

And as the stillness of the night wrapped around me, infusing into me with every drop of this world's cold a glimmer that grew in my chest like the faint flame of an ember ignited by the blowing winds, I felt that this cold was not just a physical sensation, but an entity trying to seep into my limbs, testing my patience, examining my resilience, and slowly creeping in to besiege me and occupy my heart. And yet, there was still something inside me that resisted, a small, stubborn thing like the faint flame of an ember that refuses to be completely extinguished despite all the stillness surrounding it.

I closed my eyes to search for warmth within me, feeling for it between my ribs as a drowning person searches for a life raft, but I found only scattered fragments, miserable, dispersed memories, echoes of a life I once lived that ended suddenly, now just a pale image looming before me without my being able to touch it, appearing with more coldness in its wake. Six, leaning on me then, represented a final sign I perceived that I was not alone. I felt her calm breathing, her stillness which resembled my own, as if together we had become part of this deserted place, a fixed image in a world that no longer changes. She didn't move, we didn't speak, and I didn't ask her if she felt the cold as I did, because I knew the cold that inhabited me was different, harsher, more deep-rooted, and more extensive in my soul than the mere coldness of the air around me.

I had no choice but to draw my feet to my chest in a desperate attempt to regain some warmth, but the coldness continued to seep into my sides like creeping water slowly submerging me. Then my breaths began to condense in the air, creating a thread of fog that reflected a part of me, disappearing with every exhale before quickly vanishing before me. The entire world had become warm except for me, as if I were the only one stuck in a cold gap between life and death, a place where no one feels me, and from which I cannot later escape. Realizing this pushed me to lower my head until it touched my knees. I felt my weight doubling, as if I were slowly turning into an inanimate object with no ability to move or speak. Then I closed my eyes again slowly, not because I wanted to sleep, but because I no longer found a difference between wakefulness and slumber. I wasn't tired, but I was exhausted in a deeper way, a way that rest cannot fix, a way that makes closing my eyes akin to surrendering to the fact that I no longer had enough strength to stay awake any longer. And soon I felt myself drifting towards a different void, where there was no sound or movement, not even cold or warmth, just a stillness that extends forever, as long as I refuse to resist it.

(9)

Now, for no logical reason for it to happen, I am standing in a wide corridor under an intensely pure golden light, so pure that it overpowered everything I had seen before since our fall on that dark planet. I hesitantly raised my gaze upwards and saw the blue sky as I had once imagined it, clear without polluted clouds, sending a warm feeling into the atmosphere akin to that which we had almost forgotten while struggling against the cold and the gloom. I didn't fully understand how I got here, or when I moved from the darkness of the previous days to the heart of this quiet illumination, but something inside me clung to this scene as if it were all I ever wanted.

I was standing amidst an expanse encircled by a celestial calm, feeling beneath my feet a level ground with no trace of cracked roads or the rubble of buildings. It prompted me to whisper to myself without a sound: Is this another dream? But it seemed purer than the dreams I was used to, more coherent and clearer. Then I looked forward, and my eyes fell upon a wide glass gate, its frame painted a pale color leaning towards blackened silver. At its top, an emblem I knew well was hung on its stone wall. It was the emblem that marked the school's entrance in a passing time you'd think had died with all we lost during the journey. Seeing it now was like an unrepeatable honor. Then I remembered how we used to pass through this gate reassured, running towards its halls at the beginning of each day, caring for nothing but the upcoming breaks and the faces of the sisters around us, or my previous moments of contemplation accompanied only by this same quietness.

My memory was stimulated by something resembling a dream-like glimmer, making me wonder: Is this the same place?

I walked a few steps forward, my eyes searching for any familiar sign, but all I saw was the place's silence and its radiance, which accompanied me as part of the light and the memories. I stood for a minute, scrutinizing the details that had receded from my memory a long time ago: the edges of the gate, the smooth marble path leading to the inner yard, the high windows that used to overlook us from the direction of the Hall of the Sun, and my painting hanging in the corridor. Everything around me was elegant and clean, contrary to the gloom and mud my senses had been saturated with for an immeasurable, though short, time. It seemed to me at that moment that I had returned as a child to her familiar sanctuary after an arduous journey, as if the world outside had disappeared and become a mere illusion.

I began to move with steps closer to caution, expecting a sudden disappearance of the light or a collision with another, less merciful vision that would turn this dream into a nightmare. But the place remained quiet, and only the sound of my breathing was the sole melody tickling the school's space, so much so that I could almost hear my pulse inside my ears whenever my longing for this atmosphere, full of an old security I had lost, intensified.

And as I was stepping in stunned silence, two warm hands suddenly extended from behind me and covered my eyes carefully, depriving me of the stunning view for a single moment, unsettling me to the point that my heart leaped—not in terror, but with an astonishment difficult to describe. I stopped in my place, my breathing growing more tense and my hands searching for something to hold onto. I didn't see the face behind me, but the warmth of the touch and the familiarity in its movement put my soul at ease despite the surprise. In seconds, I raised my hands and gently wiped those strange, familiar hands from my eyes, before slowly turning around. It was then my eyes fell upon her. It was Star Four, standing as close as could be to me, wearing a tender smile that had always accompanied her, with a glance that almost declared: Of course you guessed me.

My eyes widened in the next moment, as if a whole entity of longing had exploded in my chest. Four? How and when? I began to stare at her features, which hadn't changed much; indeed, the glow of the light made her more radiant, while her eyes reflected an effusive tranquility. I couldn't bear this flood of emotion. My voice choked, and I felt the burn of tears leaping from my eyes without permission. It was beyond my endurance. Between what we were living through outside and the misery of the separation between her and us, and seeing this warm face I had missed since the first day of our tragic journey of survival, my brokenness appeared like a storm of acrid, yet inherently delicate, crying. I didn't care about anything else. I threw myself into her arms without thinking, like a child who had stumbled in the darkness and suddenly found her mother.

Four locked her arms around me. I buried my face in her chest, catching her scent which takes me back years, and I cried. I cried as I had never cried before, a cry filled with all the horrors I had faced, and with every loss I had lived in the past days. In return, I felt her gentleness mixed with a silence that knew how to pat my deep wounds as usual, as if her presence in itself was the medicine I was hoping for. Long moments stretched on as I was lost in her embrace, unable to speak or ask, but confident that she was aware of all the pain I had carried in her absence. Little by little, the light around us seemed to grow warmer, surrounding us like a white bubble that pushed away all the scenes of destruction and loss we had lived through. I didn't need to speak; it was enough for me that she was there for me to cry with complete freedom for the first time since the ship fell with us on the desolate planet. I had returned to her in a second world that allows a tired heart to collapse in peace between her arms.

The moment I raised my eyes towards her face, my pulse quickened with confusion, as if I were seeing myself, but a more tender, intelligent, and calm image. Her features were almost identical to mine, but there was that serenity in her gaze and confidence in her smile—things that separated us like a thin hair. She is my sister and my twin, the other me with whom we grew up sharing joys and sorrows as well as features. How many times have I looked at this face and seen myself in it, and asked it in silence if it understood all that was going on inside me without a single word, until I imagined that we were partners in a beautiful secret since the moment of birth, a secret no one understood but us. It called me today, after I had been away from her all this time, to see her again with familiar features, sprinkling a cloud of desolation on me. And in another part of my heart, a sharp pang of grief possessed me as I recalled the reason for our separation. It was nothing but my weakness back then and my inability to stand bravely against Three and her unjust decision to expel Four and Two from the ship. How I regretted my silence then, and how I allowed her insistence to steal my sister and my twin from me, and to throw us both onto paths that do not meet. I don't know if I would have even found her amidst this world, or if she was lost to me forever. Fate wanted then to test my fragility to the end, before it suddenly turned and gathered our scattered pieces in an impossible meeting in this world of dreams, a meeting that, if not for its mercy, I wouldn't have been able to see her again.

"It seems you really missed me."

I held my breath for a second before answering her, to say, possessed by a feeling of burning for what we had missed: "My longing surpassed what you can imagine. I can't believe I let Three throw you out of the ship like that. If only you had stayed there, maybe..."

Four nodded her head like someone hearing a speech they expected, then closed off my plea by saying: "There's no use in discussing the matter now after it has become a past that cannot be changed. All our talk will only make things worse as usual and bring more troubles that we can do without."

I then found myself trying to object, but she preempted my protest with her usual gentleness, looking at me as one who smiles at a sad situation and continuing: "Look at what will shine in our future instead of ruminating on the past. Somehow, this meeting is, most likely, the last between us. if we truly want to invest this moment, let's talk about deeper and more important matters than memories that won't change anything in the present."

There was a kind of strange firmness in her words, a feeling that made me wonder: Had she folded away all her pains to leave me a chance to exit my misery? I surrendered to that quiet tone and listened to her completely, realizing that, despite all our losses, she was capable of granting me a moment of peace that doesn't care about what happened, but about what we can do. Perhaps that's why I loved her to this extent, and perhaps for this reason also I felt that I still needed her by my side. A light exploded in her eyes; it wasn't a visible light so much as an intimacy I feel in the eyes of my sister whom I missed, as if she were affirming to me in silence: Let's live this moment without digging up wounds that won't change anything.

(10)

I didn't know how we had picked up the middle of the conversation, or how much time we had spent sitting side-by-side. It seemed clear that Four was immersed in describing her daily life with Two and Seven in a faint light that resembled a glimmer of twilight seeping in from high in the sky, clear, without calamities or hardships. It even seemed I glimpsed her face light up during her words whenever she spoke of those moments she had lived, interspersed with light, unending laughter. After a break where she paused her speech to breathe, she continued in an amusing tone, despite her eyes being filled with a touch of sorrow: "...We felt as if we were living in a world less chaotic than we imagined, that is until

321

you two would drift towards the world of stories, but each in her own way: Seven dives into the finest details, her eyes jumping between the lines as if preparing to live every experience herself one day, while Two seeks to detach from her surroundings and takes refuge in contemplating tales from ages past, believing that interpreting what time has left behind might grant her a lesson or wisdom to illuminate her reality."

Every word that came from her was carving the details of pictures I hadn't witnessed, coloring them as if she were telling a tale lost between collapsed metal walls. I recalled in my mind the impact of the calamities on us who were stuck inside, and how life outside must have seemed much freer to them, despite the danger. I leaned my back against the wall behind me as Four continued: "And for a moment, I expected the two to come out at me waving books as if they were defensive weapons, as if my skinning of a rabbit resembled a heavy artillery attack like the army's. And what made matters worse was Star Two's scream that filled the air when she saw me. Oh, how I wished I had turned the rabbit into a fancy dish before that. And the funniest part of all this is that we were sitting under the fuselage of a dilapidated aircraft, sheltering in the shadow of its wing from the rain, on a journey to find an aircraft. It wouldn't have been any use anyway; I realized that after the chatter about jet engines and space rockets. When I think back on the scene, I feel as if I were a cook in a space engineering squad, stranded in a low-budget science fiction movie!"

She sighed gently as she continued: "I sometimes felt I was the only one sensing the real danger, because Two and Seven were always acting with spontaneity, or let's call it simplicity, amidst ruins that were no laughing matter."

Here she waved her hand as if pointing to a vague horizon. I turned towards her, awaiting the major details. A bitter look flashed across her features, then she continued: "...And after we reached the aircraft's core, we thought it might be the greatest lifeline. The engines weren't intact, but..."

She stopped in the middle of her sentence suddenly. I also felt that tremor beneath my feet, as it seemed the ground began to crack. Then the light around us flickered, and the edges of the scene began to burn with creeping cracks like black threads. I looked at Four, her eyes wide with speechless astonishment, as if the dream itself were pulling us to its end without preamble. I called to her cautiously. She gave me no more than a quick glance in my direction, then extended her arm to me in a futile attempt to hold onto me or to hold onto the dream that was collapsing. And although I opened my mouth to ask her to finish the story of the aircraft, everything around us began to shatter like glass split by an overwhelming light.

(11)

My chest tightened with an unknown burning, and before I could utter another word, my lungs expanded to catch my breath as the light was once again overpowering, almost erasing our images. A creaking sound, as if the school walls were shattering from above, and I was ready to follow the collapse at any second. Spontaneously, my gaze fell to my palms, and I found the necklace Six had given me, glittering again between my fingers. I didn't fully understand what had brought the necklace into this dream, but something inside me insisted that I give it to Four. I looked at my sister as she should be, my twin whom the days had lost, and my heart fluttered with old emotions like longing, remorse, and a yearning that had never subsided. With them, I said, as if the words were flowing from within me with a heat I could not restrain well: "I want to give you this. Six was longing to see how you would look in it, and she did so through me. But at the same time, it made me feel beautiful for the first time. That's why I wanted to share this feeling with you."

I took stumbling steps forward amidst the cracks and flickering lights, protecting the necklace in my palms from fading or falling. Then I placed it gently around her neck, and I murmured as I adjusted the chain to settle it: "It's yours now."

The light spread around her as if celebrating the gift. The ceiling above was still emitting a crackling that threatened its collapse at any moment, and the floor was shaking beneath our feet until it seemed cracked like glass about to explode. But I forgot all that when I noticed a sparkle that touched her calm skin. Four raised her hand to touch the necklace, and amidst all that vibration and blind noise, I saw light tears in her eyes—not a loud cry, but a deep gratitude through which she smiled. Then she said in a faint voice, almost mixing with the noise of the collapse: "Yes! It's beautiful on me, and on you. How could it not be, when we resemble each other, as we always have before."

I took two steps back to see the whole scene: Four wearing the necklace, making the broken lights around her shine brighter, reminding me of the days when we stood with one heart and two separate bodies. Then I caught her sad smile. At that moment, I felt as if time were bidding us farewell together with its final silence. I was about to say something else to calm her, but I was struck by a new storm of sounds, as if white dust had erupted from every direction. I screamed at her: "Will we see each other again?"

And her reply came quickly, quiet and harsh at the same time: "It's difficult. This world is vast, and ruin fills its every corner to a degree that you can never distinguish its features. And I don't really think I will return. Once this dream ends, I will most likely disappear forever, or perhaps I will be born again. Who knows."

My ribs trembled under the weight of her words, and I remembered in that moment that our reality is harsh and sick, but my existence in it connects me to something living that I must detach from to stay with her. As I took my last breath, I realized that I wanted to stay with her more than I wanted to continue a futile journey in a worn-out world that would lead us to no result. Perhaps escaping together in this dream is more merciful than living alone outside it.

Four began to fade with strange speed, as if the burning wind in the place were erasing her image little by little before, I could copy her final features. I hesitated for seconds before my every step was pushed by an immediate loss, but I felt a longing pulling me towards her despite what was happening to my feet. I made a hard effort to move towards her as the cracking beneath us intensified, and gradually I crawled to her position. With every step I crossed, I felt I was losing a part of my body and of the warmth I had forgotten in her arms. The end came faster than I expected. Nevertheless, I was able to finally reach her to embrace her, to hold her with all the strength I had left. The scene around us narrowed as if shrinking, and my panting was mixed with a suppressed sob. Then I heard her whisper in my ear: "But they need you out there, in reality."

I scowled and closed my eyes, refusing to believe it.

"There's no one left to need me. It's a journey of being lost, and journeys of this kind don't need a leader. That's because its fate is known and its end is certain: that we surrender in some corner amidst the ruin, and remember every beautiful moment that accompanied us during that futile journey as a conclusion."

She wanted to reply, but the storm of light destroyed everything in my vicinity. I felt her grip disappear from between my arms as if a wind were snatching it with silent violence, but I kept clinging on, even if it was a melting illusion, even if I was unable to save her or to grasp any extra second with her. Then I fell to the ground as she disappeared, and I broke into silent weeping as I held the necklace that had fallen from her while she was fading. For a moment, the void around me seemed to swallow the school, leaving the dream's walls to fall in the form of white crumb-like remnants. Then it swallowed the crumbs themselves. I knew then that my turn would be next.

The words completed and the dream ended. And that was before she could tell me what really happened to the aircraft.

Chapter Eight:
The Chrysanthemum Wreath Makes the Sky Bloom

We return to continue the main story from the end of Chapter Five – And as we are accustomed, from the tongue of Star Seven, our genius, creative writer, the writer of this story.

(1)

We were lying under the shade of that tree. It was nothing but a dilapidated-looking tree, but here it stood, majestic in an inexplicable way despite the war. I raised my gaze through the gaunt branches and saw them swaying in a breeze that hardly resembled the gentle rustle I had known before. And yet, it seemed to me like a true sanctuary amidst this ruin that had covered everything.

I pressed the palm of my hand on the dry ground, trying to feel some kind of pulse beneath this ash. I found only a petrified hardness, and I wondered: How did this tree manage to emerge from under the ground and break apart that rock to stay alive and grow? I don't even know if its roots are still able to absorb water and life from beneath this hard surface. I just saw it, exactly like us, stubbornly continuing to cling to the thin thread of life, relying on a mysterious legacy of strength, as if refusing to be erased from the memory of the destroyed earth. Then I raised my head slightly and saw a familiar scene looming from a distance: corners of the ruins of a great city that had once rivaled the sky in height, scattered in the surroundings like pained, stone-like metal pieces. I blinked my eyes and began to stare into the emptiness of the sky. The shadow of sadness continued to weigh on my chest whenever I remembered the faces that had departed, until I fought back the tears with another question: How is it that I did not die with them? Is it fate or blind chance? And can I survive alone, like it?

Amidst these thoughts of mine, the tree rustled a few remaining leaves above my head, as if it were nodding for me to continue. I felt a light breeze caress my cheek, a breeze saturated with the smell of ash and of rain that had stopped. And yet, there was a hidden warmth in it, returning a pulse of hope to my heart. I felt a strange gratitude, as if a kind spirit had whispered in my ear: There is still time to survive. There is still a way to return.

Its image is fixed in my mind: a tree with a pale trunk, one that any storm could uproot, yet it survived all the storms. This idea is what made me a little stronger. I wrenched from the bottom of my exhausted body the ability to rise. Even despite the fatigue in my limbs and my broken foot, there was still something inside me pulsating with life, screaming: Get up! We can get out of this desolate world, for the earth will not abandon you, just as it did not abandon this tree.

My breaths were heavy, hurting something in my lungs each time they passed, but the idea of survival remained gleaming in my mind like a small glimmer piercing the darkness. Yes, the Stars are no longer as bright as they were; many of them have left us. But if this shaky tree is able to cling to life, then we can too. I secretly smiled a smile that didn't fully form on my lips, but it eased my pain. I don't know how much time passed as we lay under this thin shade, nor do I know how tomorrow will come or if we will see it. But, in this moment, we are still here.

With this, our fourth day on Spoiled Paradise reaches its midpoint: a speck of hope that I cling to, however trivial it may seem. And in the corner of my mind, I see the stricken ship waiting for me, and I know I must move forward at some point. We may stumble or fall sometimes, but as long as this tree reminds us that life is renewable, even in the worst of conditions, then we too are capable of facing the unknown fate that awaits us.

(2)

And in other moments, the silence passes between us as if it will never end, settling over the place like a red curtain that blocks any light of hope. Star Two is sitting beside me, escaping her feelings this time by sitting on the opposite side of the tree. As for Star Thirteen, she is perched at Four's head, patting her forehead, as if her touch were capable of bringing back life. Four is still lying before us. Perhaps she is alive, but she is sunk in a deep coma. We have no choice but to wait for her return. I try to breathe deeply, but my chest tightens with an indescribable fear whenever I see her, and a tremor strikes me when I contemplate her pale features. My sweaty hand clutches the hem of my skirt like someone clinging to a straw, and I feel the turmoil of my heartbeat, as if my heart wants to scream out a prayer, but I possess only silence.

It's the first time I've seen Thirteen so quiet like this while working, her eyes fixed on Four's face, trying to pull her from her world with words she does not utter. And Star Two, for her part, has not spoken a word, contenting herself with her eyes shifting between Four and me, imprinting her gazes on each of us without comment. No one wishes to break this silence lest it awaken a harsh reality: What if Four never opens her eyes again? I closed my eyes and leaned my head against the trunk behind me, pretending that the silence itself is a story we are reciting in our hearts, that with our will alone, we can bring the pulse back to Four. Is it an illusion? Perhaps, but here we are, betting on a deep-seated feeling that Stars have an extraordinary ability to cling to life.

Thus, the three of us sit in a mixture of prayer and silent hope. Only our breaths separate us from potential death. We watch for her slightest movement, or a quiver of an eyelid, or a sudden gasp that would signal her return from the darkness of absence. Time passes very slowly, as if stuck in a net of bewilderment, and every minute seemed to us like a full year. Every now and then, I raise my eyes to the distant sky behind the cracked canopy of the tree, hoping for deliverance or a sudden mercy, while I glimpse Thirteen's pale face, desperate in her attempts to keep Four hanging by the last thread. I rest my hand on her shoulder and feel her slight tremor, and I realize that what we are doing now is everything, and nothing at the same time.

(3)

None of us had the ability to break this heavy silence. It was like a sacred silence, as if it were the final rite while awaiting a miracle that might happen. As we were surrendered to it, I saw a small, bold movement in the corner of the space. It was Star Two, who had remained silent as usual, but was quietly fiddling with her bag. With that action, she decided to break the stillness of the moment. Then she took out small food cans, from those metal cans that had filled the facility's storeroom before it destroyed itself. The sight of her taking them out of her bag was like the appearance of a small miracle we hadn't been hoping for, something that didn't belong to our grim reality. Then she said in a faint voice, as if seeping cautiously from a throat that didn't wish to disturb the place: "It's better if we don't die of hunger too."

She then paused for a moment, stared at the contents of her bag again, then turned towards me and extended her hand with something completely different. It was my old recorder, the small device we had found earlier on our first tour among the remains of the aircraft's contents, the one Two had unintentionally destroyed. I raised my head to her and saw her calm eyes staring directly at me. Then she said in a deep tone, her voice barely above a whisper: "Four... she fixed it for you."

I felt my heart stop for a moment. My eyes went back towards Four, lying there like a corpse. And yet, she was here; she had thought of me, worked for me, fixed something I loved, and hadn't even told me. My mouth clamped shut, and I couldn't say a thing. I felt the words were heavy and incapable of expressing what was going on inside me. Four deserved another thank you, one more time among the hundreds of times I hadn't said "thank you" to her aloud. Before I could find the words, my hand moved involuntarily towards my bag that was beside me. I took out an old disc from among the ones I had collected earlier, checked it quickly to make sure it wasn't damaged, then inserted it into the trembling device between my fingers, pressed the button, and waited.

At first, we heard nothing but a simple buzzing sound, but it soon transformed into a warm voice filling the place, narrating an old human story, a story I don't know who wrote, but I had always felt it was written as a message for us specifically, and not for them. I closed my eyes. I felt comfort for the first time in a long time, as if the story's voice had become the only thing capable of pulling us away from this land, from this reality that is swallowing our souls.

(4)

I don't know where to begin or how to conclude, but I will say what must be said, because I have lived long enough to see wars spreading like the plague across the decades. I was a sergeant in the US Army during World War II, and fate led me to the streets of France, Belgium, and Germany. I fought believing we represented the good side against Nazism, until I realized a bitter truth: in wars, there is no good side, but rather interests, intertwined blood, and many lies.

Today, as an old man, I am currently watching the world collapse anew, but this time on a level I didn't think possible even in my worst nightmares.

After the fall of Berlin in our war, my country entered a new conflict with Japan. Then after its defeat, division began to seep into Asia, until Japan, as had happened with Germany before, was turned into northern regions subject to Moscow and southern ones loyal to us. The Cold War continued for decades, its trenches stretching across Europe, Asia, and the Middle East. Behind the Soviets lined up both Beijing and Tehran, while we took shelter with NATO, Europe, Japan, and some Arab nations.

The years passed and the fire lay dormant under the ashes, until the moment China decided to invade Taiwan to obtain its protected technologies. Washington thought it would settle matters quickly, so it struck Taiwan with a nuclear bomb in an insane step it took for the first time in its history. The result was that Russia, the descendant of the Soviets, joined China in a major alliance, and with them, Japan and Iran, while we aligned with NATO, Korea, European nations, and some of our Arab allies. The first thing China did after its anger over our striking Taiwan was to seize control of an American nuclear warship, then bomb the Guam base, thus lighting the fuse of the Third World War, or the Nuclear World War.

Perhaps you are wondering: Why am I telling you this?

Because I have seen what wars do to people. I have seen comrades of mine return to their homeland as fragments in flag-draped coffins, and I have seen soldiers from the enemy, who were children not yet of age, throw down their weapons and run in search of any shelter to protect them from death. All the wars I fought were but a repetition of a single grindstone, turning in all our heads, driven by politicians and arms dealers, while we believe we are fighting for homeland or freedom or justice—illusions whose appearance is repeated over the decades.

And if you were to ask me: Who is right? China or the United States?

I would answer you: No one.

Each side calculates its figures, then comes out and claims to be the official spokesman for justice, humanity, and absolute peace. But the truth is that it is a war for interests and power, a war whose calculations have proven its returns are worth its losses. But when cities tumble under nuclear fire, no one will care about a flag or a slogan. If you have the choice, however limited, do not be fuel for this war.

And what can we do? I tell you, from my long experience: raise your voices in refusal. Do not believe the slogans that justify the killing of innocents. Support the victims who are trampled between the wheels of conflicts. Teach the coming generations how wars usually begin with a great deception, that there is no heroism in destroying cities and killing people, and that there is no real enemy except for he who exploits our emotions and our souls to achieve political and commercial gains we do not see. In World War II, I believed I was fighting to liberate the world from fascism—we all believed the same. But I returned with memories too harsh to bear, and I saw how our leaders exploited the victory to reinforce their political and economic influence. Today, I see the scene repeating with the same lie, but on a larger scale, and with nuclear power. Believe me, when the bombs rain down, it will not matter if you are American, Chinese, Russian, or a mercenary of war. Everyone will burn in the same fire.

And perhaps you ask: How will this war end, in my opinion?

Most likely, it will end like its predecessors: with a treaty of submission after comprehensive ruin that achieves the victor's gains, or with an annihilation that might not even leave us a chance for regret, after we can no longer find a drop of water to drink or a meal to eat. But there is a scenario that might surprise you all: that the peoples awaken from the illusion of slogans and reject these massacres. I do not have a certain answer, for history repeats itself and rarely learns from itself.

My final message to you is this: Never think that taking up arms is a path to honor, or that launching nuclear missiles guarantees security. Rather, know that those who move the pieces on the chessboard do not enter the field with us. We are fuel for their gains and their conflicts. If you truly want to serve your homelands, build in them a dignified life, not new graves. And if you want to stop the madness of war, begin by refusing to be herded behind it. Every bullet that is fired, and every bomb that explodes, kills with it a part of our humanity.

Hear this from a man who survived the old war with his body, but continued to carry its scars in his soul: War devours minds and hearts, and turns us into beasts and ghosts who regret every single shot fired. Do not wait for the moment when it is too late. If there is a glimmer of hope, it is in our collective refusal of this madness, and in the belief that a peace, however difficult it may seem, is a thousand times better than a war that will not leave one stone upon another.

This was a recorded message from Jonxxn Kexxck, a former sergeant in the US Army. Perhaps these words of his will find listening ears before the glow of life is extinguished on *this planet. We now continue the recording with a story he had written down after World War II about his tank.*

The sound of the recording began to fill the place again, this time with a distant story, coming from a time that no longer exists, flowing as if from a world that had not yet known ruin. I listened for a little, closed my eyes, tried to imagine us far from this shattered life, far from this burning planet, until I almost forgot for a moment that death surrounded us on all sides. Then I heard Two's voice, worried and agitated: "Thirteen! Something is happening!"

I opened my eyes quickly. Her voice was agitated in a worrying way that made my heart pound fiercely. I moved closer to Four, stared at her, and saw her chest rising and falling at an unnatural pace. Her breaths were ragged, heavy, as if she were catching the last remnants of air from the world around her.

Thirteen dropped her food can then and rushed towards her immediately, pressing on her chest, then feeling for her pulse. I too approached her, barely feeling my pain as I dragged my injured leg, driven by a deep feeling of fear, as if I were about to lose my own breath as well, and not just another one of us. Thirteen's eyes were flooded with tears. She pressed harder on her chest, both her hands trembling. Every movement from her was screaming that she wasn't ready for this moment. She said in a trembling tone: "Four, wake up! Please!"

My heart began to race madly. I wanted to scream and demand that she wake up too, to tell her about the school, about the Engineering Squad, about what we built together, about the space rocket, and about the device she fixed for me, about the memories I hadn't told her about yet, and about the stories we hadn't finished telling. I moved closer to her face, held her cold hand, and screamed with all the strength left inside me: "Four, don't go! You used to fix everything for us! Please, fix yourself now!"

Two was standing behind us, silent, as if all of life had stopped within her, awaiting the final judgment. Meanwhile, Thirteen continued to press without stopping, her strenuous effort making her bones fail, her breaths coming out charged with despair. But Four's chest remained completely still, ignoring all our attempts, and her eyes remained hopelessly closed. Then Thirteen suddenly stopped moving, as if she had comprehended the truth. Her hands remained on Four's chest, as if time had also stopped in this moment. She raised her head towards me very slowly. I saw in her eyes a collapse deeper than I expected. She shook her head weakly, saying in a broken voice: "I... I can't bring her back."

The words seeped like a cold dagger into my heart. With them, Thirteen collapsed to her knees and said nothing more. I realized then that the world had changed forever, and that a part of us had departed with her. I felt those burning tears flood my face, my body crumbling to the ground beside her, unable even to scream. I had nothing but to whisper with intense bitterness as I held her cold hand for the last time: "Why did you leave us behind? How will we survive without you?!"

Then Two advanced silently and touched my shoulder lightly, as if telling me that time was up, that nothing would bring Four back now. I looked up at her with despair and saw her hiding her eyes, looking away, as if she couldn't bear to look directly at death. Finally, amidst the silence that had returned to erase all of our existences, I slowly let go of Four's hand and moved away from her. That was the moment we all admitted the bitter truth: Star Four had left us forever.

And when we had completely surrendered, I looked at her face again, amidst the tears and disappointment, and noticed something small I hadn't seen before: her lips were forming a quiet, delicate smile, a warm smile the likes of which I hadn't seen since we landed on this grim planet. All the sounds around me stopped, and the world became nothing but a faint music in my ears, as calm as a breeze from distant days. Perhaps Four was seeing something more beautiful in another world that we couldn't see. And perhaps she departed having known that we would continue the path, that she hadn't truly left us. A strange feeling of tranquility seeped into me then, despite the pain. Her smile was her final promise, as if she were telling us in silence that death is not the end, but the beginning of a new life.

(6)

Although the matter was over, I still found grief creeping into my depths for the loss of Four. Before me, Two looked as if she didn't know the meaning of mercy. As soon as my tears had dried, she adjusted her sitting position with a stern simplicity, as if she had just been waiting for me, as if there were no way for grief to disturb her composure. Then she proceeded to call a sudden meeting without prior warning, involving us in it, presenting her plan to us as if she carried no trace of emotion. In that moment, I felt our hearts swinging between pain and astonishment, and I wondered how a soul could ignore a tragedy with such coldness. Then she broke the silence that had almost suffocated us, saying in a serious and harsh tone: "We don't have time to cry. What happened, has happened. If we don't move quickly, we'll lose more of us too."

I looked towards her with hesitation, while Thirteen seemed more understanding of this behavior of hers, as if Two were holding herself responsible, and this is what responsibility imposes on a person—to ignore the pain or hide it well. Despite that, something inside me did not approve of her action. She continued, but in a quieter and steadier voice: "We will now split into two groups."

I slowly raised my head towards her, as did Thirteen. We both held deep questions, and a hidden anxiety and fear we couldn't hide. Two advanced a little while holding an old, torn map, which she carefully took out of her bag. She spread it before us with great care on the dry, cracked ground and held the two ends of the map with her hands to prevent it from flying away with the weak wind that caressed the place from time to time.

"Thirteen, you will go immediately to the ship. Check on the stars who remained there and bring back the survivors."

Then she pointed with her finger to a specific spot on the map, her eye gleaming with resolve and clarity, as if she had drawn every step in her mind before uttering it. She continued in a confident voice: "You will head with them to that point in the middle. It's supposed to be a central army camp, but it will be destroyed like the rest of the city."

She fell silent for a moment, during which she seemed to be gathering what words she had left to answer the questions drawn on our faces. Then she raised her head to us and continued: "This military map I found indicates the presence of a number of military emergency shelters near it. This warehouse was apparently one of them. During that time, Seven and I will search for another shelter and work on rehabilitating and reactivating it. Let's hope we find one as intact as the last. When you reach the camp, just send up a light into the sky, and that's how we will reunite with you."

Her words gradually faded amidst the silence that had once again taken control of the place. We stared together at that torn map, as if it held some salvation, or perhaps another catastrophe, that none of us could clearly understand except Two herself. Finally, I couldn't contain myself. I looked at Two and said with clear hesitation, fear dominating my tone: "And if all the shelters are destroyed? What will we do then?"

Two turned towards me with a reassuring calm, and without showing the slightest doubt in her quiet, confident eyes: "We will find one. Those military shelters were designed to resist. That's why I'm confident we'll find what we're looking for."

I didn't reply, just contented myself with a simple nod. I wanted to believe her, to cling to her words despite everything. Then I felt a light movement beside me; it was Thirteen getting ready to stand. She gave us a calm look and tried to smile as she said in a voice through which she tried to hide its trembling: "This is a good plan. So... we'll meet again soon?"

Those simple words, despite their simplicity, carried so much hope, so much pleading, and even some fear she couldn't hide well. Then she turned directly towards me, perhaps noticing my absent-mindedness and anxiety, and added with gentle encouragement: "Won't we, Seven?"

I raised my head towards her and smiled a faint half-smile as I answered in a quiet and hesitant voice, which I tried to make carry some reassurance: "Of course. We'll meet again soon."

After we finished our words, I noticed Two taking a carefully folded white paper out of her bag. I watched in astonishment how she began to draw a new map with unbelievable speed and precision, its lines orderly and clear, as if it were printed, not from the memory of a person exhausted by fatigue and fate. Her fingers continued to move with amazing speed, while I followed the details of the places we had passed before appearing with perfect clarity, as if we were still there, amidst every turn and detail. I couldn't resist the curiosity, so I asked her with clear wonder as I stared at the paper: "How were you able to remember all those details?"

Two didn't raise her head towards me, but remained focused on finishing what she had started, and answered in a quiet, faint voice, as if addressing the paper before her and not us: "It's the world of a story I loved. How could I not remember all its details?"

When she finally finished, she extended her hand with the new map to Thirteen, who took it with clear gratitude, seeming to draw some courage and confidence from it. She looked at us after contemplating the map for a moment. Her features then seemed more firm and less anxious, so she said with resolve and certainty: "We'll meet again soon, so be careful."

Then she set off quickly, quickening her pace, as if she feared she would turn back if she looked behind her again, leaving behind a new silence that settled between me and Two. We remained standing silently for moments, watching her recede. When she disappeared from sight, I looked at Two, realizing that the time had come for our next step, perhaps the most difficult in our journey so far.

(7)

Contrary to what I had expected, Two sat down quietly beside me, her steps as light as ever when she approaches me. In a single moment, I felt her head lean to rest on my shoulder, while a calm, pure smile, devoid of any worries, crept across her face. She closed her eyes, as if by doing so she were reclaiming a peace we had lost long ago, and she whispered to me in a quiet, warm voice I was not used to from her: "Finally. Alone again."

Annoyance quickly rose inside me. It was repulsive to make Thirteen go alone in this way, to hurry her steps, to rush her, just so we could be alone for a little while and she could rest from the burden of the journey, while the other bears the weight of everything. I couldn't stop myself from expressing this, so I replied to her immediately in an accusatory tone whose sharpness I didn't try to hide: "So that was your plan from the beginning?"

She didn't open her eyes, just smiled a slightly wider smile. Her voice came out quiet, confident, carrying the nature of a confession, as if in her view she hadn't done anything wrong: "Didn't I tell you before that I don't care about anyone but you? And that this journey means nothing to me as long as you are by my side."

Her words struck me with a deep confusion, in which the feeling of annoyance mixed with warmth, and perhaps with some foolishness that I hadn't understood her intention earlier. I remained silent for a moment before replying to her with hesitation: "I remember that well, but it seemed as if you were just getting rid of Thirteen."

She laughed a faint laugh I barely heard, then lifted her head from my shoulder for moments, during which her eyes met mine, before returning to her position and saying: "And that's what I was actually doing. I wanted us to sit together, just you and me, for one last time before everything ends."

I didn't understand the truth she had revealed, so I asked her cautiously: "But... aren't we going to some shelter?"

She was silent for a longer moment this time, as if thinking about her answer, or perhaps she was gathering her courage to be honest with me about something more dangerous. Afterwards, she opened her eyes, but she kept looking at the emptiness before us, then she whispered as if confessing a sin she had committed: "If there really were a shelter, why, in your opinion, are we still sitting here? I just made it all up."

I couldn't restrain myself this time, so the words came out of me with an emotion unlike me, filled with anger, admiration, and astonishment all at once: "What a sly and wicked star you are!"

She smiled again with deep relief, as if my words were nothing but a hidden compliment, and her eyes closed again in peace, before she replied quietly and with a confident voice that carried an unshakeable conviction: "And do you think she will find anyone there? I don't think so, but she will find a solution somehow. In the end, everything that happens in this world, as long as you are here with me, doesn't concern me."

After those words, we sank into a deep silence, while her head still rested quietly on my shoulder, as if she had fallen asleep, reassured by my presence near her. As for me, I fell into a deep confusion between the desire to scold her and a strange joy at being the only precious thing in her eyes. And although I was annoyed, and that was clear in my voice which had risen unintentionally during our conversation, this annoyance began to fade and gradually turn into an inner warmth I couldn't deny. And so, despite everything I felt, I could do nothing but be still, just be silent, while I listened to her calm breathing as she slept on my shoulder, thinking that perhaps, really, we are having our last session together, before the world around us ends.

(8)

Time passed with a deadly slowness under that old tree, which seemed as if it were the last remnant of life on the face of this dilapidated planet. Its branches swayed quietly with a light, cold wind, carrying with them mysterious whispers of endings and secrets we did not yet know. I sat still beside Two, both of us silent, each supporting the other as if the world around us no longer existed. But soon, faint sneezes coming from Two in intermittent periods, which she tried hard to suppress and hide from me, caught my attention. At first, I ignored them, thinking it was just a fleeting effect of fatigue or cold, but something inside me insisted on the contrary, insisted that there was something bigger, something Two didn't want to tell me. A full hour passed in that state, a heavy silence broken from time to time by the sound of those sneezes, which grew clearer and more worrying.

And at some point, Two lifted her head from my shoulder, sighed deeply, then stood up deliberately and calmly, and began to silently check that she had enough food and water in her bag without turning to me. I silently watched her move very slowly, as if trying to plant her feet on the ground so as not to fall, and I noticed her hands as they trembled while gripping her bag. I wanted to ask her, to talk to her, but the words remained stuck in my throat.

And despite her condition, and my own condition which didn't allow me to walk for long, Two insisted that we leave together on an adventure. She paid no attention to my objections or to my broken foot, which made every step I took feel like a whole journey of pain. Instead, she just gave a faint smile, as if by doing so she were telling me that my staying alone under this tree was more dangerous than the adventure itself. In the end, I had no choice but to surrender to her quiet insistence, leaning on her, feeling grateful that she had stayed by my side until this final moment.

We moved together quietly and unhurriedly. I was worried she would face me again with a false smile and tell me she was fine, but she continued walking without looking at me, until I couldn't bear this anymore. I took her hand, stopping her from walking. She turned towards me with silent astonishment. I looked directly into her eyes, trying to hide my fear which was clear from the trembling of my voice: "We're stopping here for a rest. You don't look well at all. You should have had Thirteen check on you before she left alone if your condition was this bad! I knew very well that letting her go alone was a very bad idea."

Two almost opened her mouth to say something—perhaps to be honest with me, perhaps to confess something she was hiding—but she suddenly stopped, as if something frightening, some secret, prevented her from speaking. I saw this hesitation of hers directly in her eyes, and my heart clenched because of it. After moments of silence, she smiled again, that faint smile which hides a thousand pains and a thousand secrets behind it, and said to me quietly as she gently squeezed my hand: "Don't worry about me. I'm still happy despite what's afflicting me, because you are here by my side now, and that's all that matters to me. Come on, remove this worry from your forehead... What do you say we listen to something while we walk? What surprises do you have inside your bag?"

The smile never left her face, but this time it was weaker than any time before. I felt my heart slowly tearing apart inside me, as if a part of me began to seep away and disappear. The idea of losing her struck me with a terror I had never felt in my life before. I wanted to refuse, wanted to scream in her face and force her to stop, but something in her eyes, in that sad gaze wrapped in her smile, made me surrender. I carried out her request in silence and began to search in my bag for something with which we could break this bitter atmosphere. This time it was a different disc, bearing a title that seemed as if it would carry the final piece of the human story that no longer existed: Humanity Stands to Confront the War Government.

I took the disc out of my bag with a trembling hand, inserted it into the old recorder, then gently pressed the play button. Two was listening with interest, still holding my hand without letting go, despite the clear tremor of her fingers. And I, in turn, listened to the voice coming from the disc, and began to think in silence: How did our lives become like this? How did we come to be walking on the land of this strange, destroyed planet, as if we were created only to witness the story of the humans that had passed?

When we resumed walking, at first, I was the one relying on Two for my steps, because of my foot which made every step feel like the stabbing of a knife into a bone that has not yet healed. I was leaning on her shoulder, trying not to make a groan that would betray my pain, while she held me by my waist with one hand and carried the recorder with the other. Heavy words emanated from the device, accusations between the rebels and the government. But Two, although she was following the story closely, was just staring at the road with tired eyes. As time passed, I began to notice a strange trembling in her body. Her shoulder would tremble slightly under my hand, and the rhythm of her breathing had become completely irregular. Whenever I tried to speak to her, she would nod her head and continue walking, as if something were occupying her more than justifying her apparent fatigue. Then suddenly, after a few more minutes of silent walking, I felt a greater pressure on my arm, until she almost collapsed onto me. I bent down unconsciously to carry her weight as best I could, and I exchanged the role of supporter with her unexpectedly...

(9)

(Recorded speech of the Free and Just Humanity Squad - New York, United States.)

Terrorism?! Is that what the government calls us, we citizens who decided to defend this homeland after we saw it being crushed under the feet of the corrupt?! We're soldiers who fought the battles and saw with our own eyes that all we were told about victory was a glory of lies?! If this is the definition of terrorism in your view, then what about you? If we are the terrorists, then who is the real terrorist? Is it the one who fights to protect his people, or the one who sends the sons of his nation to their deaths in a war in which there is no victory? The one who demands freedom, justice, and peace, or the one who crushes them all under the treads of tanks with his stubbornness? The one who stands with the people, or the one who trades in them for his own interests?

We have seen this play before, many times. This same government that accuses us of terrorism was talking about fighting terrorism decades ago, when it led its armies towards the Middle East, claiming it was liberating peoples from corruption and tyranny for the sake of a few pennies. It told us then that it was fighting for freedom, but it left nothing behind but destruction. Now, the roles have been reversed.

This time it's here, in the streets of the United States itself. So, will the outcome change, I wonder?

We are not fighting for ourselves alone, but for all those who cannot raise their voices, for those who lost everything under the rule of this murderous dictatorial regime. And we repeat it for anyone who still doubts our intentions: We are not supported by any foreign power, nor are we subject to any hidden agenda. We are not part of this global madness, and we are not a tool in the hands of any international party. We are just American citizens who decided to say: Enough! We do not seek to spread chaos, but are trying to stop it before it devours everything. For this war, if it continues, will devour the United States as we know it, and there will be nothing left for governments to fight over. We are not enemies of this homeland; rather, we are the hand trying to save it before it drowns completely. For this reason, we are here. And for this reason, we will not retreat.

We have come out today to declare to all who still doubt our strength: Our movement is no longer confined to New York alone. The administration of the state of Texas has decided to officially join our movement. This is not just a small battle in New York as some believe, but a widespread revolution, because the people have begun to awaken. They have begun to realize that this government no longer represents them, and that remaining under its authority means annihilation.

No matter how they try to suppress us, no matter how they strike us, no matter how they label us as traitors or terrorists, we will remain standing. Because we alone have the courage to speak the truth, and because we alone will be able to save humanity from this insane war. We are fighting for something bigger than ourselves, for something politicians cannot understand. We are fighting for the human being. We know the war will end, no doubt about it, but the question is how. Will it end with total destruction? Or will it end with a revolution that reclaims what was stolen from us? We have chosen our path, and now, you must choose yours. The government will tell you that you are safe, that they control the situation. But open your eyes. Do you see safety? Do you see stability? Or a nation falling piece by piece into the hands of the Soviets?

We, the Free and Just Humanity Squad, have thrown the last lifeline for the homeland. For anyone who wants to save what remains, we are here. For anyone who refuses to be fuel in a war that serves no one but those controlling the strings, we are here. For anyone who believes that freedom is not bought or sold, we are here. And we will remain here, and we will not stop. Despite everything that befalls us, we will continue, because we are the only ones who see the truth, we are the only ones who dare to face reality, we are the only ones who will be able to save humanity, and save the United States from itself. Either we stand today, or we are buried with this homeland under its rubble tomorrow. And the choice is yours.

Welcome, dear viewers, to new news coverage. Moments ago, you followed with us the speech delivered by what is called the Free and Just Humanity Squad from the heart of New York City, which called for an escalation of their movement against the government. To talk about this speech and its impact on the domestic stage, we are joined by retired Colonel Richard MacKenzie, prominent military analyst. Welcome, Colonel MacKenzie. As we all saw, the speech was filled with strongly-worded messages towards the government, and even explicitly accused it of leading the country to ruin. How do you see this speech? And what are the motives behind it, in your estimation?

"Let me first clarify that this group is trying to win over public opinion with grand claims, but the reality is completely different. The speech exploited the anger of certain groups, like soldiers, and headlines like freedom and justice to cover their true intentions, which may be linked to schemes of a malicious nature. Their use of terms like revolution and saving from chaos is just a cover to try and destabilize the country's stability under flimsy pretexts to serve our enemies."

But they assert in their speech that they are not supported by any foreign power, and that they represent the voice of the people. Did this statement not resonate with some segments that see clear shortcomings or narrow interests in the government?

"Let's not overlook that any armed group or organization that wants to grant itself legitimacy will, of course, deny any external support, and this is an old game. The government, according to our information, has evidence indicating the existence of internal and external parties that benefit from stirring up conflict and destabilizing stability. As for accusing the government of shortcomings, this is normal. No government in the world is free of flaws, especially in a difficult time like this. But the solution is never war and rebellion and turning city streets into arenas of conflict."

And what about their accusation that the government previously dragged the country into destructive foreign wars, and is now bringing the battle home to fight the citizens themselves?

"This is a one-sided narrative! We know that the United States has faced huge security and political challenges over the past decades, and that military decisions do not stem from the whim of one person or a specific faction, but from entire institutions, a Senate, and a Congress. Portraying it as if the government is deliberately grinding down the people is a damaging oversimplification of reality, and I believe what this group is doing is a systematic distortion of state policies..."

Apologies for the interruption, but we have just received images confirming that the US Army has indeed begun to mobilize. There are reports of armored military units being sent to New York to support police and riot control teams, and to other areas witnessing activity from this group. What is your comment on this development?

"This decision was expected. We are talking about a direct threat to internal security, and about a speech that incites the masses to adopt violence and destabilize state institutions in a time of war. It is natural for the government and the army to deal with the matter seriously and firmly in accordance with the law. A state like New York cannot be left at the mercy of a group that claims to be the savior and threatens to ignite more tensions. In the end, the army's primary mission is to protect national security and the safety of the citizens. Let me direct a simple message: In times of crisis and turmoil, the arena is filled with rumors and exaggerations. My advice to you is not to be swept away by enthusiastic headlines and fiery speeches without verification, and always remember that the homeland is going through a sensitive phase, and that any ~~irrespon. befxxx oxxexxxxxx… xxxxx…~~

(11)

I bent down unconsciously to carry her weight as best I could, and I exchanged the role of supporter with her unexpectedly. She said then in a faint, hoarse voice, as she struggled to catch her breath: "It's alright... I can still continue..."

I didn't believe her, but I could do nothing but accompany her, trying to drag my broken foot, and at the same time provide her the support she had been providing me. This seemed absurd: a person who can barely walk trying to support another who is fighting exhaustion, walking on a final tour without a goal. And we were both wondering in secret, how long this scene would last before we collapsed together.

Around us, the scene looked like a painful painting: we were stumbling in the semi-frozen mud, and a strange voice coming from another world was talking about the army mobilizing, and the people being torn between cries of freedom and oppression. I screamed internally: Isn't it strange that we, two stars from a different world, are witnesses to the chaos of humans? Then I remembered that chaos was never exclusive to humankind.

I was living this moment for the third time. I saw the wilting seeping into Two's eyes with every step, and I was about to ask her again what she was suffering from. But this time, I felt her hand slipping from my waist, and suddenly, her full weight shifted onto me. With my obvious weakness in the broken foot, I stumbled first. I tried to resist being dragged down, planting my good foot in the ground so as not to fall, but Two's body collapsed completely. In the blink of an eye, I was dragged down after her, our bodies losing balance completely together. I fell to my knees first, then Two, who had already preceded me to the ground, her exhausted body colliding with the sand and mud. I heard a muffled groan escape from between her lips, as the recorder fell from her hand, making a final noise before it fell silent.

I felt nothing but my racing heartbeat and my urgent desire to hold her, ignoring the pain in my foot which flared up like a torch inside my bones. I feared she would not get up again. I crawled towards her, encircling her shoulders with my arms, panting as if I had been running in a long, endless race. I saw her eyes were shut tight for a moment, catching her breath with difficulty, before she slowly opened her eyelids, gathering what was left of her consciousness to murmur in a barely audible voice: "Sorry."

I placed my palm on her cheek, wet with the water of the earth or perhaps with tears—I could no longer distinguish—and whispered in a voice trembling between fear, anger, and pity: "Don't apologize. Just stay with me."

She didn't reply, didn't say anything to explain what she was truly suffering from. But I felt that our shared moments were shrinking and fading, as if some counter had begun its countdown to annihilation, and that we were inside a spiral we could no longer stop. I reassured myself that I would get her back on her feet, even if it required me to drag her with my right hand and drag my broken foot behind me with the other arm. But when I tried to pull her up, a sharp pain flared at the site of the fracture. I let out a faint, helpless cry, followed by an overwhelming wave of frustration. I am helpless, and so is she. We are both completely helpless.

I knelt beside her, holding her head to my chest. The recorder's sounds still echoed, hoarse and distorted, over a collapsed body. Everything on this earth seemed to be breathing its last breaths. No escape for them and no refuge, except each other. In that moment, I realized something important: even if humanity repeats its mistakes, and even if everything around us is heading for annihilation, I will continue to hold Two's hand with all my might, as if with this simple act, I am able to protect us from an inevitable disappearance. This was my last means of resistance, a mad desire to continue the journey, whatever the cost.

(12)

Then suddenly, as we were on the ground, Two let out a light, feeble laugh, closer to a suppressed bitterness. She then looked towards me without any sign of astonishment in her eyes, as if she had actually been waiting for this scene to be repeated somewhere in this shattered world. She raised her eyebrow sarcastically and said in a low voice covered by a mixture of indifference and sadness: "Those humans, they're doing it all over again, as if history teaches them nothing but how to repeat their mistakes with greater artistry."

She swallowed, and she almost followed her words with a harsher protest, but she contented herself with taking a deep breath, trying to rein in the anger or grief that lay behind her eyes. She turned her face slightly forward, observing the horizon whose borders we could no longer distinguish, as if reviewing in her imagination images of endless human battles whose details she had never stopped hearing. Then she followed up in a tone closer to someone talking to herself: "Here or there, inside the borders or outside, what's the difference? If humans want to burn their houses, they always find the suitable pretext to light the fires just so they can boast of the ashes. What a tragedy. They possessed all the potential to spare themselves this fate. I've told you before about those measures, about real possibilities for establishing peace, but they were incapable, or they refused. In the end, leaders won't give up their power, nations won't surrender their sovereignty, and humans prefer the noise of destruction and change over the silence of building and stability."

Then, as if remembering something that sparked a note of sarcasm in her voice, she added faintly: "They throw accusations haphazardly and fight over a murderous rule, when they are only killing themselves with a slow death, each according to their own justification. That's why I don't have to cry for one who sets fire to his own home and stands silently contemplating it as it crumbles. My only consolation is that we might finally witness another collapse to add to the long list of this planet's collapses. And whenever a world explodes, another is born in spite of it."

She concluded her speech with a lengthy sigh, then her eyes roamed the ground searching for something, perhaps for a sense of hope she didn't find. She raised her head towards me, and I saw in her eyes the remnants of a great sorrow and disappointment: "Am I angry with them? No. I'm just tired of re-watching scenarios that time has left behind. And maybe I even feel a little pity for them, as they still haven't realized they are walking towards an abyss of their own making."

Her words hung in the air, and within their folds was a bitterness and an old acceptance of this recurring human drama. She remained still for moments, as if bidding farewell to a humanity she had never fully believed in. Afterwards, she averted her face, leaving me with a confusing feeling between admiration for her tranquility and anxiety over that terrible conviction she holds: that humans are condemned not to learn until it's too late.

(13)

Not many minutes had passed since we collapsed together, Two and I, before I felt strange symptoms invading my body: a light dizziness enveloping my head, shortness of breath, and a cold numbness creeping into my fingers. Those sensations weren't entirely new to me; rather, they were a sign, later confirmed by my sneezes, that I had read repeatedly in Two's face. I knew immediately then that my time, like hers, had become shorter than I expected. I looked towards Two who was leaning on me, trying to snatch her breath from the air. Her trembling palm was still pressing my fingers with tension as if to reassure herself I was here, her eyes half-open, a faint glimmer within them dying just as my anxious soul was dying. I tried to swallow my tears and my sneezes so as not to spoil the rest of the moments with Two, which perhaps wouldn't exceed the blink of an eye on the timeline. Then, unintentionally, I murmured in a quiet, hoarse voice, my tone as if I were begging her for an answer other than the one, I knew: "We're going to die soon... aren't we?"

But she didn't answer immediately. She sighed first, her chest rising and falling with difficulty as if she were fighting a battle to breathe. I looked at her, my heart convulsing with both terror and pity, as it seemed to me, she was mustering all her remaining strength to speak. When she finally spoke, her words came out choppy, weak, but they carried a strange narrative quality: "Have I told you before... how much I love the ridiculous stories humans tell about themselves?"

I froze in my place—a strange sentence in such a trying situation. She continued her words as if she hadn't noticed my astonishment: "Since the earliest ages, they began searching for power. They thought that through it, they could build a civilization far from ruin. So, they made catapults first and armored the horses, then they turned to iron, fire, and gunpowder. Then they began to justify it to themselves: This is an eternal war for the sake of good versus evil. But, every time, that power fell into the wrong hands, dragging everyone into a bigger mire. When do you think they realized how stuck they were in a vicious circle of violence?"

For a short moment, I forgot the pain in my foot and the numbness in my hands, and I became engrossed in thinking how her features were closer to a wandering soul narrating a tale from an ancient memory. I composed myself and replied to her with desperate bitterness: "If they had realized that, they wouldn't have reached nuclear war. In the end, they are the reason for everything that happened to them: that sinful nature of theirs led them to destruction."

Two stopped talking immediately, as if my phrase had awakened something hidden within her. She closed her eyes for a moment, then opened them with clear exhaustion, and our gazes met. She seemed to be laughing a choked laugh in her core: "You know, Seven... we Stars... are not as different from them as we imagine."

"What do you mean?"

Her head rose slightly from my chest, and she caught her breath with difficulty to utter her words, as if they were a final piece of her soul: "I have never told anyone this... I am not a Star from this era of the Stars, but from the previous era. We were older and greater stars than you can imagine. I was Star Two during it as well, and no one else knows this except the Sun, our first star. And no one would believe it if I told them."

My eyes widened in astonishment. I tried to comprehend, but the universe around me seemed to be shrinking, and the sound of the wind grew louder against the ground. Two continued with a feeble narration: "One day, a great celestial war broke out among us for control of the universe. And Star One was the one who won in the end and forced the rest into submission. All those stories we tell about the previous era are a lie I created myself, which everyone believed—that we saved the universe from chaos, when in reality, we were the primary cause of its occurrence. Later, I secretly moved to your era, to rewrite our history, as the new Sun wanted..."

Silence fell for moments until I expected she had been extinguished before she could finish, but her lips moved slowly, fighting death: "All those victories and shining values... We wanted to convince everyone that the previous era was heroic and saving… while we... and I personally... were the ones who started the catastrophic celestial war."

I didn't fully understand how she could be a survivor from a bygone era, or how she rewrote the events. It seemed greater than my ability to comprehend in this miserable state. But the pain in her voice was sincere, telling of a long life of hidden sins. I realized then that I had never truly known Two despite all the time we spent together. Or rather, I had only known a floating shell of her character. She concluded her speech with what she whispered, the last of the strength she had left: "Even in the end... I couldn't... fix this universe..."

I extended my hand to hold hers, which was growing colder and colder, but she couldn't continue speaking. She gasped one single time, as if drinking in her last breaths. I begged her to cling to any possible atom of life, but her head tilted back with a frightening quietness, coming to rest on my chest as it had before. I saw a fleeting look in her eyes, as if she were recalling distant scenes—a giant sun swallowing older stars, a war fading into the darkness of space—until her eyes went dim forever.

Silence settled, and the sound of the world around me was suddenly cut off. I could no longer hear or see anything but the terrible void that her absence created. I tried to say her name, to call her from through life: Two! But my voice stuttered in my throat and turned into hot cries of tears that poured down without stopping.

I held her still body, shook her shoulders with my trembling hands as if trying to wake her from a brief stumble, but my calls became an echo in a deaf world. Despite all our sorrows and the gravity of the fate we had escaped together, I could never have imagined that death would separate us this quickly, and in a moment stained with secrets she had revealed, which I was not ready to contain. Darkness suddenly clamped down on my thoughts, and I collapsed beside her without moving. And I remained there, holding her to my chest unconsciously, while the cold darkness enveloped us, and the gunpowder-saturated air consumed us. I knew my own end was approaching, that I might not even be able to cry any more than that, but my tears didn't stop, not even when they mixed with the remnants of pain on my face. All I could do was cling to her frozen hand, closing my eyes to avoid looking at a reality in which I had lost the dearest person to me, she who was my sister, my mirror, and my supporter, taking with her a secret bigger than all my stories and beyond my endurance, leaving me alone in the unknown before a truth I do not dare to comprehend.

I don't remember the amount of time I spent kneeling beside her, for all of time had become a dark, featureless face, as gray as the sky left behind by the destruction of humans around us. I thought I would sleep there forever, holding Two's empty body, and let life go on without us. But something inside me kept pulsating despite the brokenness. Perhaps it was that small hope she had bequeathed to me as she was leaving, or her memory which still demanded that I stand.

With great difficulty, I dragged my knees from the mud and forced myself to get up. I had to continue on the path as Two had done before, even if it was without a destination or a purpose. The map we carried, its usefulness had vanished as I had lost it, and the principle of survival itself had become feeble in my head. But I continued walking, like one who had lost their mind and no longer had a choice but to imitate their past until the end. I took slow steps, stumbling over rocks I couldn't see and miserable fragments digging into my mind. Even my chest would tighten with every breath, and my feet would betray me every few seconds, but I resisted, even if through sheer stubbornness, lest I feel that I had failed her. However, after only a few meters, I lost what was left of my balance, and the world spun in my eyes.

I didn't realize I was before a small field of chrysanthemum flowers until I collapsed upon it. I fell on my face, and the scent of the lush flowers amidst a dead ruin enveloped me. I felt a sense of warmth wash over me despite my impact with the ground, as if the chrysanthemums were embracing me with a final tenderness, or a lament for the turmoil of my soul. I looked with half-closed eyes at the distant horizon, and suddenly, everything we had been through flashed in my mind, especially that moment when our ship fell here. How that collision was like a hammer striking the edifice of our dreams, shattering our certainty that we were safe in space.

And now?
Now I know, in our last moments in this world, that our fall was not lost in the void.

For perhaps we, like humans after their annihilation, were not forgotten, because the ruin they left behind remained a living witness to their existence. Our ship here, and the wreckage of the Stars scattered on this land, will become a legacy to remind whoever comes next that we passed through here one day. Inevitably, a silent sound will remain after us to confirm that we had existed, even if our memory is buried in a land that does not hear.

I moved with difficulty, pushed some flowers from my face, and turned my head to the sky, and saw the sunset. Then I whispered words that began to come from my heart, as if they were a final testament for a story that always accompanied us:

The feeling of being lost was the best thing we experienced on this planet, or at least, it was for me. For with every step, we took searching for a way out, we harvested a story that consoled us, gave us the lessons we needed, and even adorned the darkness of perseverance for us. Perhaps the fall wasn't as random as we first thought; perhaps the journey itself was the story we would present to you, O Mother Sun.

What led me to think this way is that this experience carried, deep within its folds, the answers to all the questions that had come to us up above. But no one else cared about such things; no one cared about anything except trying to survive in the darkness and returning to your light. Were we previously this reckless to embark on a journey of this kind? Dull of feeling? Lacking experience? Perhaps you, O our story that accompanied me and Two all that time, and even the rest of the Stars, to record all that befell us on the surface of this planet, are wondering which stars you are talking about. Us? But we were never worthy of playing that role. And now, we have departed. No trace of our existence remains but the wreckage of a ship and you, both left as a legacy for the coming Stars, so they might realize that the world outside also carries meanings of sorrow, and that it is intensely dark.

The world outside is nothing but a vibrant life of being lost, and its inhabitants are in no better state than you up above. Perhaps you will realize it's time to return to the sky without argument, for writing stories is nothing more than a long solace, an unending lament, and much that should not be conveyed to a lofty lady like her, through you, O Stars. So, return whence you came.

I felt as if my soul were summarizing all its weight in these sentences, and it was freed from burdens greater than my ability. My head stopped spinning, and I no longer felt the pain or the wind; I no longer felt them in my broken foot. I then closed my eyes, surrendering with a strange tranquility. It was a final moment in which I knew that the farewell had arrived in the simplest form, amidst a field of white chrysanthemums, on a planet that no longer perceived us. There, I sealed the tale of our ship, our story, and the tragedies of every star who accompanied us. I had nothing left then but to leave for them a flower from our legacy in the heart of the ruin.

(15)

*(The **original draft of the novel** ends on the previous page — this is just an additional ending attached to the draft; you can skip it if you've had enough of the work.)*

I run lightly through the wide corridors, my steps hitting the ground with a speed that reveals an excitement I cannot restrain. There was almost no one in my path, as everyone was busy with the final preparations, while I had only one destination: the library.

I push the door open with a rush, as I always do when I'm excited about something, and I find her there, sitting at the large table as I expected, her head resting on her arms, and my book open in front of her. Her gaze is absent, and boredom is drawn on her face as if she were stuck in a whirlwind of endless thoughts. I stopped at the entrance for a moment, then jumped towards her with clear enthusiasm: "The ship will take off shortly for a diagnostic flight to ensure its safety before the adventure begins. Aren't you coming with us?"

She slowly raised her head. Her eyes met mine, and unexpectedly, she stood up and approached me before encircling me with her arms in a strange, uncharacteristic hug from her. I felt a slight tension in her body, as if she were trying to hide something I shouldn't see. She held her breath for a moment, then whispered: "That story you wrote, make sure no one reads it before you all leave."

I raised an eyebrow with slight surprise, answering her jokingly: "My latest story? It might be tragic and silly, but it seems you liked it, seeing as you finished it."

370

She took a step back, and the trace of the hug vanished quickly, but she didn't smile as usual. Instead, she fiddled with her fingers for a bit, as if trying to choose her words carefully before saying: "It's good. It has a special flavor. And most importantly, you've convinced me. I will definitely accompany you on that adventure."

Then, while avoiding my gaze directly, she asked in a hesitant tone: "Do you really think we might fall on planet Earth?"

"Its surface might seem catastrophic, but it's much better than falling on Jupiter, for example!"

She looked at me for a moment, then nodded with resignation, as if reluctantly accepting the idea: "You have a point."

And I didn't know back then that those words, which were said with indifference, would carry an unwritten prophecy, and that my latest story... was not just imagination.

To be continued?